Don't miss any of the acclaimed
Kate Jasper mysteries . . .

ADJUSTED TO DEATH

A visit to the chiropractor—who has a corpse on the examining table—teaches Kate that a pain in the neck may be pure murder . . .

THE LAST RESORT

Kate muscles her way into a ritzy health club to investigate a murder—and finds that detective work may be hazardous to her life!

MURDER MOST MELLOW

Kate teams up with a psychic to solve a murder—and the message channeled through is crystal clear: Butt out or die . . .

continu...

P9-DIZ-275

FAT-FREE AND FATAL
Kate takes a vegetarian cooking class where a student is found murdered—and she must find the killer before she's dead meat herself!

> "Jaqueline Girdner triumphs again."
> —Janet A. Rudolph, *Mystery Readers Journal*

TEA-TOTALLY DEAD
Kate attends a dysfunctional family reunion—and someone turns the homecoming into a homicide . . .

> "Jaqueline Girdner has another winner . . . a delightful
> sleuth . . . fiendish fun."
> —Margaret Lucke, author of *A Relative Stranger*

A STIFF CRITIQUE
When the most egotistical author in her writing group is murdered, it's up to Kate to find the killer—before he can plot a sequel . . .

> "Very funny and entertaining . . . essential reading."
> —*Mystery Week*

MOST LIKELY TO DIE
The Class of '68 Barbecue brings back memories for Kate . . . and proves that high school reunions can be murder!

> "Entertaining . . . enlivened by Girdner's gentle wit."
> —*Publishers Weekly*

A CRY FOR SELF-HELP
A New Age guru is pushed to his death—and Kate must find a killer who's acted out some very negative emotions . . .

> "Offbeat, tongue-in-cheek, and endlessly appealing."
> —*Publishers Weekly*

And don't miss the newest Kate Jasper mystery,
MURDER ON THE ASTRAL PLANE,
now available in hardcover.

DEATH HITS THE FAN

✙

JAQUELINE GIRDNER

BERKLEY PRIME CRIME, NEW YORK

DEATH HITS THE FAN

A Berkley Prime Crime Book / published by arrangement with the author

PRINTING HISTORY
Berkley Prime Crime hardcover edition / April 1998
Berkley Prime Crime mass-market edition / April 1999

The Penguin Putnam Inc. World Wide Web site address is
http://www.penguinputnam.com

ISBN: 0-425-16808-5

Berkley Prime Crime Books are published
by The Berkley Publishing Group,
a member of Penguin Putnam Inc.,
375 Hudson Street, New York, New York 10014.
The name BERKLEY PRIME CRIME and the BERKLEY PRIME CRIME
design are trademarks belonging to Berkley Publishing Corporation.

PRINTED IN THE UNITED STATES OF AMERICA

10 9 8 7 6 5 4 3 2 1

To the real life members of Sisters in Crime and Mystery Writers of America for their support, kindness, good advice, and good humor. And not a back-stabber among them!

❦❦❦❦❦❦❦❦❦❦❦❦❦❦❦❦

IT'S CROSSOVER NIGHT AT
FICTIONAL PLEASURES BOOKSTORE!

7:30, THURSDAY EVENING,
FEBRUARY 29TH

Come, meet some of the finest crossover artists writing today, successfully combining the genres of science fiction and mystery:

S.X. Greenfree, author of *CIRCLE OF DEATH*, "Beautifully constructed and executed. A masterpiece of mystery and conscience."

Ted Brown, author of *REVENGE RITES*, "A passionate . . . disturbing story."

Yvette Cassell, author of *A SMALL DETECTION*, "A delightful tale of whimsy and old-fashioned sleuthing."

❦❦❦❦❦❦❦❦❦❦❦❦❦❦❦❦

PROLOGUE

I would blame God for the unfairness. If I believed in him anymore. I would reach up into the stars, pull him down, and beat him until he felt the kind of pain HE has inflicted. But that might be too easy, too kind. And I don't believe in God anyway. But human evil, yes, I believe in human evil . . . (diary excerpt, pg. 296)

ONE

"But the whole idea of a leprechaun posing as, as . . . as Nero Wolfe!" I was insisting. I steered my old brown Toyota through the splattering rain toward the bookstore where Wayne's friend was hosting an authors' signing. "It's so silly. Leprechauns don't solve crimes, they make shoes for elves or something. I mean, at least Greenfree's character makes sense—"

"A clairaudient alien left on earth four hundred years ago makes more sense to you than a leprechaun armchair detective?" Wayne asked, his low voice polite even as he challenged me. But there was a smile beneath that politeness. I could tell.

And, no, Wayne and I still weren't married. But it wasn't for lack of trying. After our Wedding Ritual seminar we'd decided that a tango wedding was the ticket. Sensual and beautiful. And possible for both of us: Wayne who wanted formality, and I who wanted a quick fix. But it takes two to tango, and neither one of us knew how. So we took a tango class. Makes sense, right? But for some inexplicable reason the tango teacher, Raoul Raymond, decided to fall in love with me. Me! Ms. short, dark, and A-line. How he could fall in love with me while matched with the lovely Ramona, his tall, sleek, and sexy dancing partner, was a mystery to me. But apparently Raoul didn't need any rational motivation. Or encouragement. So Wayne and I quit the tango class.

Unfortunately, that wasn't the last of Raoul. He knew where we lived. And he'd been showing up there at odd hours, his wild curly black hair flying above his rolling eyes as he made grabs at my hand in order to kiss it and swear undying love. He was about as attractive to me as the skunks under our house at that point. And even less attractive to Wayne.

"But Greenfree's Beth Questra *feels* real," I went on, trying to forget the tango in all its twists and variations as I made the turn onto a straight, tree-lined lane leading to downtown Verduras. "At least to me. And it's so cool when she finds the guy that's killing all the female law students and then gets all the women together to take care of him—"

"Kate, you just told me you hate all that vigilantism, at least when it's *male* vigilantism."

Damn. Wayne had something there. Ted Brown's hero, Demetrius Douvert, was yet another alien left on earth (three hundred years for this poor guy) who used his clair*voyant* skills to track down the evil doctor/scientist who was killing the poor through free medical clinics. But somehow it bothered me more when Douvert dealt the deadly blow to the wrongdoer in the end. *Was* it because Greenfree's sleuth was female?

I shook my head. Mostly to clear it. At least Greenfree's sleuth wasn't a leprechaun. Or a skunk. Skunks no longer seemed cute to me either. Skunks had taken up residence under our bedroom at the beginning of that rainy winter, pulled out our heater vents and made themselves cozy. Aromatically cozy. And then their mating season began, at least that's what the skunk man told us. And aromatic turned to bursts of choking gases floating up through our abused heater vents as the skunks argued. We'd nailed up the five access holes we'd found sometime in late January at midnight while the skunks were out shopping or whatever skunks do at night, bless their nocturnal little souls. But the skunks were undeterred, using their tiny paws to tear off airflow screens for instant access, screens Wayne and I couldn't have yanked off by hand without tools under any circumstances.

The skunk wars had begun. They tore off screens. We nailed them up. They tunneled under concrete. We blocked the tunnels. They got better uniforms, equipment, and weapons. We were not winning the war.

"Well, who did you like best?" I countered, wrenching my mind back to the present once again. Or at least the fictional present. "Greenfree or Brown?"

Wayne paused to give the question serious thought.

Unfortunately, his pause gave me all the time I needed to worry some more. About Ingrid, my friend in need. Well, at least she was a neighbor. Why I'd thought she was actually a friend, I still hadn't figured out. She'd called me from down the street, sometime during the middle of the skunk wars, to tell me that her live-in boyfriend was abusing her mentally *and* that she was afraid physical abuse was soon to follow. So I told her to come and stay with us. What are friends for, after all? I guess to drive you crazy, among other things. So she moved in, along with the skunks. And along with her little yapping terrier, Apollo. My cat, C.C., took one look at Apollo and swiped my leg, claws extended, before reducing Apollo to a yipping mass of hysteria. Which laid him out right alongside Ingrid in mood and temperament.

And then Ingrid's boyfriend, Bob Xavier, showed up. And

was none too gently escorted out by Wayne and myself. Repeatedly.

So Wayne and I had left the house that last night of February, only too glad to shut the door on skunks of all sizes and get in the car to drive through the pelting rain to the Fictional Pleasures Bookstore in Verduras, owned by Wayne's old friend from law school, Ivan Nakagawa.

"S.X. Greenfree is the best writer, it's true," Wayne said after a few more moments of thought. And Wayne ought to know. He wrote, too. He'd even had a few short stories published which, happily, didn't feature either aliens or leprechauns. Or skunks. "Her plotting is perfect, her characters believable . . ."

"But?" I asked. I could hear the word in his silence.

"But Brown's got more passion going for him," he finished.

"Male passion," I pointed out.

"True," he agreed. "But I appreciate Yvette Cassell's leprechaun and his trusty female investigator, Peggy, more than you do. So it isn't just a male/female thing."

We still hadn't agreed on the three writers' respective literary merits when we got to the store a few blocks later. But the discussion had left me energized. I could almost forget my worries. One thing I loved about Wayne was his willingness to engage in verbal sparring on an intellectual level. Another was his refusal to engage in verbal bashing on a personal level. Wit *and* kindness are a rare combination.

So I gave Wayne a big hug when we got out of the car. And I followed it up by kissing his kind, homely face as the rain splashed the top of my head. I looked up into his eyes—what I could see of them under his low brows—and at his cauliflower nose. Fondly. Maybe we could have a wedding that focused on a discussion of fiction.

"Getting wet," he muttered, then kissed me back quickly before grabbing my hand to lead me to the store. The quick kiss was enough to make me wish we were home again, in the bedroom—skunks, tango teachers, and neighbors in need notwithstanding.

We tore through the rain toward the bookstore. But before we even got in the door, we were stopped by a picketer. He said nothing, just stared at us as he held up his sign. He was a small, paunchy man with burning blue eyes, wet, cropped brown hair, and a matching beard that must have been at least a foot long. How he could stand out there in that downpour was beyond me, but I decided not to ask. The picketer's sign read simply "Science Fiction = Demonic Poisoning." That was enough of a message for me.

So we swerved around him and into the doorway of Fictional Pleasures, feeling a welcome blast of heat as we entered. And then we heard the sound of someone screaming.

Not a human someone. And not an alien either, although she was lime-green with flashes of red, yellow, and blue. It was Polly Morphous Perverse, PMP for short, the bookstore's parrot.

"*Squawk, scree,* cash or charge, no literary merit," PMP greeted us from atop her perch behind the walnut sales counter.

"Hi, PMP," I whispered back.

Ivan Nakagawa waved from his place at the cash register and smiled a quick smile that made his eyes disappear into the rest of his bulldog face. Ivan always looked like an Asian gangster to me. Maybe his rough features and flattened nose were the commonality that had pulled him and Wayne together as friends. Or maybe just the fact that they were both plenty smart—but far too uncontentious to have stayed in the field of law.

"Wayne, Kate," he welcomed us softly as he walked around the counter. "Glad you could make it."

Ivan tilted his head at the rows of teak folding chairs he'd set up in the small foyer between the counter and compli-

mentary tea urn, the only space in the simple white-walled
room not crammed with hand-designed, floor to ceiling
wooden bookshelves arranged in library-style rows to the
back of the store. Bookshelves filled to the brim with fictional pleasures from literature to horror to romance, and
everything in between.

Unfortunately, the chairs for the audience were not as full
as Ivan's bookshelves. In fact, only one chair was occupied.
A statesmanlike individual who looked to be in his early
seventies sat front row and center, his pinstriped back
straight as a book spine. But there were a few other people
over by the tea urn: a gray-bearded man talking with a
younger, well-built African-American man, and a voluptuous fifty-something woman dressed in Mao-style pajamas
beside them, frowning at whatever they were saying.

Something moved in the rows of bookshelves and I
caught a glimpse of yet another possible customer, a lanky
young woman with long red hair who peered out at the rest
of us. I'd seen her behind the shelves before, always lurking,
her face usually buried in a book.

"Want a bag?" PMP squawked. "Pretty bird. Nice signature. Oh, will you shut up!"

Marcia Armeson, Ivan's second in command at the store,
rushed down the center aisle that led through the shelves
from the storeroom in the back, camera in hand, ready to
take pictures of the stacks of books set out on the authors'
signing table. Her thin lips tightened with concentration in
her fragile face as she moved forward for a shot of an open
book.

"Be lucky if I sell a tenth of them," Ivan whispered by our
side. "The authors have already signed an awful lot of stock.
But still, I understand. It's a wet night. Can't really expect a
crowd."

"I understand, I understand," PMP agreed with another
squawk and a familiar sigh. Ivan's sigh.

Then I heard a high, ringing voice coming from the store-room.

"I'm telling you, it's a real bummer to be short. I take my number at the fu-fuddin' deli, and then they call it and don't even see me. I mean . . ."

Ivan squeezed his eyes shut for a moment. This time he didn't seem to be smiling. His expression was more one of pain. Or perhaps prayer.

"I guess it's time to begin," he announced softly as he opened his eyes again. The three prospective customers at the tea urn took their seats in the front row. Wayne and I sat behind them. But the redheaded young woman stayed where she was, unmoving, behind the wooden book-shelves.

Ivan walked down the center aisle to the back of the store, and I heard the low rumble of his words as he spoke. But then the front door opened with a blast of cold, moist air and all I could hear was the sound of rushing footsteps. I turned to see a slender moon-faced woman with oversized eye-glasses running in. She looked around as if confused for a moment, circled the chairs uncertainly, passing the authors' table slowly as she eyed the display of books, and then an-other burst of speed took her to the second row to sit with a thud one chair away from Wayne.

"Sounds cool," came the same high, ringing voice I'd heard before. Which of the three authors waiting back there did the voice belong to?

I didn't have to wait long for my answer.

All three authors came trooping down the main aisle in front of Ivan. The first one to emerge was male, with a long, morose face and even longer dark hair tied back in a pony-tail. I was pretty sure he wasn't the owner of the voice. Un-less he had delusions of daintiness. He had to be Ted Brown. And he certainly wasn't short. Nor was the next one short, though she was definitely female. She was tall and elegant, a swan in flowing blue silk that suited her sleek, well-groomed persona. I would have bet she was S.X. Greenfree. Because the last in line had to be Yvette Cassell, the creator of the leprechaun sleuth. She was under five feet, no bigger than a leprechaun herself, with a narrow face, sharp nose, and close-set eyes under tinted glasses, her hair drawn back in a ponytail, not unlike Ted Brown's, with short uneven curls in the front.

"Damn, damn—I mean, darn notes," Yvette, if it was Yvette, exclaimed, her high voice ringing before her like an announcement as she stooped to pick up a piece of paper she'd dropped.

A moment after the trio finally reached the authors' table and sat down, each behind their respective pile of books, Ted Brown smiled. And I was surprised to see his morose features transform themselves into something handsome. Something sexy even.

"Look," he said, "a gift from a fan," and pointed at a jewel-encrusted bracelet sitting in front of S.X. Greenfree's books.

"Oh my," the elegant woman cooed from behind the books. So, she *was* S.X. Greenfree. Or else she was in the wrong seat. "Who?" she asked and surveyed our small crowd.

When no one answered, she smiled, picked up the bracelet, and winked. "Well, whoever you are," she said, "thank you. And *you* may call me Shayla."

Ivan cleared his throat and introduced the authors briefly, telling us that each would do a short reading.

He nodded toward their table and Yvette popped up like a marionette.

"I'll go first," she said and launched into a long and loving biography of her sleuth, Lovell, and his assistant, Peggy. And an even longer synopsis of each of her seven published books.

S.X. "Shayla" Greenfree picked up the jewel-encrusted bracelet from the table and fingered it with a small smile on her face. Then Yvette picked up her most recent book and opened it.

"Chapter One," she began, her voice ringing through the small store. "'A client for you, Lovell,' I insisted, peering into my boss's glaring face. 'A paying client . . .'"

Shayla opened the clasp on the bracelet and slid the jewels slowly onto her wrist.

"'And don't tell me we don't need the money,' I warned," Yvette read on, "'You haven't spun any gold since . . .'"

Shayla closed the bracelet around her wrist with a snap. Her face pinched for an instant. Was the bracelet too tight?

"'No elves are getting you out of this one, Lovell,'" Yvette continued. "See, we did need the money. My boss had expensive tastes for a leprechaun—"

"Kate, I . . ." Shayla interrupted.

Kate? I thought. She can't mean me. Was there another Kate in the audience? I looked more closely at Shayla for a breath, but I was sure I didn't recognize her. At least, pretty sure. The face of a far less elegant woman flashed before my mind's eye, but then it was gone. And Shayla wasn't smiling anymore.

"Cash or charge, hot sex, *scree*," PMP cut in.

Yvette glared at Shayla and PMP, and I looked quickly back at our reader. But I could see Shayla's face flush in Yvette's periphery. Shayla let out a small cough and her eyelids began to droop as Yvette went back to her reading. Was Shayla actually falling asleep?

"'I hoped our client *had* money,'" Yvette continued. "'It was hard to tell from the way she was dressed . . .'"

Yeah, I answered myself, Shayla *was* falling asleep. And sure enough, S.X. Greenfree's whole upper body pitched forward onto the authors' table as Yvette read on.

The gray-bearded man in front of us jerked up in his seat, clearly startled by Shayla's sudden drop. But the younger, African-American man beside him put a hand on his shoulder.

"She's probably asleep," he whispered gently. "This happens sometimes when Yvette gets going."

Or feigning sleep, I thought. Damn, that was rude. Suddenly, I wasn't so fond of the great S.X. "Shayla" Greenfree. The most I could have said for her was that she had the grace not to snore.

After what had to be a good twenty minutes more of Yvette's reading, however, I was coming to understand Shayla's reaction. And suppressing a yawn myself.

"End of chapter Three," Yvette finally finished.

I roused myself to join in the small hand of applause, more out of relief than anything else.

Yvette turned to the fallen author next to her.

"It's your turn now, Shayla," she said, her ringing tones surprisingly good-natured. "But I'll try not to sleep through *your* reading."

That got a laugh, followed by an even bigger laugh when PMP added, "Stoo-pid bird, shut up, *scree-scraw*."

But Shayla, S.X. Greenfree, didn't move.

Yvette tapped her colleague's shoulder, a look of concern on her narrow face now.

The man with the gray beard got out of his chair hesitantly.

"Shayla?" he asked.

Then more urgently, "Shayla?"

As the man started for the authors' table, Ted Brown shook Shayla's shoulder, then pulled her by that shoulder straight up in her chair.

Shayla's face was tinted a delicate shade of blue. Perfectly matched to the flowing silk that draped her inert body.

TWO

"Shayla!"

Now the gray-bearded man screamed her name, the syllables pelting the silence inside as loudly as the rain was pelting the small bookstore outside.

"Shayla, oh Shayla!" he kept on as he rushed toward the authors' table.

My brain felt sodden. The elegant and prolific S.X. Greenfree was tinted blue and unblinking in her seat, Ted Brown's hand frozen on her shoulder. The whole store was stone-still. Only the gray-bearded man seemed to be in motion.

And then the black man leapt up to join him. And finally, Ted Brown stepped back to collapse into his chair as the other two men rushed around the table to pull S.X. Greenfree away from her seat, away from the table with all of her books, and stretch her out in the small space left open on the floor. Kneeling, each man felt for her pulse, one at her neck and one at her wrist. The bearded man put his ear over

Shayla's mouth, then lifted his head to stare down at her. The younger man pushed past him and put his own mouth over Shayla's as he pinched her nostrils, breathing slowly into her mouth. But even I wondered if the effort was futile. Could someone that color be alive?

The bearded man seemed to agree with my unspoken opinion. He watched for a few more moments, shaking his head, then rose unsteadily to his feet, shuffling backwards until he bumped into the end of a bookshelf.

"Dear God," he murmured. "Dear Lord." He didn't seem to know the rest of us were in the room. Maybe he didn't even know *he* was still in the room. He put his head into his hands for a moment, then pulled on a chain around his neck and freed the jade stone that had been hidden under his shirt. "What will I tell Scott?" he asked no one in particular as he held the green stone.

There was a clatter a seat down from Wayne as the moon-faced woman in the oversized glasses sprang into action. She jumped from her seat and ran to the bearded man, averting her eyes as she detoured around the authors' table, Shayla, and her would-be resuscitator. When she reached the bearded man, she grabbed his arm, turning him toward her with a yank.

"Dean!" she said loudly, looking him in the face.

Dean just stared through her, still holding the jade in his hand.

"Dean," she said more softly. "It's me, Zoe. Zoe Ingersoll, remember?"

Dean's eyes focused on hers slowly.

"Zoe?" he said, as if trying out the word on his tongue. Then he shook his head and tears appeared in his eyes.

"Zoe," he murmured thickly. "It's Shayla. She's dead."

"Are you sure?" Zoe asked, the blinking of her eyes speeding up under her glasses. Only then did she glance back where Shayla lay. And even at that, only for a moment.

She shivered and punched her fist into her hand before quickly turning her head back, twitching her eyes at Dean's again.

"Yes," Dean assured her. "Oh, Lord yes, I'm sure," and then he began to cry in earnest. Zoe put her arms around him, tentatively, not holding him close, but holding him all the same.

Who were these two? I eyed Dean. He had weathered skin under his gray beard, a straight nose and dark eyebrows. He was of medium height and build, not handsome nor unhandsome. Other than the relative darkness of his brows compared to his gray beard, he was unnoticeable. Except for his tears.

Zoe, on the other hand, was more striking, partly because of her rounded face atop her thin body. She might have been a "Miss Peach" cartoon character. And partly because of the exquisitely embroidered vest she wore over her sloppy jeans and turtleneck. But mostly because of her frenetic energy. She was still blinking rapidly behind her oversized glasses. Sadness, concern, confusion? I couldn't tell.

What was the relationship between Zoe and Dean? Were they—

"She's not dead!" shouted the statesmanlike man who had been in the front row from the beginning. He was standing now, waving his pinstriped arms. "It's the bracelet, can't you fools see? Take off her bracelet!"

"Vince, Mr. Quadrini," Ivan murmured, advancing on the pinstriped man. "It's okay. Everything will be okay."

"Okay!" Vince Quadrini whirled on Ivan. I updated my age calculation on Mr. Quadrini to late, not early, seventies as I looked into his face. It was a good-looking face, with a long, rounded nose and solid features under wavy gray hair, but still strained and showing its age as Mr. Quadrini turned on Ivan.

"Okay, okay?" he demanded. "The greatest writer since Kornbluth might be dying, and everything's okay?"

Mr. Quadrini was right. Everything was not okay. I could see it in the face of the man still working on Shayla. He was pressing on the author's chest with two hands now, hard and fast, his dark features desperate. Shayla, S.X. Greenfree, was dead. She had to be. And she had called me by name while she was falling asleep. Only, she hadn't been falling asleep. My heart lurched as if I were the one receiving CPR. Had Shayla been dying all that time? Dying and ignored as Yvette read on and on. I looked up at the ceiling, anywhere but at the woman on the floor. The white ceiling was luminous suddenly, shining—

I felt Wayne's hand on mine, and realized my hands were shaking. I drew my head back down slowly. Why had Shayla called my name? Had she known she was dying? Had she been crying out for help? But why me? Unless someone else was named Kate . . .

I shivered and looked beyond Dean, where Marcia Armeson stood as still as a photograph, holding her camera. Her delicate features looked tight and meager in their evident unhappiness, however fashionably framed in elaborately waved black hair. But then, Marcia always looked unhappy. She jerked her head to look at Shayla, then jerked it back toward Ivan, before whirling around to run down the center aisle toward the storeroom, her designer jeans nothing more than a flash as they disappeared.

"Hey, you!" Yvette called out. "Where the fu-hell are you going?"

It was a good question. A very loud, good question. But there was no answer from the back. Yvette looked past Shayla's empty seat at Ted Brown.

"Shouldn't we stop her or something?" she demanded.

Ted just shrugged his shoulders, keeping his eyes straight ahead, his morose face pale and immobile.

"But what if she's, like . . ." Yvette waved her small hands in the air. Leprechaun hands, I thought irrelevantly. No bigger than a child's. "Holy shi-shick, what if she's destroying evidence or something?"

Ted made no response. Yvette looked down at the man still trying to resuscitate Shayla. Evidence? What did she mean by "evidence"?

A gust of wind shook the glass doors at the front of the store. Then rain splattered their surface as if in answer.

"Lou?" Yvette whispered urgently, looking down now in Shayla's direction, but the man who must have been Lou just kept pressing on Shayla's chest. Hard.

Ivan put his hand on Mr. Quadrini's shoulder. And I disengaged my cold hand from Wayne's warmer one and got up slowly, very slowly, too dizzy to do otherwise, before bending over the folding chairs to question Ivan.

"Ivan?" I hissed.

The owner of Fictional Pleasures jumped in place, startled by my sudden whisper, then looked back at me.

"Is she . . ." Somehow, I couldn't say "dead."

"I don't know, I don't know," Ivan groaned miserably. Why had I thought he'd know, anyway? Why couldn't my mind seem to function? "Maybe Lou can revive her—".

"Take off the bracelet!" Mr. Quadrini yelled again.

Ivan began to turn back to the pinstriped man.

"Who's Lou?" I asked quickly before Ivan could complete the turn.

"Lou Cassell, Yvette's husband," Ivan told me, putting his hand at the side of his mouth as if to shield his words from the others. "Lou comes to all her signings. A very supportive spouse. Very caring."

I looked past Ivan at the man trying to save Shayla's life. He couldn't have been over thirty. He had to be at least fifteen years younger than Yvette. And he was gorgeous, with a body like Adonis and skin the rich brown of shiitake mushrooms. This was Yvette Cassell's husband? A man with large golden-brown, tiger-shaped eyes and high cheekbones above a mustached, sensual mouth—

He rose slowly as I was cataloging his physical attributes. But his sensual mouth wasn't smiling. He closed his golden-brown eyes for a moment, then shook his head.

"No!" Mr. Quadrini objected. But his voice was quavering now.

And then that gorgeous younger man turned to Yvette.

"She's gone," he said, his tone clear and high, astonished. He shook his head again, harder, took a breath, and reached out for Yvette's hand. Yvette grabbed his large dark hand with her small light one, eyebrows raised over the rims of her tinted glasses. Lou stood still for a moment, head bowed. Then he looked up again.

"Someone needs to call the paramedics," he said.

"I'll call," Wayne offered quietly. He stood up and patted my back gently, as if for permission.

I nodded and he made his way down the row of chairs and turned toward the phone.

"And the police," Lou added, his tone deepening. His gorgeous features looked angry now. Fierce.

"The police?" Ivan said, looking as dazed as the rest of us. "The police?"

Wayne picked up the phone by the cash register. I could hear the low rumble of his voice against the rhythmically pounding rain and Dean's quiet weeping. Mr. Quadrini let out a sob as the heater kicked in with a roar of hot air.

I wanted to do something suddenly. Shayla had called out my name. And she was dead. But what could I do?

"I don't know, I don't understand," Dean mumbled through his tears. He cradled the jade stone in his hand. "What will I tell Scott?"

"Oh, jeez, Scott," Zoe muttered, pulling back abruptly from Dean. "Scott."

I wondered who Scott was. And who was Dean to Shayla? And Zoe . . .

"Who's the man with the gray beard?" I whispered to Ivan.

"Dean Frazier, a friend of Shayla's, I think. And the woman was her friend too, Zoe something," Ivan told me, his voice a whisper.

His thug's face looked a little more relaxed now. Ivan liked to gossip. Maybe that was how I could help, engaging Ivan in his favorite pastime. Well, second favorite, next to reading. He had to be shaken, an author dying in his book-store. An author who had called out my name. An author who— I wouldn't think about that, I told myself.

"And what about Mr. Qua—" I began.

But the voluptuous woman in the Mao pajamas rose from her chair, pushing it back emphatically and loudly, before I could finish my question.

"Can't be," she stated brusquely. "Let me help, she can't be dead." She looked toward Lou.

Lou just stared back at her, then shrugged.

For a breath, she stood there, straight and tall, her head still turned toward Lou. All I could see from behind her was her large, lush body, and her salt-and-pepper hair in a French roll held together with carved ivory pins.

The store heater let out another roar of hot air, and the woman marched forward to kneel by Shayla's body, taking the author's pulse, but differently than the two others who'd preceded her. Gently, she felt Shayla's right wrist at three places. And then her left wrist. She even felt Shayla's ab-domen. Finally, she frowned and rubbed her own thumb against her forefinger before standing again and straighten-ing her spine.

"Can't be," she repeated, but more quietly now, as if to herself. She tapped her heels on the floor and turned back toward Ivan. She was a lovely woman with creamy white skin and large, hazel eyes. Large, worried hazel eyes.

"Phyllis Oberman, she's an acupuncturist," Ivan whispered to me. "She's into romances."

I felt a hand on my arm and whirled around, my heart pounding louder than the rain on the roof. But the hand was Wayne's.

"Sorry," he said.

I took his hand and squeezed it in a not-guilty verdict.

"Made the calls," he added tersely.

"Thanks," Ivan whispered and sighed.

PMP echoed his sigh and we stood listening to the mixture of rain, heat, weeping, and the distant hum of traffic.

"The bracelet!" Yvette exclaimed and the symphony of sound was shattered.

She bent over, her fingertips almost touching the jewels gleaming around Shayla's wrist.

But Lou leapt in front of his wife, blocking her, lifting her back into a standing position.

He whispered something to Yvette, something I couldn't hear. But I could hear Yvette's comeback clearly enough.

"Poisoned?" she sang out. "So, you think Shayla was poisoned?"

"I sincerely hope not, but—" Lou stopped mid-sentence. "Yvette, keep out of this, please."

Yvette looked around, eyeing each of us in turn. Did she think we were suspects in one of her books? *Had* Shayla been poisoned? Murdered? A familiar sick feeling began in my stomach and climbed into my chest. Please, I thought. Please, not another murder.

"Who put the bracelet there?" Yvette demanded, hands on her tiny hips.

But no one answered her. Not even PMP.

"Honey, no one's going to 'fess up,'" Lou told her, his words coming faster now. "This is no prank—"

"Someone must have seen something," she insisted, patting his arm as if he was her size and she was his. His tall, well-built body was beginning to vibrate with frustration. I knew the phenomenon well, having observed Wayne in the same state more than once.

"Did anyone see who put the bracelet on the table?" Yvette plowed on.

Suddenly I didn't feel cold anymore. I was beginning to feel unbearably hot. I felt sweat bead on my brow and wondered if I looked guilty. And wondered once again why Shayla had called my name.

"Perhaps we should all sit down," Ivan suggested. "A moment of harmony—"

"No." Yvette cut him off without a glance. "Someone must have seen something. And once the fu-fuddin' police get here, we won't be able to share what we know. If Shayla was murdered—"

"Maybe she just had a heart attack," Lou interjected reasonably.

The shrill sound of a nearby siren seemed to spur Yvette on.

"Maybe, maybe," Yvette conceded, speaking more quickly. "But maybe not. And we probably only have a few minutes . . ."

We had less than that. Yvette was in the middle of ordering us all to tell her exactly what we'd seen, when a wave of cold, wet air crashed through the doorway of the bookstore, carrying with it a uniformed man, a uniformed woman, and a load of medical equipment. The paramedics had arrived.

An agony of efficient activity later and the paramedics had reached the same conclusion as Lou Cassell had. The same as Dean Frazier. The same as Phyllis Oberman. Shayla, S.X. Greenfree, was irretrievably, irrevocably dead.

"Who owns the store?" one of the paramedics asked.

Ivan raised his hand, hesitantly. I didn't blame him for the hesitation. I shivered in spite of myself.

"*Scree,* police procedurals, last row," PMP offered helpfully. "Oh, shut up."

Maybe Ivan could claim the parrot owned the store.

But the paramedic only glanced at PMP and then her eyes were back on Ivan.

"Police been called?" she asked sternly.

Ivan nodded.

Dean turned his head away and moaned. Mr. Quadrini was not as quiet about his feelings, however.

"Why are you asking about the police?" he demanded. "What is it that you're not saying?"

The paramedic put up her hand, but Mr. Quadrini wasn't as easy to ignore as PMP.

"Was it the bracelet? What . . ."

I opened my mouth to ask Ivan more about Mr. Quadrini. But he was way ahead of me.

"Vince Quadrini, Shayla's super-fan," Ivan whispered my way, shielding his mouth with his hand again. "Bought all of her books. Came to all—"

And then suddenly, a figure came flying out from behind the bookshelves, running toward the door, red hair streaming behind her. The young woman who'd been lurking. I'd forgotten all about her. I'd have bet we all had. Until now.

"Not so fuddin' fast!" Yvette shouted and ran to block the redhead's trajectory.

Yvette blocked her all right. The hard way. The two women went down in a heap and then I saw legs kicking. Long legs in knee-high boots and shorter legs in Reeboks. Lou was there a moment later, pulling the younger woman up off the floor by the collar of her flannel shirt. The redheaded woman couldn't have been too many years over twenty. And she was clearly frightened, her oval eyes wide and off center in her freckled face. Frantic.

The two paramedics moved toward the trio cautiously.

"No, no," the young woman whimpered. "I gotta leave now."

"Why, are you our murderer?" Yvette demanded calmly, on her feet now. Her tinted glasses were askew, but her tiny hands were firmly in place on her miniature hips. She peered up into the younger woman's face. "Go ahead, tell me why you killed her."

"Me?" the woman said. Her full lips fell open for a moment; then she gulped as if swallowing the enormity of the accusation. "Me? No way! She was my hero. I read everything she wrote." She rubbed her flanneled arms convulsively.

"Who?" I asked Ivan urgently.

"Don't know her name," he whispered back, urgency in his tone, too. "But she's always in the store. I think my son, Neil, knows her." He brought his hand up to his temple. "No, I do know her name. It's Winona, Winona Eads—"

And then another wave of cold air poured through the door. This one brought the police. At least I assumed they were the police. A woman and a man in uniforms different from those of the paramedics, and another man in a well-made gray wool suit. A man who was smiling widely.

Ivan sighed and made his way to the smiling man in the gray suit while the uniformed officers glared at the rest of us, then shook the smiling man's hand before leading him back behind the sales counter where they whispered in frustratingly low tones.

"I understand," PMP sighed. "Of course."

"It was murder, you know," Yvette announced loudly.

The smile didn't waver as the gray-suited newcomer turned toward Yvette.

"And you are?" he inquired, his voice warm and obliging. Friendly even.

Was it murder? I surveyed our group, wondering what this man saw to smile about. The two paramedics who remained halfway between Shayla and Yvette? Yvette herself, and Lou Cassell, standing side by side at the end of a set of shelves containing apocalypse fiction and horror, now seemingly completely fused into couplehood despite their differences? Winona Eads, her oval eyes still wide with fright? Ted Brown, morose and unmoving in his author's seat? Dean Frazier and Zoe Ingersoll, clearly not a couple but still somehow allied at the end of another set of shelves? Vince Quadrini, senior super-fan? Phyllis Oberman, voluptuous acupuncturist? Ivan, Wayne's old friend? Or maybe the one who wasn't visible, Marcia Armeson, Ivan's second in command, now missing in action?

And Wayne. My Wayne. I grabbed his hand and willed the strength of his body to seep into mine. And mine into his.

Then I looked back at the smiling policeman. He looked familiar to me. Something about his dark eyes reminded me of our unwanted houseguest's boyfriend, Bob Xavier.

I shook the thought out of my head. Now I was seeing doubles.

The policeman cleared his throat.

"Now people, I want all of you here tonight to think positively," he declared. "I'll be here to help you through this difficult situation. Let me introduce myself. I'm Captain Cal Xavier of the Verduras Police Department."

ꓔHREE

✦

Captain Cal Xavier?

Damn. No wonder his eyes reminded me of Bob Xavier's, the man Ingrid had been living with before she moved in with us. The man she was afraid of. The man Wayne and I had repeatedly escorted from our living room. The man whose last words to us had been, "I'll get you guys for this."

How many Xaviers could there be in Marin? Especially Xaviers who looked alike. Captain Cal Xavier was older, but he had the same dark flashing eyes as Bob, the same neatly shaped nose with a rounded tip, even the same springy hair, mustache, and brows, except that his were graying.

Was he Bob Xavier's cousin? Brother? Father? My heart beat harder with each guess. And he was here to investigate S.X. Greenfree's death. The woman who had called out my name before dying.

I felt Wayne's hand return my squeeze sharply. Had he noticed the resemblance, too? I kept my face forward, but let my eyes travel for a quick look at my sweetie's face. Wayne scrutinized the police captain, then flashed me a return look, with one brow raised high enough to expose a glint of panic. He'd noticed.

"Now I hope you'll all help me out here," Captain Xavier was continuing, smile unabated, his booming voice filled with enthusiasm. "We have a job to do and with everyone pitching in, we'll get it done."

No one said "amen," though his words seemed to cry out for some kind of affirmation.

It didn't really matter if Bob Xavier was related to the captain, I told myself, nodding all the time, hoping I looked like someone who was ready to pitch in and help. Hopefully, Bob Xavier hadn't bothered to mention his troubles with In- grid to his relatives. Or to mention where she'd sought sanc- tuary. Or who'd given her sanctuary. Even if he had, he probably wouldn't have mentioned our actual names. I swal- lowed. Hopefully. Somehow, my self-lecture wasn't helping to slow my pulse any.

"Well, all right, then," Captain Xavier concluded. "Let's all start in by introducing ourselves—"

"Hey," one of the uniformed officers cut in. He was a small round man with what looked like a permanent sneer on his clean-shaven face. He put one hand on his hip. "Shouldn't we at least establish death, cordon off the body, that kinda stuff?"

Captain Xavier's smile faltered for a moment, but re- turned in full force.

"Very helpful, Officer Dupree," he commented, his voice booming as if in commendation, though I would have bet that his tone was just about as sincere as my helpful nods were. "Why don't you and Officer Gilstrap just do that?"

They did. Officer Gilstrap was female, about four inches taller than Dupree, well-built with a face that showed all the emotion of a marble paperweight under her fringe of blond hair. Blue eyes unblinking, she headed toward the para-

medics, engaging them in whispered conversation as
Dupree left the store for purposes unknown. The captain
brightened up his smile some more and continued speaking.

"So, perhaps we can arrange these chairs in a nice little
circle," he suggested cheerily.

"I'd be glad to," Ivan offered and scuttled out from behind the sales counter. "Where's Marcia?"

"Where's Marcia?" PMP echoed. "Where's Marcia.
Never here when I need her. Oh, well. *Scree-scraw*. Cash or
charge."

But Marcia Armeson *was* there suddenly, appearing like a
genie from the bottle of the back aisle. She sauntered toward
the rest of us with a show of nonchalance that matched her
designer jeans but not the tightness of her clamped lips.
Whatever she'd been doing in the storeroom before, she was
a dutiful employee now, helping Ivan arrange the folding
chairs into a circle with a minimum of clattering and a max-
imum of efficiency. Actually, the circle ended up being more
of an oval, the chairs skirting the authors' table, and Shayla's
body behind it, just as carefully as the humans had.

Once the seating was arranged, one of the paramedics
gathered up equipment while the other listened to the
squawk of a hand-held phone, and then they rushed back out
into the night, letting in another blast of cold, wet air. Captain Xavier swept his arm toward the group of chairs.

It was amazing how easily everyone dropped into those
teak folding chairs. Maybe it was the captain's charisma at
work. Yvette Cassell started to protest, but Lou laid a restraining hand on her arm and they both sat down. Ted
Brown took his place beside them without a word. Zoe Ingersoll led a still dazed Dean Frazier to his seat, before taking her own. Even Winona Eads sat down, though still
rubbing her arms convulsively. When Marcia, Ivan, Wayne,
and I took our own seats, Vince Quadrini collapsed into his.
Only Phyllis Oberman, the acupuncturist, remained stand-

ing, straight and tall, staring into Captain Xavier's eyes as if there was a secret there she didn't understand.

"Madam?" Captain Xavier offered with another expansive sweep of his arm, and Phyllis clumped into the circle, seating herself and pulling at the legs of her Mao pajamas while muttering something too low to be heard. Only then did the captain of the Verduras Police Department lower himself onto one of the folding chairs as if it were a throne. King Arthur of the Knights of the Round Table, minus the table.

"Well now," Captain Xavier boomed. "The first thing on my agenda is to get to know you each a little better. Why don't we just go around the group, introduce ourselves, where we're from, and how we knew Ms. . . ." He turned to Ivan for help.

"Ms. Greenfree," Ivan whispered, his voice husky, his Asian bulldog features flat, face drained.

"Of course, Ms. Greenfree," the captain echoed, beaming as if at a prize student. "An author, I understand."

"A great author," Mr. Quadrini put in, his voice loud but quavery. For a moment I worried about Mr. Quadrini. He seemed too old for the game we were playing, whatever it was. His body was shaking in his pinstriped suit, really shaking. It was cold again in the store, all the heat sucked out by the many trips in and out the front door, but not that cold. Was he having some sort of attack?

"Perhaps, you might introduce yourself first, then, sir," Captain Xavier suggested.

Mr. Quadrini straightened up in his chair, clasping his trembling hands together. "My name is Vincent Joseph Quadrini. I'm the owner of Quadrini and Associates Realty. I knew Shayla Greenfree as a fan—"

"Do you live here in Verduras?" the captain interjected, his voice and face friendly.

"What?" Mr. Quadrini jumped. "Oh, Verduras. No, I live

down the way in Hutton. Anyway, I just wanted to say that Shayla Greenfree was a truly gracious woman, and a truly great writer—"

"Damn-darn, she wasn't all that great," Yvette threw in. "I mean she was pretty flippin' good, but not great. I mean Ted here did the whole alien-left-on-earth shtick first, right?" She turned to Ted. He shrugged his shoulders, his long, morose face impassive. "I mean, she wasn't even that original—"

"I beg your pardon," Mr. Quadrini threw back, his face suddenly red under his well-groomed wavy hair. "I'll be blunt. Neither you, Ms. Cassell, nor you, Mr. Brown, was even in the same class with S.X. Greenfree. She was a *real* writer, a truly brilliant woman, and for anyone to say different is just, just . . ."

"Irreverent," Zoe put in helpfully, diffidently. Then her round face pinkened and she looked down at her lap.

Zoe's terminological helpfulness wasn't making any friends for her with Yvette or Ted, that was for sure. Yvette's tiny head had reared back with Quadrini's blunt evaluation and even Ted's gloomy face had showed a spark of something, annoyance maybe.

"Yes, irreverent, exactly," Mr. Quadrini continued with a small bow of his head Zoe's way. "Thank you, young woman. That is exactly the word I was searching for, irreverent—"

"Oh, come on," Yvette began. "All this *real* writer shi-stuff is—"

But Captain Xavier interrupted her with a raised hand. And I was glad he did. Mr. Quadrini was out of his chair now, his hand balled into a fist. More than twenty years ago, when I worked in a mental hospital, I'd run group therapy sessions in the violent ward where the interaction was friendlier than in this group. Of course, the patients had been on medication. But still—

"And your name, if you please," the captain asked, turning his high beams on Yvette.

Yvette gave her name and her husband's name, as Mr. Quadrini sank back into his chair. Then she began to talk about her leprechaun-sleuth series but the captain interrupted once again to ask if she or her husband lived in Verduras. Strike two. She and Lou were also out-of-towners. For what it was worth. And the territorial information seemed to be worth something to Xavier. Though I wasn't sure exactly *what* it was worth.

"She really was a good writer," a wistful voice put in before Yvette could continue. The captain turned his head toward the speaker. "I'm Winona Eads," she added quickly. "I live in Morris, and I, I . . ." Tears came into the red-haired young woman's eyes as she struggled to go on. The heater belched hot air as if in sympathy. "How could she die? She was like . . . like, really cool and no way, no way . . ."

The front door opened again and Ivan's seventeen-year-old son, Neil, bustled in with the cold air. I would have known he was Ivan's son even if I hadn't met him before. He had the same bulldog features as his father, however much younger he was.

"Hey, Dad, what's the deal?" he demanded. "There's a cop car and—"

But his flow of words stopped abruptly as his eyes flickered to the group in the circle of chairs and fastened on Winona Eads.

"Hey, Winona!" he cried in concern. "What's the matter?"

He rushed around the chairs toward the redhead, but his feet stopped and his eyes widened as he took in the sight of Shayla Greenfree's body stretched out behind the authors' table. The room was quiet for a moment except for the splatter of rain outside.

Then he tried again. "Hey, what's the deal—?"

"There's been a . . . a . . ." Ivan struggled, keeping his voice low.

"A most unfortunate incident," Captain Xavier finished for the bookseller. "And who might you be?"

"Huh?" Neil answered. He looked back at Winona, at his father, and then back at Shayla's body again. "Huh?"

"My boy," Ivan growled, closing his eyes for a moment before he got up and walked over to his son to put a fatherly arm around him. "Listen, Neil, why don't you go on home? We need to work things out here—"

"No way," Neil replied, a familiar bulldog expression replacing his wide-eyed one. "Mom said—" He stopped himself mid-sentence and looked back at Winona.

Ivan removed his arm with a sigh known to parents of teenagers all over the world.

"I understand, I understand," PMP put in.

"Winona, are you okay?" Neil asked, squeezing his way into the circle of chairs to take his place beside her. He patted her freckled hand tentatively.

"Neil," Ivan tried again, raising his voice.

"I'm sure your son's presence won't harm our process," Captain Xavier boomed benignly. He smiled in Neil's direction.

"Who the hell is he?" Neil demanded of his father.

"He's the captain of the Verduras Police Department," Ivan answered quickly, a high note of warning in his usually low tone. "Please, Neil, will you cooperate?"

"Sure, Dad," Neil answered more quietly, looking around the group. "But what—"

"Shayla wasn't just a writer," a deep, quiet voice interrupted suddenly. Everyone's attention shifted toward the gray-bearded man with his jade pendant still cradled in his hand. His eyes stared out from beneath his dark brows beyond us, focused on something visible only to him. "She was a human. A kind and compassionate human, though she

had her problems, Lord knows. And a friend. Don't you understand? She was a person. Zoe knew her, she can tell you."

"And your name?" Captain Xavier asked softly.

"Dean Frazier," the gray-bearded man answered suc-
cinctly.

"Dean's a friend of Shayla's," Zoe added, turning her
head to the side as if embarrassed. She pushed her oversized
glasses farther up on her nose. "Well, really a friend of
Shayla's husband, Scott Green. Oh phooey, I mean he *was* a
friend of Shayla's. And Scott. Or is, of Scott. Or . . . whatever."

The dead woman had a husband? Suddenly, the meaning
of Dean's words were real to me. Real like the woman lying
on the floor. Not just an author. A real woman with real
friends. And a husband. Damn. I felt the pressure of immi-
nent tears behind my eyes. For a woman I didn't even know.
But others had known her. And probably loved her. Who
was going to tell her husband she was dead?

Zoe Ingersoll introduced herself briefly, then went on. "I
was a friend too, I guess. Maybe you'd say an insignificant
other." She rolled her eyes. "Of Shayla's, I mean," she finished up awkwardly.

The group was silent then. No one else volunteered any
information. So the captain began asking each of us formal
questions. Ted Brown identified himself as a fellow author.
Phyllis Oberman simply as a reader. And Marcia Armeson
said she was the store manager.

When Captain Xavier got to me, I decided on the name,
rank, and serial number approach. "Kate Jasper," I said. "I
live in Mill Valley. I'd just read Ms. Greenfree's books, and
Wayne and I know Ivan—"

"Holy shi-shift! Shayla called out 'Kate' right before she
fell over!" Yvette yelped, popping out of her seat with the realization. She pointed her finger at me accusingly. I glared
back at her. I knew there was a reason I didn't like the lep-

rechaun lady. "Didn't Shayla, huh?" she insisted, looking to her husband, Lou, for support. He looked down at the floor. "I mean, like she was—"

"I heard her say 'Kate' too," I cut back in, keeping my voice as calm as I could, while everyone's eyes turned toward me. Everyone's but Dean's. He was still focused on the unknown. "But I don't think she could have meant me. As far as I know, we'd never even met before."

Captain Xavier gazed at me. Somehow his smile didn't look as congenial as it had before.

"Well, Ms. Jasper," he began, his booming voice sounding like thunder now. "Do you have a reasonable explanation—"

Officer Dupree came marching through the door at that moment, looking more officious than official with a roll of yellow crime-scene tape in his hands, along with tape and scissors and other implements of construction. I was grateful for his interruption. And for the cool air he brought with him. My face felt hot. And I was beginning to sweat again. Captain Xavier hardly glanced over as Dupree circled Shayla's body with the crime-scene tape and then began on the authors' table. The captain was still looking at me. And his smile seemed to have awfully big teeth all of a sudden.

"And can you tell me just why Ms. Greenfree called out your name, Ms. Jasper?" he asked.

"No!" I answered in frustration. I had to opt for honesty. I didn't know what else to do. "I don't know why she said 'Kate.' Maybe I reminded her of another Kate she knew. Maybe I *did* meet her and don't remember. If I knew, I'd tell you. It's driving me crazy."

"Huh! It'd only take a short putt, not a drive," Yvette muttered, dropping back into her seat. I kept myself from turning her way, afraid that a truly murderous impulse might show in my face. By this time I hated Yvette Cassell, leprechauns, and all things Irish, for that matter.

"Wayne Caruso," came a low rumble from my side. The heat of my anger cooled a few degrees when I heard my sweetie's voice. At least I didn't hate *everything* Irish anymore. "Mill Valley. Fan, and friend of Ivan's. Mr. Frazier, did Ms. Greenfree have a friend named Kate?"

"What?" Dean said, his eyes finally focusing. Focusing on Wayne.

"Did S.X. Greenfree have a friend or relative named Kate?" Wayne expanded.

"No," Dean answered slowly, wrinkling his forehead in thought. "Not that I know of. Though I wouldn't necessarily know. You might ask Scott. Just in case."

And then I remembered the dead woman and her husband again, and the flame of my anger was extinguished completely.

"Well, think about why she said 'Kate,' Ms. Jasper," Captain Xavier suggested mildly.

I nodded. As if I could stop thinking about it.

The captain went on then to ask us all what we had seen.

And then the reality of S.X. Greenfree's death really seemed to hit the fan, in the form of Mr. Vincent Joseph Quadrini.

"She died!" he shouted. "She died in front of all of our eyes! It was the bracelet. I said it was the bracelet, but no one would listen—"

"And just why are you so sure the bracelet was involved in Ms. Greenfree's death?" Captain Xavier interjected quickly.

I was beginning to see the method in the man's friendliness. It was all too easy to forget he was a policeman. A policeman investigating a suspicious death.

"Because . . ." Mr. Quadrini sputtered. He raised his pinstriped arms. "Because . . . because she put it on and then she was dead."

"How about you, Ms. Cassell?" the captain went on. "Did you see who placed the bracelet on the table?"

It was nice to see Yvette in the hot seat. She just shook her head, squirming in her chair, keeping her small mouth closed for a change. Xavier turned to Ted Brown next. Who also shook his head. And to each of us in turn. But no one had seen the bracelet. Or admitted to it, anyway. Not until Ted had pointed it out. Not even Marcia with her camera. No matter how many times he asked, the captain of the Verduras Police Department got the same answer. Nothing. PMP had a few words to say, but not about the jeweled bracelet. Or about anything else that the captain wanted to know, for that matter. And he wanted to know an awful lot of things: about our movements, our times of arrival, our relationships. All he did find out for sure was that no one in the room actually lived in Verduras.

But if any of this noninformation bothered Captain Cal Xavier any, it didn't dim his radiance. He was still smiling broadly a couple of hours later when he politely asked each of us to give our full names and addresses to Officer Gilstrap, then left the bookstore after a warm handshake for every one of us. As he shook my hand, I couldn't help but notice his resemblance to Ingrid's troublesome ex, Bob, again. And to see the curiosity in those dark Xavier eyes.

Officer Gilstrap took our names, addresses, and phone numbers one by one, with Officer Dupree by her side checking our drivers' licenses, shaking his stubby finger and warning each of us not to leave town.

Only Ivan, Marcia, Neil, and Winona Eads remained as fellow survivors of the signing when Wayne and I were finally given permission to leave.

"Help me figure this out," Ivan whispered as we were almost to the door. "Help me find out what happened, who killed her."

"But maybe it was just a heart attack," I protested weakly, praying as earnestly as an agnostic can that it *was* just a heart attack. Or anything natural. "Everything will be all right—"

But then I really looked into Ivan's eyes. There was desperation there. "All right" wasn't going to be enough. Wayne stood behind me, wisely silent.

"I know I shouldn't ask," Ivan sighed finally. "I understand."

Wayne gave his friend a hug and then pulled the door of the Fictional Pleasures Bookstore open to the elements.

"I understand," PMP repeated and gave us a wolf-whistle as we ran out into the nonfictional pleasures of the rainy night.

And it *was* a pleasure to feel the cold rain again. I stood for a moment by the Toyota, leaning my head back, feeling the wet splatter of freedom on my face. And then we climbed into my old car for the ride home.

Wayne didn't say anything as I drove.

"But I *didn't* know her!" I burst out when we were almost home.

"Of course," Wayne answered quietly, but a quick glance was enough for me to see the worry in his homely face. "I know that, Kate."

"But will they?" I asked.

Neither of us had answered my question by the time I pulled into our driveway, splashing and popping wet gravel. I was suddenly grateful to be home. I lowered my head into my hands for a moment just to feel that gratefulness. Home to safety. To warmth. To peace.

Wayne put his arm around my shoulders as I pulled my keys from the ignition. And a woman with a perfect, compact body came hurtling down the front stairs in our direction, blond hair streaming out behind her.

"Skunks!" she screamed.

FOUR

It was Ingrid, of course. Home: safety, warmth, peace. And Ingrid. How could I have forgotten Ingrid? Not to mention the skunks.

She'd reached the Toyota by now, her long, frosted blond hair and bangs flattening in the rain, her lace bodysuit and leggings plastered to her perfectly formed body. I snatched a glance at Wayne, wondering how the sight of the baby-faced diva of aerobics wet to the near-nude had affected his hormones.

But Wayne's brows had lowered in a glare that made his eyes invisible. I didn't have to see his eyes, though, to guess that the sight of Ingrid, no matter how well-formed, stirred more feelings of frustration than lust in his heart. Luckily for me. Especially since Ingrid had confided that her primary goal in life was to snag a "really super-rich guy," one who wouldn't insist on a prenuptial agreement like her former boyfriend, attorney Bob Xavier, had tried to do. And Wayne was super rich, all appearances to the contrary. He didn't flaunt the inheritance that he had come into when his former employer had been murdered. The only sign of his affluence was the aging Jaguar he still drove. And I'd come to realize that he drove that car as a kind of penance for his self-perceived failure to protect his former boss. The same way he drove himself to keep his former employer's restaurant-cum-art gallery empire alive and well.

"Ooh, Kate, this icky smell came up through the heater vent!" Ingrid announced loudly enough to hear through the rain and windshield. She curled her upper rosebud lip in revulsion. "It was really gross."

Apollo, her terrier, yipped in agreement from her side. The rain had plastered his fur to his little body too. But Apollo looked more like a drowned rat than a god in the rain. No wonder my cat, C.C., had intimidated Ingrid's dog so quickly. Apollo was probably smaller than C.C. under all that wiry fur.

Wayne removed his arm from my shoulders with a low groan. I felt like doing more than groaning, but Ingrid seemed as much a force of nature as the rain by now, so I stifled my inner screams and got out of the car. Slowly, taking a big wet breath, willing myself to ask her to leave.

"It smells really, really bad, Kate," she went on before I could speak, batting her wet eyelashes at me. At me! "So, can you fix it?"

I shrugged my tense shoulders. Ingrid claimed to be looking for an apartment. But she hadn't found one. Could I throw this orphan out into the cold rain? Easily. With my own two hands. But would I? Should I?

"First Bob, and then the skunks," she moaned. "I mean, why me? I'm almost thirty, you know. All I want . . ."

I didn't have to hear the rest. I knew, I knew. Super rich. Happy trophy wife. Really cool house. Etc. I still hadn't decided if Ingrid's latter-day Jayne Mansfield, blond bimbo persona was an act. She had a degree in mathematics. I'd

seen the framed proof with my own eyes when she'd un-
packed upon arrival at our house. Maybe the degree would
help her with finances if she snagged that super-rich guy
after all. And she did work for a living, teaching aerobics. At
least she was honest about her primary goal in life. I hadn't
needed any more convincing after the day I'd overheard her
on the phone with a friend saying, ". . . oh yeah, feminism,
my mom was into that . . ."

The skunk smell got stronger as we walked up the front
steps. And Ingrid's stream of words grew too, beating on my
head as incessantly as the rain, but not nearly so pleasantly.

". . . the living room isn't all that comfortable, you
know . . ."

"Maybe some of your other friends might have more, um,
comfortable accommodations," Wayne put in hopefully.
Quietly. Turning his head aside as he spoke.

But turned head notwithstanding, he couldn't miss the
wide-eyed, little-girl-lost look with which she answered his
suggestion. Nor could I. By the time we got to the open front
door, I knew I wouldn't ask her to leave. Not tonight anyway.

Our guest futon was spread out in the center of the living
room floor, made up with our best sheets, the handmade
wood-and-denim couch pushed to the back wall beside the
pinball machines, pushed against the overflowing bookshelves and houseplants that were there first. Before Ingrid.
B.I. And yes, it smelled like skunk.

Wayne and I flopped down in one of the swinging chairs
suspended from the wood-beamed ceiling to listen to Ingrid
in the skunk-scented room. At least we could bask in the
warmth of our own house as our houseguest described the
incredible shock of skunk on her uniquely sensitive nostrils.
After a few more minutes of description, though, we agreed
to do a flashlight search to see how the skunks had gotten
back under the house. Not that either of us knew what to do

if we found their new entryway. Block it up in hopes they were now outside? But if they weren't, we'd just be blocking them in. Still, the search got us out of the living room and Ingrid's presence. And back into the cold and wet night air.

So each of us held a flashlight and made our way around the house, shivering, then startled each other when our respective beams met near the back porch. Neither of us had spotted the skunks' secret staircase, though.

"So?" I said, looking up at Wayne in the rain.

"You okay?" he said back.

And then we were holding each other, neither of us okay, but better in each other's water-logged arms. I wondered if this was how Cathy had really died in *Wuthering Heights*. Catching pneumonia while mooning around in the rain.

"Oh, sweetie," I began and then we heard banging sounds from the front of the house. Skunks?

". . . damn well do what I say!" came crashing around the house.

No, not skunks.

". . . told you what I wanted," a higher voice replied. Ingrid's.

Well, maybe big skunks. Great big human skunks.

". . . got friends this time, and . . ."

The voice had to belong to Bob Xavier.

Wayne and I rushed around the house, back to our own front yard. The voice did indeed belong to Bob Xavier. He stood at the bottom of the stairs. And this time he had backup. In one hand he held the leash of a German shepherd. A German shepherd who was looking oddly bored by all the excitement, while Apollo yipped from behind Ingrid's well-muscled calves. But Bob had more than a yipping terrier behind him. Actually, he had two hulking men. Bob was a nice-looking man when he wasn't in a rage, with well-trimmed hair, beard and mustache, and those dark Xavier eyes. A civilized-looking man. The same couldn't be said for his companions, though. One of the hulks had long, greasy strawberry-blond hair and an eye that looked either extremely swollen or sewn together. The other guy had both of his eyes, but was missing a few teeth. And a few points of IQ, judging by the goofy grin on his face.

"Whaddaya gonna do?" Ingrid challenged from the open doorway. "Kidnap me? That's a federal offense, you know."

The goofy grin faded from the face of the guy with the missing teeth. Maybe Ingrid had a degree in law too.

"Hey, I'm talking here!" Bob replied. "All right? All I'm saying is that you can stop messing with me this way. You're driving me nuts!"

He wasn't the only one. Actually, kidnapping Ingrid didn't seem like such a bad idea—

"Excuse me," Wayne growled from my side. "It's time for you to leave now."

Bob Xavier whirled around, rage evident in his dark eyes. "You!" he shouted, pointing. "What right have you got—"

"Kate," Wayne cut in quietly. "Call the police."

I almost protested. Was I supposed to call the police because I was female, while Wayne stood off the three men because he was male? But this was no time for a divided front. I started up the stairs cautiously, ready to turn and help if Wayne needed me. He didn't.

"Listen, man," Bob put in, quieter now. "I'm just trying to talk to Ingrid, okay? That's all—"

"Please leave now," was all that Wayne said. Softly and firmly.

I'd just reached the top stair when Bob sighed, "Okay, man, we're outa here. For now, anyway."

I turned and watched as the three men and the bored German shepherd piled into Bob's vintage Mercedes and roared back down the street. Of course, I realized. That's why Wayne had told me to call the police. Bob Xavier might risk his right to practice law if he were arrested. Not to mention prosecuted. I told my body it could stop producing adrenaline. Not that it listened.

Because the drama was not quite over yet. Now Ingrid was crying.

"I don't know," she sobbed. "I just don't know. Maybe I should leave. All the trouble I'm causing you guys . . ."

Wayne and I held our respective breaths, hopefully.

". . . but that would just be giving in," Ingrid finished up.

Our breaths whooshed back out, along with our hopes. We walked into our skunky house, saying goodnight quickly to Ingrid. It was late. Very, very late.

After a long hot shower had warmed our chilled bones, we lay side by side in bed, flat on our backs, staring out the twin skylights into the storm.

"Was it murder?" I whispered to Wayne finally.

"Well," he whispered back. "Since you were there—"

"Wayne!" I yelped. I couldn't believe he'd said it.

"Sorry," he offered a few minutes later, in a voice so sincerely miserable that I rolled over to hold him again. And stealthily, under cover of the pounding rain on the skylights above our bed, and the scent of skunk from the heater vent, we loved away each other's misery.

The rain had let up by the next morning when we finally got up late, neither of us having thought to set the alarm the night before. The sun was shining on our soggy, skunky house. Unfortunately, Ingrid was still there. I would have preferred the rain. Especially since Wayne and I had concluded in frantic, pre-breakfast whispers that Bob Xavier had to be related to Captain Cal Xavier.

The three of us sat at the kitchen table, eating Whol-ios and soy milk at ten o'clock. No sugar. No honey. No fruit. Wayne had offered to make his melt-in-your-mouth, dairy-free crepes for breakfast, but I'd resisted. If nothing else, I was hoping a steady diet of soy products might drive Ingrid away. But soy just seemed to fuel Ingrid's energy.

"I don't understand this vegetarian thing, Kate," she was saying. "And anyway, just 'cause you're a vegetarian shouldn't mean poor Wayne has to suffer . . ."

She offered him a sympathetic glance. He declined it and took another bite of Whol-ios, swallowing with solidarity. And difficulty.

". . . Teaching aerobics is really hard work—"

The phone rang. Wayne and I both jumped up from the table, but I was faster. I'd picked up the receiver before he'd even made it from the kitchen through the doorway to my dining room/office.

"Kate, this is Ivan Nakagawa," the soft-spoken voice on the other end said. I took a deep breath. I was betting he didn't have good news. "The police have visited us again. I'm fairly certain they believe Shayla's death was, well . . ."

"Murder," I supplied much less gently than I could have.

"Murder?" Ingrid echoed from the kitchen table.

Damn. I should have kept my voice down. I plopped into my old Naugahyde comfy chair. And my cat, C.C., hopped into my lap, clawing my thighs ecstatically. Her favorite position. Luckily, my Chi-Pants were tough.

"Captain Xavier came by this morning, just as I was opening the store," Ivan went on.

My body tensed as Ivan emitted a long sigh, PMP screeching something about apocalypse in the background. C.C. yowled, turning her little black-and-white face up to mine resentfully. I willed myself to relax, to be a more comfortable scratching post.

"The captain asked a lot of questions," Ivan went on.

"About us?" I whispered.

"About you, about Wayne, about everyone . . ."

"Is that Ivan?" Wayne asked from behind me.

I jumped in my chair. C.C. gave my thighs one last swipe and leapt off in disgust.

"Let me talk to him," Wayne demanded, his voice a hoarse growl.

"Captain Xavier was friendly," Ivan went on. "But I . . ."

"In a second," I hissed, hand over the receiver, motioning Wayne away.

And then the doorbell rang. Ingrid got up from the kitchen table. I wasn't about to let her answer the bell. I shoved the telephone receiver into Wayne's hand and sprinted toward the door. Wayne was right. He ought to be the one to talk to Ivan. The bookseller was his friend, after all.

I was puffing a little, but I did beat Ingrid to the front door. So much for aerobics, I thought triumphantly, and yanked the door open, expecting a FedEx delivery.

The package on my doorstep was small, but it wasn't FedEx. It was Yvette Cassell.

The deerstalker cap she wore today obscured most of her narrow little face. But her height, or lack of height, gave her away. And if stature wasn't enough of a clue to her identity, there was always Lou Cassell standing behind her, an embarrassed smile on his sexy brown face.

"Just call me Watson," he muttered and looked skyward.

"Okay, Watson," Yvette agreed, loud and clear, taking a step inside.

"May Holmes and I come in?" Lou asked belatedly. "Yvette has some theories she wants to share about the—"

But Lou didn't finish his sentence, as he looked behind me. I turned. Ingrid, of course. Ingrid with an open-mouthed look of curiosity on her baby face. My own mouth went dry. My mind did equations. If Ingrid equaled Bob Xavier, and Bob Xavier equaled Captain Cal Xavier, would anything we said get back to the Verduras Police Department? Everything? Suddenly, Ingrid was looking less like the houseguest I was planning to evict than a potential blackmailer.

"Incident," I finished for Lou.

"Pee-yew," Yvette put in, stepping past us as if I'd asked her to. "It smells like shi—"

"Skunk," I finished for her.

"Oh, skunk," she said, removing the deerstalker to reveal mashed curly hair, and her all-too-inquisitive eyes behind her tinted glasses. "Have you tried ammonia?"

"Huh?" I answered.

"Then, there's always bright lights. The little mothers hate bright lights . . ." Yvette went on, stepping into the living room. She was in one of the swinging chairs, still giving me skunk advice before I could open my mouth again.

Lou threw his arms into the air, but I saw amusement and fondness in his face. Was it possible that he liked his intolerable wife? Even loved her? I sighed and motioned him in.

Lou sat next to Yvette in the swinging chair, then reached over to squeeze her tiny hand. He did like her! She turned to smile at him even as the words continued to pour out of her mouth. And she liked him back. I shook my head involuntarily. Amazing.

Ingrid sat in the other swinging chair, across from the happy couple, leaving me to sit on the floor since our only couch was still pushed up against the other wall.

". . . but probably you're best off calling the fuddin' skunk broker," Yvette finally finished.

"We already called the fu . . . the skunk man," I muttered. And needed to call him again, once we finished with our human pest problems. Like Yvette. And Ingrid.

C.C. jumped up into Lou's lap.

"Cute kitty," Lou purred, bending his own feline face over her.

C.C. was cute, if annoying, with those white splotches against her black fur, one shaped like a goatee on her chin and one like a beret rakishly balanced over her left ear. She clawed Lou's thigh tentatively. He didn't flinch. Cute but annoying. No wonder he liked C.C. He liked Yvette.

"So, I thought we could toss around a few theories," Yvette announced. Her voice was like a bell, ringing at the beginning of class. "As far as I'm concerned, everyone's a suspect . . ."

"In what?" asked Ingrid.

Luckily, Yvette appeared not to hear her. Her mouth just kept on moving.

"Now, Quadrini, I've watched him for a long time. He's one hell of a nut case if I ever saw one . . ."

"Well, I guess you'd think so after what he said about your writing," I put in, instantly ashamed of my own spite. I shouldn't have worried. Yvette went on without paying any more attention to me than she had to Ingrid.

". . . and that Winona broad, what a shick-kicker she is." Yvette shook her head. "And Ted's been weird ever since his kid died—"

"Kid?" I heard from the other room. It sounded like Wayne had finished his conversation with Ivan.

"His boy got sick and died a few years ago," Lou put in, sadness tightening his face. "It's tough when a kid dies."

"Yeah, yeah," Yvette murmured, patting Lou's hand. "Lou's brother got hit by a car when he was nine. Car killed him."

Lou's expression turned from sad to fierce so quickly, it was scary. I was glad when Wayne sat down beside me on the floor.

"It's okay, hon," Yvette told her husband softly. Gently. But then her mouth was up and chiming again. "Though neither Ted nor I could have put the bracelet there," she declared. "We were in the back room."

"You weren't in the back room the whole time—" I began. It was useless. Tossing theories around seemed to be a one-person game for Yvette. She rolled her mouth right over my interruption like a tank.

"But Marcia, the manager or whatever she calls herself, now she's interesting. She was there, on the spot, at the table. And she ran. Why did she run?"

That was a good question. But before I could wrap my mind around it, Ingrid intruded again.

"Hey, I'm in the room," she caroled. "What are you guys talking about?"

"Who are you?" Yvette demanded, glaring at the intruder through her tinted glasses.

"A houseguest," I put in quickly before Ingrid could explain herself. I didn't even want to think of the possibility of the name Xavier entering this conversation.

"Oh," Yvette said, apparently satisfied. She waved her hand, as if waving Ingrid away. I wished I could do that. "Last night—"

"An unfortunate incident," I interrupted, just as Lou interjected, "A little problem."

Yvette reared her head back and squinted at her husband. Then she turned her gaze on me.

"And you, *Kate*," she said. "Kate. Just what Shayla said before she cakked—"

"Cakked?" Ingrid murmured, her eyes widening. "You mean like, died?"

"Aren't you supposed to be at work?" I demanded of my houseguest.

She usually was out of the house by this hour. Owning my own business had the sometimes advantage of my being at home while being at work. I could do my design work, and paperwork, and supervise most of the activities of Jest Gifts from my house, only visiting the warehouse a couple of times a week to see that the gag-gifts were in order. Or usually, that they weren't. My employees called me daily. Only once or twice a day, if I was lucky, usually more often when there was a crisis. And there almost always was a crisis.

And Wayne didn't usually go into the city to visit La Fête à L'Oiel, his restaurant-cum-art gallery till afternoon. But Ingrid—

"I called in sick," Ingrid murmured with a pout. "I want to know—"

It was time to change the conversation.

"So, Lou," I interjected, smiling at Yvette's impossibly beautiful husband. "How do you happen to know CPR?"

"CPR?" Ingrid asked.

"Cardiopulmonary resuscitation," Lou told her. "I work for a chain of hospitals—"

"I know what CPR is," Ingrid told him, her petulant voice rising. "I want to know *why*—"

"Hey," Yvette cut in, putting her hand out, palm forward. "Will you let him flickin' finish?"

Okay, Yvette wasn't all bad, maybe—

Lou cleared his throat and began again. "I work for a chain of hospitals. Emergency training is mandatory, even for accountants . . ."

I lost the rest of his words. The cold slap of astonishment had stunned me. This gorgeous hunk was not only married to Yvette, he was an accountant?

"Lou, may I ask you something?" Wayne's quiet voice came from my side. Lou nodded. "Why did you stop Dean from helping Shayla?"

Lou's brown skin pinkened. "People have fallen asleep before," he muttered softly.

"Yeah, yeah," Yvette agreed with apparent good nature. "It happens. Some people aren't good listeners, so what the fu-hell? Dean's the really interesting one, anyway. Do you know what his real relationship to Shayla was?"

I realized she was looking at me. And actually waiting for an answer.

"No, I don't," I admitted cautiously.

"Huh!" she snorted. Then she leaned forward. "Let's put it this way. He had more of a relationship with Shayla's husband than with Shayla." Then she leaned back, smiling.

"All right, I'm hooked," I told her. "What do you mean?"

"Come on, honey," Lou objected before Yvette could answer. "I think Dean and Scott's relationship is no one's business but theirs."

Suddenly I was on Yvette's side. Why was Lou getting in her way? Did she mean something sexual? Or something else?

"Not when murder's involved," she replied, still smiling.

"Murder!" Ingrid squeaked.

And then the phone rang again. I let the machine take it, but then I heard my warehousewoman's voice coming through the speaker.

I had to pick it up.

"Kate, this is Jade," Judy said. Judy was still searching for the name that really matched her spiritual essence. This week it was Jade. "You wouldn't believe what's happening here . . ."

I would, and did, believe what was happening. Another crisis. One box of shark earrings for the attorneys was missing and the new shipment had just arrived with half of the sharks hanging upside-down. Right in time for spring sales. (We always sold a lot of shark earrings in spring. I was never exactly sure why.) And that was just the beginning of Judy's news.

Twenty minutes and too many crises later, I got off the phone. Lou and Yvette were gone. But Ingrid still remained.

"Why are you guys acting so weird?" she was demanding of Wayne.

Wayne took my arm and hustled me down the hallway to our bedroom.

"Ivan wants us to look into this," he hissed, once the door

was locked behind him. "So I told him I'd call Ted Brown, maybe Mr. Quadrini—"

"I'll talk to Zoe and Winona," I offered eagerly.

"Kate," Wayne warned with a plea in his voice, "this is dangerous. It's not a game. Don't be like Yvette—"

"Like Yvette!" I yelped. "How can you—"

The doorbell rang again.

This time Ingrid beat me to the door. But when I saw who was standing there, I was just as glad. I turned to slink away. Too late.

"Ah, the lovely Ms. Jasper," Raoul Raymond sighed and slithered his way past Ingrid.

FIVE

"Ah, *mon amour*," Raoul murmured, grabbing my right hand.

I snatched it back and executed a quick tai chi backstep. He was about to kiss my hand. I knew from experience. And it hadn't been a pleasant experience.

Raoul Raymond had looked good from a distance when he'd demonstrated the tango with Ramona. He was tall, lean, and lithe. A man who could have been anywhere between thirty and fifty, with wild curly black hair, an extravagant mustache, and large rolling eyes that reminded me more than anything of hard-boiled eggs with brown irises painted on.

But close up, his combination of lechery and lunacy was not as appealing. And his eyes kept changing color. Today the painted-on irises were green. Colored contact lenses? And I was beginning to doubt that he was even Latin-American. His accent changed as often as his eye color.

"Since when is *mon amour* Spanish?" I demanded when I'd stepped out of grabbing range. "I thought it was French."

"Ah," he replied, shrugging his shoulders in a fluid movement that might have been Continental or Latin-American, or Yonkers for all I knew. "I am a man of the world."

As Ingrid might have said, "Yuck."

But Ingrid wasn't saying "yuck" or anything else. She was staring at Raoul with the frank interest of a dog watching a package of hamburger go by. Could Raoul Raymond be super rich? He drove a new red Porsche, it was true. But could tango-teaching pay that well?

"I have waited so long to see you again," he declared, both hands crossed over his heart, eyes raised to heaven. All he needed was a lily and he would have been elegant in a silk-lined coffin. "I asked myself if my memory could even hold your image. Your spark, your verve, your—"

I squinted at him. His eyes were no longer rolled heavenward. What had stopped his recitation of my charms? Ingrid, of course. My houseguest had walked around from behind Raoul to stand at my side. I didn't think she was interested in protecting me, however.

"And who is your most dee-lightful friend, Ms. Jasper?" Raoul inquired politely after a moment of intense contemplation, an accent back in place. What accent, I couldn't have said.

"Ingrid Regnary," Wayne answered from behind me.

My jump was not nearly as graceful as Raoul's, but it wasn't nearly as high either. His eyes had been so fixed on Ingrid that he hadn't seen Wayne coming any more than I had.

"Think it's time for you to leave," Wayne added as my heart rate braked back to normal.

"Right," agreed Raoul, turning smoothly toward the doorway, his hands in the air.

"I'll walk you down," Ingrid offered sweetly.

• • •

" 'I'll walk you down'?" I repeated incredulously to Wayne half an hour later as I steered my Toyota toward Ivan's. We had waited to make sure Raoul was truly and safely off the premises before taking off for Fictional Pleasures. "Do you believe it? As if Ingrid's not in enough trouble with Bob Xavier, she wants to get involved with Raoul Raymond?"

"He's a male, drives a Porsche—" Wayne pointed out.

"But what about his wife, Ramona?" I demanded.

"Are you sure Ramona *is* Raoul's wife?" Wayne asked.

"Well, isn't her last name Raymond too?"

"But are either of them necessarily using their real names?"

That stopped me. Raoul's eyes weren't real. His accent was phony. Why should his name be real? Or Ramona's? And, actually, they hadn't acted much like husband and wife, sensual tangoing aside.

"But still," I insisted. "One minute, he's telling me he loves me and the next minute he's practically kissing Ingrid's hand. He was just flirting!"

"Are you jealous?" Wayne inquired mildly.

"Jealous!" I protested, but, but . . . I would have been happy to never see Raoul Raymond again as long as I lived, even in future reincarnations, but still, his all so obvious and nimble transfer of affections had sparked something in me that, well, maybe bore a faint resemblance to jealousy.

I laughed aloud. Jealousy. I was jealous.

"You know, he might just take Ingrid off our hands," Wayne added, his voice hard with a ruthlessness I hadn't imagined he could muster. But then, I wouldn't have imagined I'd have been jealous of Raoul's wandering affections, either.

"Ingrid gone," I murmured blissfully as I turned onto the

tree-lined lane that would take us to downtown Verduras. "Damn, I do love you, Wayne."

I saw him blush out of the corner of my eye. But there was a little smile along with the painful blush. I reached over to squeeze his well-muscled thigh before parking in front of Fictional Pleasures, banishing the thought of all the unfinished Jest Gifts paperwork waiting on my desk at home. As well as the crises, waiting to spring. I wasn't letting Wayne do this alone. We were a team.

"Where's suspense?" PMP screamed as we opened the bookstore's door. "Cash or charge. *Scree-scraw.* I understand."

Ivan came out from behind the sales counter to greet us as we crossed the threshold, hugging Wayne first, and then me, with a grip that came close to squeezing the Whol-ios out of me. I was beginning to feel more like a life raft than a friend. One about to burst.

At least it was warm at Fictional Pleasures today. And quiet, except for PMP. I lifted my eyes to enjoy the play of sunlight on the rows of wooden bookshelves. It kept my gaze from the authors' table, still in place with its stacks of books, and surrounded with crime-scene tape from the night before. Though Shayla's body was mercifully gone.

Ivan had set up a few of the folding chairs near the tea urn, along with a little table holding a tray of pastries. He motioned us to sit.

"I bought them fresh from the health food store's bakery," he assured me. "No white flour, no white sugar, no dairy."

He didn't have to convince me. I could smell the raspberry filling oozing fructose into the ozone. And the rich whole-wheat crust. Whol-ios were just a memory as my bottom touched the familiar slats of teak and I reached toward the tray.

"I thought they might provide a little harmony while we

talked," Ivan said softly, taking his own seat and handing me a cup of herb tea to accompany the pastry.

The carob-almond tea was a perfect contrast to the sweet-and-sour fruit flavor of the raspberry filling. And I could taste almond in the crust too. Vegetarianism at its most decadent. I forgave Ivan for his too-tight hug instantly.

"So . . ." Wayne prompted, untouched by gluttony, a lone cup of tea in his hand.

Ivan sighed.

PMP sighed.

I was ready to sigh too, despite the pastries, when Ivan finally leaned forward and began to speak. Quietly.

"Captain Xavier believes Shayla's death was murder," he began. He took a deep breath.

Suddenly the pastry didn't feel so harmonious inside me anymore. I'd guessed that Shayla had been murdered, but hearing it confirmed was still a shock. Or an aftershock, at least. Especially hot from the lips of Captain Cal Xavier.

"How?" asked Wayne.

Ivan sighed again, looking down at the floor.

"Captain Xavier asked me to consider the details confidential," he replied. "I'm not really supposed to share."

Wayne and I waited. I figured it wouldn't be long. Ivan's need to confide was as palpable as the oversweet smell of raspberry.

Ivan sighed again. Then he raised his head to look around him. No one was here but us and the bird.

"Apparently there was some kind of mechanism in the jeweled bracelet," he whispered. "When Shayla closed the clasp, it triggered a series of poisonous injections from the syringes inside."

I remembered the way Shayla's face had pinched when she'd snapped the bracelet closed. And her one word. *Kate.*

Raspberry jam began oozing its way back up my digestive tract.

"And the captain and I agreed whoever placed it on the authors' table had to have been one of the people present that night—"

"Who has access to syringes?" asked Wayne. Clearly, he'd already figured out that the bracelet was the murder weapon. Mr. Quadrini had been right. Shayla had put on the bracelet, and then she was dead.

Ivan looked down at the floor again. I couldn't see his face, but his shoulders were radiating evasion. And something that looked like guilt. What was he hiding?

"Well, lots of people have access to syringes," he mumbled. He lifted his head, but then I saw the evasion in his flat, round features too. A sick little butterfly fluttered in my stomach right below the pastry. Ivan was Wayne's friend. I hadn't even thought of him as a suspect, but that look—

"I mean, Marcia's ex was a doctor, and Phyllis Oberman is an acupuncturist," the bookseller went on, his voice going faster and higher. "And Dean's an anesthesiologist."

"Who had motive?" Wayne demanded brusquely. I shot a quick glance his way. Wayne's face was cold now, angry. He'd noticed Ivan's obvious dissimulation, too. When a friend asks for help, it's better if that friend shares his information with his would-be helpers. And Ivan wasn't sharing well.

In fact, Ivan looked like he was going to sigh again, but PMP interjected with a shrill whistle.

"I just don't know," Ivan groaned miserably. The misery, at least, was real. I was sure of that. He clasped his hands together. "I feel like I should know, of all people. The only strange thing that's been going on is, well . . ." He stopped and looked around again. It was still just us and the bird. And we were all getting impatient. "I've wondered if Marcia's been stealing books," he finally whispered, so low it took me a moment to realize what he'd said.

But PMP picked it up right away.

"Stealing books, stealing books!" she screamed. Ivan whirled around to glare at the bird. She whistled and chirped, "Stooo-pid bird, shut up." Was it my imagination, or was there a real apology in her chirp?

"Go on," Wayne told Ivan, his interest evident in the tilt of his body.

"First editions, from my special collection," Ivan whispered, his voice even lower. "Too many to be a random thief. At first, I thought I'd just remembered incorrectly, but the inventory kept coming up wrong. I even tried hiding the more valuable ones, but they're still disappearing." He leaned back in his chair, shaking his head, eyes glazed. "But still, I can't believe it's connected with Shayla's . . . oh dear, you know what I mean. I've asked myself how it could be. And Marcia. Well, Marcia, she's not all that bad."

Only bad enough to make life a misery, I thought, especially for a man like Ivan who most of all wanted everyone to agree, everyone to be comfortable, everything to be in harmony. Thievery and murder wouldn't fit into his well-constructed escape into fiction.

"Anybody besides you know where you hid them?" Wayne kept on inexorably.

Ivan got that evasive look again. But then he shrugged his shoulders and the look was gone. "My son, Neil, but you know Neil. He's a good kid. He can't. He wouldn't—"

"Who else had a motive to murder Shayla?" I asked, unable to bear Ivan's misery any longer. I could even smell it in the air, over the scent of raspberry and books.

"Well," he said, a welcome gleam of gossip in his eyes again. "There were the other two authors. And Ted did do the alien psychic routine first—"

"Did Shayla steal his idea?" I asked. "Did it make him mad?"

Ivan wrinkled his forehead. A gossip he was, but not easy with serious accusations.

"No, I don't think so," he finally replied. "No to either question." He shook his head. "They were similar ideas, but people come up with similar ideas all the time. How could Ted be angry? All ideas arise from the same life source, the same archetypes. And Adams and Smith did their alien sleuths before either Shayla or Ted. Though Shayla was more successful than any of them. But still, I just can't believe—"

"How about Yvette?" I demanded. It was too hard to listen to Ivan arguing with himself. I knew neither side would ever win. "Is she nuts or what?"

Ivan smiled gently. Affection, for Yvette? "Nuts, maybe," he agreed. "But in a highly creative way. And very prolific. She and Lou are a wonderful pair. He supports her all the way."

Lou—there'd been something about Lou. Then I remembered. It'd been nudging my subconscious all the way over.

"Wasn't Lou's brother killed in a car crash or something?" What if the driver had been Shayla? My pulse beat a little faster. It was far-fetched, but what if—

"That's right," Ivan told me, his head tilted, wondering why I was asking. "Lou still gets upset about it. They were both kids when it happened."

"Did they ever catch the driver?"

"They didn't have to," Ivan answered. "The driver was killed too. He was drunk. Very, very sad."

"Any relation to Shayla?" I tried desperately.

Ivan shook his head. "I doubt it. He was a German tourist."

So much for that idea. I settled back into my chair and sipped tea, thinking.

Wayne took over. "How about Mr. Quadrini?"

"Quadrini's an odd one, all right," Ivan said. "He's rich, but deeply unhappy. No inner peace. His wife died of cancer a few years back. That's when he became obsessed with Shayla, I think. But in a perfectly gentlemanly way."

"Obsessed?"

"No, no. Not really obsessed. I used the wrong word."
Ivan shook his head again, thinking. "Just a real fan. He
loved her work more than he loved her, maybe that's the best
way to put it. He's certainly not some kind of stalker."

He took a sip of his own tea before going on.

"Now Winona is the one who *seems* the oddest," he told
us. "She's always here in the shop. She buys a few books,
but not many. I think she really reads most of them here in
the aisles so she won't have to buy them. But I expect she's
just poor," he finished up. "And that's certainly no crime."

Damn. Ivan could just about handle the prosecution *and*
the defense of any suspect. What a loss to the legal world.

"How about Phyllis Oberman?" Wayne suggested.

"She doesn't come in very often," Ivan said, looking serious again. "I know she's never attended an authors' signing
before. And all she ever reads are romances. At least, that's
all I've ever sold her." He shook his head. "But once again,
that's certainly no crime."

"No crime! No crime?" I heard from behind me.

At first I thought it was PMP. But it was Marcia Armeson,
her thin lips stretched into a grimace as tight as her designer
jeans. "Ivan doesn't want to believe anyone could have done
something as unharmonious, as uncouth, as real-life murder.
But someone did, and I'm not gonna get hung for it, that's
for sure—"

"So, who do you think—" I began.

"I don't think, I know," Marcia said with a sudden enig-
matic smile. "And—"

But a customer entered the store before she could finish.
A mild-looking woman of about my age who was interested
in something with "real literary merit."

Ivan took his place behind the sales counter.

"Who?" Wayne challenged Marcia as Ivan suggested
literarily correct books in a suitably subdued tone.

Marcia only smiled back at Wayne. "It's just an idea. And

I'm not setting myself up for a slander charge until I'm sure," she told him. Then she turned away pointedly and left to rearrange some books a few aisles over. I looked at Wayne's frustrated face sympathetically. It would be hard to question a head of wavy black hair or the rear end of a pair of tight jeans.

But I followed her anyway, quietly.

"Is it okay if I use the restroom?" I hissed into her ear once I was by her side. I wanted to see her unrehearsed reaction. I did.

She whirled around, arms flailing, then dropped them to look into my eyes suspiciously. But finally, she just nodded. There was no way she was going to bar my access to the storeroom. I'd been there many times before. But her eyes tightened before she turned back to her books. Was I her suspect? A shiver ran up my arms. I hoped not. She was not a woman I wanted to tangle with.

But she was a woman I was incredibly curious about. That's why I was heading for the storeroom, full bladder notwithstanding. What had she been in such a hurry to hide back there the night before? If anything. She'd probably just run to the restroom to be sick.

I scooted down the main aisle to the back before she could change her mind.

But all I saw is what I always saw in the storeroom of Fictional Pleasures. Books. In carts, in stacks, in boxes. And atop the highest stack of boxes, a large, precariously balanced two-wheeled handcart with a wicked-looking metal scoop-end. I found the door to the little office Ivan and Marcia shared. I jiggled the doorknob. Locked. I longed for burglary skills, but had to settle for a trip to the restroom and an empty bladder.

The literary customer was gone when I returned, and Marcia was talking, her fragile features lit up with pure malice.

". . . Zoe and Shayla weren't all the good friends they pretended to be," she was finishing up. "I'm not as stooo-pid as some of the rest of the folks around here."

Was Zoe the one she suspected?

"And Dean and Scott and Shayla were in some kind of weird threesome—"

"Now, Marcia," Ivan objected, butting in at exactly the wrong time. Why did he have to be confrontational now? No wonder he never made it as an attorney. No sense of timing. "I never quite understood their relationship, but Shayla, Dean, and Scott were all genuinely fond of one another. You could see it in the way they treated each other. Almost like a family."

"Huh!" Marcia snorted, turning on her heel. "Some people never see what's in front of their faces."

"So what's in front of your face?" Wayne asked gently.

"Wouldn't you like to know." was her only answer, and then Marcia disappeared down another aisle. Just as another customer came in, a young man this time.

Ivan motioned us to stay where we were as he got up to wait on the man.

I looked at PMP, willing her to ask, "Where's Marcia?" but the bird remained silent. Well, it was certainly no crime, as Ivan would say.

After Ivan had loaded the young man up with an unexpected armful of Mary Higgins Clark, he sat back down with us again.

"Do you really think Marcia has an idea who the murderer is?" I whispered to Ivan. I didn't like Ivan's manager much, but still, if she kept talking the way she was, her health was going to be in serious danger.

"Probably not," Ivan answered slowly. He closed his eyes for a minute. "You see, Marcia likes to think of herself as unique. Special." He could have been speaking about one of his kids. Maybe that's how he saw her, I realized. "And with all this, this . . . you know, she's getting a lot of attention."

As long as she didn't get the wrong kind of attention, I thought.

But then Ivan was talking again.

"I think we might be able to reach some consensus about dealing with this situation if we were all to get together tomorrow," he suggested.

I groaned inwardly. Sharing the experience of murder was not an exercise I was fond of.

But Ivan pointed out that the next day was Saturday. If we were going to gather a group, it probably was the best time. So, reluctantly, Wayne and I agreed, and then escaped into the weak February sunlight, but not before Ivan had slipped me a typed list with the address and phone number of each and every member in the group. But it was Shayla I couldn't get out of my mind as I pulled the Toyota back onto the street. She was the one person we really hadn't talked about. What was her relationship with her husband, Scott? And with Dean? And Zoe? And who was she, besides the famous writer, S.X. Greenfree?

"I wonder what Shayla was really—" I began, a few blocks later.

"Kate," Wayne announced quietly, "I think we're being followed."

At first I thought he was joking, but a glance at his rock-like face convinced me he wasn't.

I started to swivel my head for a look.

"No, look in the rearview mirror," he ordered.

I did. Wayne was, after all, a former bodyguard. This was his area of expertise. And when I looked into my rearview mirror, I saw a battered, old, red VW bus behind us.

Just for fun, I took a turn off the main road. The bus took the turn too.

I drove back to the main road, keeping an even speed with

difficulty. I could still see the red hulk behind us. Then I saw the local health food store where Ivan had picked up our pastries. I jerked the wheel, pulling into the parking lot with shaking hands. What the hell, I told myself, I wanted a tofu burger for lunch anyway. We walked into the store nonchalantly. I got my tofu burger. Wayne chose a soba noodle salad and ratatouille for himself. I made him promise not to show Ingrid our food. We'd eat in the car and come home empty-handed, thus reducing her to a further diet of Whol-ios and soy milk. I didn't even mention the old VW as we stood in the checkout line and returned to the parking lot with our purchases. But it was still there, parked a couple of rows away.

We watched the bus from the rearview mirror as we scarfed down health food. I couldn't see any face, just the front bumper. No one moved. No one got out of the bus. No one got in. And when I pulled back out of the parking lot, the old VW was with us.

"Should I try to lose the van?" I asked Wayne. As if I could. "We have to go home sometime."

"Probably knows where we live anyway," Wayne replied glumly.

So I drove home slowly as the VW bus followed us, even turning down our street, only passing as we wheeled into our driveway. Then it was gone in a flash of red.

Wayne and I turned to each other.

"Did you see his face?" I demanded.

"No," he said. "And the license plates were covered in mud."

"Oh."

We were both completely spooked. Who had followed us? And why?

We were still asking each other unanswerable questions when we walked into the living room.

Ingrid was there. I'd actually forgotten about her.

But we had another visitor too, Bob Xavier.

And for once, he wasn't yelling.

SIX

❦

But what was Bob Xavier doing in our living room, anyway? The threat of police intervention had been enough to drive him away last night. What was different about today?

Bob smiled broadly and got up from the swinging chair. Ingrid stayed where she was, huddled on the floor, arms around her crossed legs, an orphanlike stare on her baby face. Apollo was next to his mistress, quiet for once. I wished he'd at least yip at Bob a little. Actually, Bob was looking quite handsome today, his dark eyes gleaming with pleasure, his white teeth gleaming with good dental work.

"Guess who my big brother is?" he challenged, his shark's smile growing wider.

"Cal Xavier," Wayne answered evenly. Nothing on Wayne's face betrayed any of the feelings I knew he had to be having. His face was carved rock. But Bob's face was molten.

First he frowned with disappointment. But then the frown

deepened and his formerly handsome features contorted with anger.

"And that doesn't change the fact that you are unwelcome in this house," Wayne added, still calm. Still quiet.

"Listen, man, I can get you into all kinds of trouble, trouble you can't even imagine," Bob hissed, throwing up his arms. The sour scent of his anger mingled with leftover skunk fumes. "You don't know what the hell you're messing with here—"

"We know," I answered, keeping my voice as calm as Wayne's. My answer was the plain truth, even if my tone was manufactured. I knew exactly what we were messing with. A vicious bully whose brother just might like to pin a murder on that bully's enemies. I only hoped the bully in question didn't notice the tremor that was dancing its way from my brain to my extremities.

"And I'm going to call the police now," I finished up. I didn't need Wayne's cue this time. Bob Xavier was a real menace. But as I walked to the phone, a possible happy ending stopped me with one foot still in the air. I turned.

"Unless, well . . . Ingrid wants to leave with you?" Forget calm and cool. Now I was pleading. Not with Bob. With Ingrid.

I looked at my houseguest, willing her to leave with Bob, psychically pleading with her to get out of our lives. And to take the Verduras police captain's brother with her.

"Well," she said slowly, widening her eyes. "If Bob was a little more reasonable, like about that stupid prenuptial agreement—"

"Hey!" he shouted. "The agreement isn't stupid, get it? I told you before—"

Now I turned my psychic powers on Bob. Please, I thought, please be reasonable. Forget the prenuptial agreement.

Oh, sure.

"You think you can keep messing with me, don'tcha?" he blasted away, ignoring my psychic pleas. "Well, I'm talking here—"

"Not here," Wayne disagreed. "You can talk somewhere else, but not here."

Then Wayne, too, turned his gaze on Ingrid.

"Ingrid, it's up to you whether you stay, or go with Bob," he stated, the slightest quaver of a plea shaking his deep voice.

Ingrid crossed her arms, tilted her head, pushed out her lower lip, and looked up at the ceiling.

"Bob just doesn't understand me," she murmured. "Now Raoul . . ."

If she had wanted to goad her former boyfriend into a further frenzy, she'd done a damn good job.

"Raoul!" he bellowed. "Who the hell is Raoul?" Then he turned to us, reeking of rage now. "You guys put her up to this. If it weren't for you—"

"You're leaving now," Wayne told him as Apollo belatedly began to yip.

In the end, Bob left. But he was still shouting.

"I'll get you guys for this!" were his last words, trumpeted over his shoulder as he stomped down the front stairs.

Unfortunately, his old threat no longer seemed empty. It seemed full, full to the point of bursting. And I didn't want to be there when it happened.

Wayne turned to Ingrid once Bob had roared off in his Mercedes.

"Maybe it would be better for all concerned—" he began.

"Oh, please, don't throw me out," she begged, her baby-doll face shining with a thin trickle of tears. "You heard him. He's violent . . ."

I put my hands over my ears and crossed the hallway to my office. Now I was shaking with anger, not fear. If I listened to Ingrid's babbling stream of consciousness anymore,

I would get violent. Or else just curl into a fetal ball and roll away.

No, I admonished myself. No fetal-ball bowling. No Ingrid crunching. Forget Ivan. Forget justice. It was time to concentrate on survival. Wayne and I had to figure out who'd murdered Shayla. And fast. Before Captain Cal pinned the crime on us donkeys.

I turned to the telephone and let my fingers do the trudging. It was time to talk to suspects. More than anything, I wanted to get a fix on Shayla, S.X. Greenfree. I still didn't know who the woman was. Or why she'd called out my name, for that matter.

I tapped out Dean's number first from the list Ivan had given us on our way out of Fictional Pleasures. And got to listen to a very gentle, kind, and understanding answering machine. I tried the next number on the list. Winona didn't even have an answering machine. Nor did Ted. And Vince Quadrini was "in conference" according to the alert but intransigent human who answered his phone. I cursed and then remembered that it was Friday, after all. Presumably, everyone was working.

I should have been working. I glanced at the pile of Jest Gifts paperwork on my desk.

But some kind of pit bull seemed to have control of my fingers. I averted my eyes and punched in another set of numbers on the phone. Bingo. Zoe Ingersoll was in. Shayla's friend. Hopefully, her confidante. And Zoe even agreed to talk to us that evening. Yes!

I still had more than a few hours to practice work-aversion therapy before talking to Zoe. I started to call Phyllis Oberman's office.

But I had only tapped in two numbers when Wayne interrupted me.

"What are you doing?" he demanded. His face displayed as little sympathy as his voice.

"Calling suspects," I shot back, straightening my back-bone into steel and glaring at him. It was a shame I had to tip my head back to look him in the face. It ruined the effect somehow.

I waited for his sigh. For his objections. For his argu-ments.

But all he said was, "Okay."

I let my spine ease back to its normal spongy state. And told him my plans. Eagerly.

". . . and Zoe is willing to talk to us . . ."

It was then that I remembered that Wayne ran La Fête à L'Oiel Friday evenings. And it was Friday.

"Right," he said, as if he'd heard my thought. "I'll call in the assistant manager. We'll go together to Zoe's."

And then we both retreated to our respective home of-fices. My retreat was the easiest. I just had to turn my head back to my desk.

But I was too wired to deal with stacks of paper. So I shoved the piles of order forms and inventory lists to the side and worked on my new design for a cat-carrier cup for veterinarians, as my mind simmered with strategies and the-ories and fears, fears being the dominant flavor of the stew.

An hour before our date with Zoe, Wayne reappeared to ask if I wanted dinner.

I looked around. Ingrid was nowhere in sight.

"Let's go out—" I whispered.

"Let Ingrid eat Whol-ios," Wayne whispered back.

"And soy milk," I added, reaching to squeeze his hand. There's nothing like a man who can play Marie Antoinette in a pinch.

We dined on fast-food falafel and tabouleh salad, with turkey shawarma for Wayne, at the local mid-Eastern cafe on the way to Zoe's house in Tiburon.

Zoe was in the less expensive part of Tiburon, not in one of the million-dollar homes with the incredible bay views.

Hers was a pretty, narrow but tall house, painted dove-gray with white trim. We walked up the primrose- and pansy-lined cobblestone path in the twilight and for a moment, there was magic shimmering in the cool air.

I shook away the magic and rang her doorbell. Survival, I reminded myself. Survival.

Zoe answered the door, opening it about six inches and peering out, her moon-shaped face twitchy under her over-sized glasses.

"Who's there, Mom?" a voice from behind her demanded. She jumped, then answered.

"The people to talk about Shayla's signing," she threw back over her shoulder, and opened the door wide enough for us to enter. Then she laughed.

"I'm sorry, I'm all jittery from the steroids I'm taking. And I'm afraid I had a senior moment there," she told us. "Forgot all about you . . ."

But I lost the rest of her words as magic overwhelmed me once again. Zoe's living room was layered in panels and panels of tapestry that hung from the high ceiling halfway to the floor. Silk tapestries alive with swirling colors in cloth and dye and stitch and sparkles. A hanging forest of rainbow silken enchantment. I reached out to touch one of the panels, its delicately fringed bottom at my shoulder level.

A dog yapped at my feet. At least this dog was a dachs-hund, not a terrier.

"Shush!" Zoe admonished and I realized the room was not only hung with enchantment, but alive with animals. Be-sides the dachshund there were cats, six or seven that I could see right off, and a couple of parakeets in cages. And children.

A girl who looked about thirteen came walking up behind Zoe, her arms crossed. Her face was fragile, but not soft, as she glared at us. An equally fragile-looking boy who couldn't have been much more than eight wandered in behind her

with something in his hands. It was a bright turquoise piece
of paper that he was folding carefully.

"My kids," Zoe said. "Zelda and Zack, my little reasons
for living. Actually, my big reasons. The Z's were my ex's
idea. Now we can all be confused."

"Huh?" I replied, still swirling in silk.

"Mom makes these hangings for a living," Zelda explained, uncrossing her arms. "They always blow people
away."

"Beautiful," Wayne murmured. The prince was enchanted
too.

"Oh, yeah," Zoe said dismissively. "I'm so used to them,
sometimes I forget they're there. You know, duh." She
slapped the side of her head. "So, you want to know about
Shayla."

That broke the spell. The tapestries were still lovely, but
we had work to do. I brought my eyes back to Zoe. Such an
odd-looking woman with that moon face atop her small and
slender body. She wore a turtleneck and jeans, and her fine
brown hair was pulled back into a ponytail and secured with
a rubber band. Clearly she saved her experiments in beauty
for her work. Her daughter watched me expectantly.

"I'm Kate." I introduced myself quickly, stretching my
hand out to Zelda. She shook it tentatively. "And this is
Wayne."

I didn't even try with the boy. His eyes were still focused
on the paper in his hand, which was beginning to resemble
a bird. Origami?

"Oh yeah, have a seat," Zoe offered.

We sat on a couch covered with some of the same shimmering material that hung from the ceiling, only this tapestry looked as if a great many claws had added their own
artistic efforts. In a way I was glad. I couldn't have sat com-
fortably on an intact piece of art this beautiful.

Once we were seated, Zoe pulled up a chair and sat down

across from us. She wiggled her shoulders and then looked at the floor. As a cat jumped into her lap, her daughter stepped behind her like a bodyguard.

"So," Wayne began tentatively. "We, uh . . ."

His words whooshed out of him as a large marmalade cat leapt onto his lap. We were surrounded. The dachshund settled near my feet and a calico cat claimed my thighs. At least she was smaller than Wayne's marmalade. And she didn't appear to be a thigh-clawer either. C.C. could have taken lessons from her.

"That's how I met Shayla," Zoe continued, as if she'd been asked. "Through her husband, Scott. See, he's an architect, and some of the people he builds for commission my hangings." She tapped her hand on the arm of her chair and wiggled her round head on her thin neck as her son wandered through the silken forest on his way out of the room.

"Little space cadet," Zoe's daughter muttered. "All he cares about is his art projects."

"Now, Zelda," Zoe objected, but there wasn't a lot of force behind her words.

"Yeah, yeah, he's 'creative,' " Zelda mimicked, rolling her eyes. "A creative pain in the butt."

"I heard that," a thin voice replied from somewhere beyond the hangings. A voice that didn't have much more force than Zoe's.

"We're looking into Shayla's death for Ivan," I inserted. It was time to steer this conversation back on track. "I know she was your friend."

I heard Zelda mutter something behind her mother. It might have been "bitch," but I wasn't sure.

Zoe shook her head, pulled on her ear, and scratched behind it like a cat. Then I remembered Marcia talking at the bookstore earlier, doubting the friendship between the two women. What had she said exactly?

"Actually, I'm not sure Shayla and I were still friends,"

Zoe told us, with another little twitch of her shoulders. "That's really why I went to the signing, to find out, but . . ." She shook her head. Were those tears behind her thick glasses? "I guess I'll never know."

There was a short silence, the parakeets chirped, and I heard a funny humming noise. I turned and saw a hamster on the end table, spinning his exercise wheel as he climbed earnestly and endlessly to nowhere. Some of the cats were watching him too, but the cage looked cat-proof.

"Why?" I asked finally. "Why did you think Shayla—"

" 'Cause of Crohn's," she interrupted.

Another cat jumped on her lap. She arranged them side by side to accommodate both. "Now I'm Noah's ark," she commented.

"Crones?" I prodded. Maybe we were in an enchanted kingdom after all. With fair maidens and crones and . . . I was beginning to feel dizzy with the swirling hangings and moving animals. And Zoe.

"Crohn's," she repeated. "It's an inflammatory auto-immune disease, they think, that attacks certain parts of the body and trashes them completely." She stopped and rubbed the back of her neck. "You don't want to hear the details, believe me."

"But you don't die from Crohn's," her daughter declared fiercely from behind her.

"Yeah, but you're not a happy camper either, I'm telling you," Zoe went on. "You can bleed to death, but only if you're not careful. If you're careful, you get a nice, long, uncomfortable life, with constant flare-ups and a whole sidebar of complications from the medications and from malabsorption of nutrients." She rolled her shoulders impatiently. "At least it's good practice if I want to become a junkie. I have to give myself B_{12} shots—"

"But why would Shayla stop being your friend because

you're sick?" I demanded. So far, I still felt like Alice in Wonderland.

"Because she was a bitch," Zelda answered, loud and clear. Yep, I had heard her right the first time.

The dog looked up mournfully at Zoe's daughter.

"Look, you've hurt Kali's feelings now," Zoe said and laughed. "A bitch, get it?"

"Oh, yeah," I said and attempted a smile.

"Okay," Zoe went on. "Here's the thing. People don't like illness. They don't like death. And they especially don't like chronic illness. Even doctors don't like it. Makes them feel like failures. My husband sure didn't. He left me, six months after I was diagnosed."

"That's 'cause he's an asshole," Zelda explained helpfully.

"No," Zoe disagreed, playing with her ponytail now. "It's not that simple. See, people don't spurn you when you're sick if they know that you'll get well in a given amount of time. Then they help you. They want to help. But chronic illness is a different story. Good, kind, loving people want you to get well. And if you don't, it's just too uncomfortable for them. Just some people, not everyone, mind you."

"But it's not your fault!" I argued.

"Lots of people think it is, though," Zoe said seriously. "Consciously or subconsciously. They tell you that you could get well if you really wanted to. They tell you there must be a reason you're holding on to your illness. It doesn't occur to them that it's genetic, chemical. Sure, I can do symptom relief with self-hypnosis and all that jazz, but I'm no yogi. I can't just change my whole body and walk away."

"And Shayla?" I prompted. I was getting lost again.

"Oh, Shayla," Zoe murmured, real sadness in her tone now. Even grief. She looked at the floor, but I saw the moisture on her cheeks. "She really believed I could get well. She believed she could *will* me to get well. If anyone could have, it would have been her. She told me to surround myself with white light. I did." She barked in laughter. "But I was really surrounding myself in white lies. Creative denial, it's an art form."

"Shayla was an idiot," Zelda put in. Better than "bitch" at least. But probably less accurate.

"And then I didn't want to tell Shayla I wasn't getting better," Zoe went on. "I didn't want to disappoint her. It's forever, you see. There are remissions, but then there're the flare-ups, the constant inflammations, irritations, infections. And the complications. Cataracts, faux arthritis, rashes. It never ends."

She stood up, disaccommodating the two cats to their noisy distress, and began pacing the room, touching her silken hangings, one by one, as she paced.

"Then Shayla wanted me to give up my medications. 'Steroids are deadly,' she told me. As if I didn't know. But if I'm not in remission, they're what keep me from bleeding to death . . ." She pounded a fist into her palm. "I had to tell her I couldn't risk it. I'd risked it once before. There's nothing like a hospital stay to straighten out your thinking processes about creative visualization as a real solution to a serious medical condition. I wasn't going to try it again."

Her eyes glazed over as she paced. Was she reliving the near-death experience or the argument with Shayla?

"So what did Shayla say when you refused?" I asked finally.

"First it was an idea a day. Self-actualization tapes, psychotherapy, coffee enemas, you name it. And then finally the calls stopped."

"Some friend," Zelda offered.

"Oh, honey," Zoe objected. "I know you love me, but you don't understand Shayla. She really wanted me to be well. That's the irony. Her intentions were good. Of course, I'm just as tired of being sick as she was of me being sick. Only

I can't leave. It's like you're in a hotel and the only way to really check out is to really check out—"

"Mom!" Zelda objected. "Don't you dare say that."

"Honey, I didn't say I was *going* to check out, you know that. We've talked about it." Zoe sat back down, still wiggling her shoulders. Another cat jumped in her lap. "Anyway, the upshot is that other people can leave, so they do. And I think that's what happened with Shayla. She finally got fed up. I called her, but she didn't return my calls. I was pretty sure she wanted to end our friendship. I mean, duh, it wasn't like her phone wasn't working. But I wanted to be sure, so I went to the signing to talk to her."

"Oh," I said and waited for more. It came.

"See, it's hard to explain Shayla," Zoe murmured. Again there was sadness in her voice. "Some people might call her self-actualized; on the other hand you might just call her self-absorbed."

I laughed. Self-absorption did seem to go hand in hand with self-actualization. At least among those who loved to talk about it.

Zoe looked up at me and laughed, too. It was a good sound to hear.

"So when's dinner?" Zack asked, wandering back into the room, the turquoise paper still in his hands.

Zoe jumped. "When I get to it!" she snapped.

Zack looked up, clearly taken aback.

"Oh phooey!" Zoe said, hitting the side of her head. "I'm sorry. It's these damn steroids. I haven't been myself since I've been on them."

"Tell them about the lady in Safeway, Mom," Zelda said, smiling.

Zoe laughed and complied. "God, you wouldn't believe it. Here I am, walking through Safeway, telling myself to concentrate on loving kindness and this woman puts her stuff in my cart. That was fine, I told myself. I let her know about her mistake . . . with loving kindness. Then she looks in my cart and sees the yogurt with aspartame I'm gonna buy. You see, there are about five substances in the universe left that I can eat, and that's one of them. Anyway, this lady pulls out one of the containers of yogurt and shoves it in my face." Zoe got up, cat sliding from her lap, and began pacing again. "She says, 'Did you know this contains aspartame?' I pleaded guilty. Then she pushes it even farther in my face and tells me all about how aspartame causes brain tumors. I wanted to kill her. I swear, I could see her blood-bathed head in the broccoli. It was the first time I ever really wanted to kill someone—"

Suddenly, her story came to a halt. She stopped pacing too, her finger just touching one of the silk hangings. Did she realize only now that the story wasn't funny under the circumstances?

Her daughter did.

"But that happens all the time with people on steroids," Zelda intervened quickly. "All the people in the Crohn's support group have stories about wanting to kill people when they're on steroids." Her face reddened. "But of course, they never do it."

Damn, if I didn't want to believe her. Zoe wouldn't have told us that story if she'd killed Shayla. Would she?

"Who was Shayla, anyway?" I asked, wanting to end Zoe's misery. Wanting to cure her Crohn's too, just like she'd said.

"Ah, Shayla," Zoe replied. "She was a member of a magic circle. She, Scott, and Dean—"

"Dean was Scott's lover," Zelda threw in.

"Zelda!" her mother objected.

"Mom—I know about these things," her daughter told her. "Anyway, I like Dean. It was Shayla who was—"

She didn't have to finish her sentence.

"I like Dean too," Zoe agreed. "And Scott. And Shayla. I

wanted to be part of that loving circle." She sat back down in her chair and buried her face in her hands, tears streaming from her eyes.

Her daughter knelt beside her and put her arm around her shoulder.

I knew it was time to leave. If I hadn't known, there was a definite clue in Zelda's glare.

But I couldn't resist one more line as I left.

"Zoe, when all this is over, I'd like to know you better," I told her softly. "And I promise the words 'creative visualization' will never cross my lips."

She lifted her face, laughing through her tears.

"Thanks, Kate," she said. "I might just take you up on that."

Wayne and I were quiet on the short drive home.

Somehow, Zoe's chronic illness seemed worse than Shayla's instant death. But still, a hard voice nagged me: opportunity—when she walked around the authors' table the night of the murder; means—B_{12} shots meant access to syringes; and temperament—steroid-induced rage. Damn. Still, I certainly hadn't seen her put a bracelet on the authors' table that night, and I'd been watching her.

I looked at Wayne as I drove. His expression was unfathomable. But I guessed that his sympathy was stirred by Zoe's illness. Or was he more concerned about her susceptibility to murderous rage?

We were climbing the front stairs, both lost in our own thoughts, when we saw a man walking around the side of our house.

"Hey!" I shouted.

And then the figure began to run.

SEVEN

✦

Wayne and I turned and bolted down the stairs simultaneously. But we were both too late.

The man we'd seen coming around the side of the house was sprinting down the driveway now, a large figure in a trench coat and hat. Large and fast. It wasn't Bob Xavier. Too tall. And it wasn't Raoul Raymond. Too bulky. So who the hell was it?

We reached the end of the driveway just in time to see the flash of an old red VW bus, and then, even that was gone.

"But who—"

"Why—"

"What—"

We asked, and didn't answer, each other's half-formed questions all the way up the stairs to the front door.

But we stopped talking when I actually opened the door and stepped inside. Was Ingrid still here? Wayne followed me over the threshold, and we peered into the living room together.

The good news was that Ingrid was gone. The bad news was that her belongings were still present, spread all over the futon and the surrounding expanse of carpet. Still, it was nice to see C.C. nestled in Ingrid's suitcase, clawing and purring.

"Who?" Wayne began again.

We explored the possibilities. And even the impossibilities. Was the figure we'd seen running one of the people who'd been at the fatal signing? His back hadn't looked like any one of them, though. Were we even sure it was a man? Or a human, for that matter? Which led to the thought of Bob Xavier. What if he had hired the man, or whatever he or she or it was? But why? Then a worse idea dropped into the discussion. What if the running figure had been a policeman?

Exhausted, I dropped onto our old couch, careful not to bump my head on the bookcase it was shoved into. A frond from a nearby plant brushed my face affectionately.

"We have to find out who did it," I said.

"Right," Wayne agreed, dropping onto the couch next to me.

I looked into his face. Was there sarcasm lurking there? And why wasn't he arguing with me?

"Damn," I said, one last spurt of adrenaline galvanizing my exhausted brain.

"What?" Wayne asked.

"I thought I'd know more about Shayla once I'd talked to Zoe," I explained. "I thought I'd have a fix on S.X. Greenfree. That was the whole point. Who was she?"

Wayne shrugged.

"And how does her murder relate to the guy running around our house?" I added.

He shrugged again. Was he even listening?

"And what's the meaning of life?" I tested.

This time he didn't shrug. He actually opened his mouth. And then he laughed.

"What?" I asked.

"I was going to attempt an answer," he told me, shaking his head. "Third question seemed easier, by comparison."

Then we were both laughing. Hysteria, my mind diagnosed, but I didn't care. It felt good. And I was breathing again.

We snuggled and bumped and tickled each other all the way down the hall, and began pulling off clothing.

We were halfway undressed, and I was tugging Wayne toward the bed, when we heard a door slam. The front door. And then the sound of footsteps passing our bedroom. I pulled on the bedroom doorknob, just a little, and peeked out. It was Ingrid, of course, heading toward the guest bathroom.

Pheromones gave way to old skunk smells, and Wayne and I finished undressing with old-fashioned decorum, lay on our backs, and closed our eyes. I fell asleep hours later, cursing the name of Ingrid Regnary, and then remembered it was never good to curse anyone. The curse could rebound. My last clear thought was, it already had.

I woke up the next morning and turned to Wayne's side of the bed, my eyes still closed, my mind floating on amatory hallucinations. But all I felt when I reached out was the coolness of bare cotton sheets. No bare flesh. My eyes popped open. Wayne was already gone. The only trace of him was his faint scent on his pillow. I pressed my face into the cotton pillowcase for a moment, then pushed my way out of bed, feeling old, cold, and cranky.

Wayne had probably already gone to La Fête à L'Oiel in the city. Saturday was a workday for him at his restaurant-cum-art gallery. A workday for me too, actually. Everyday is a workday when you work for yourself, especially if you've spent your previous working hours in unskilled attempts at suspect interrogation instead of the prison of paperwork. I put on my old velour robe and headed toward the kitchen. C.C. yowled the minute the bedroom door opened and nagged me all the way down the hall in her ritual morning welcome.

As I walked past my answering machine, I noticed the blinking red light. In all the excitement the night before, I'd forgotten to check my messages. I turned to the machine and pressed buttons.

Most of the messages were from Judy, or Jade, or whatever her name was, from the Jest Gifts warehouse. The work week had ended for her in the normalcy of multiple crises. But then another voice boomed out over the line.

"Hello, Ms. Jasper. This is Perkin Vonburstig. I have some information that might be of interest to you." Did I detect a German accent there? All right, maybe not German, but some kind of accent, one as hard to place as Raoul Raymond's. "Ivan Nakagawa suggested I speak to you."

Then Mr. Vonburstig left his phone number.

I tapped out his number eagerly, but the only one answering it was a machine, one of those equipped with an android speaking each syllable of nonavailability clearly and distinctly.

I slammed the phone down. I'd be seeing Ivan later for the group get-together. But I wanted to know who Perkin Vonburstig was now. My fingers moved toward the telephone keypad again.

"So who was that, Kate?" Ingrid sang out from the kitchen. "He sounded really gross."

Ingrid. I withdrew my hand from the telephone and went to share more Whol-ios and soy milk with my houseguest.

"Don't you guys ever eat anything else?" she demanded once I was seated with my bowl of cereal in front of me.

"Never," I assured her, keeping my face dead serious. "Whol-ios are good for you. Three times a day. At least." Then I dug in.

"Well, I'm outa here," she told me and rose from the kitchen table with one graceful movement and was out the front door with a few more. My Whol-ios started tasting a lot better. Especially followed by a few slices of Wayne's homemade blueberry pound cake out of the freezer with some well-hidden strawberry conserves from the very back of the refrigerator.

Once I was properly fueled, I got dressed and did paperwork. Serious paperwork. Even then, every hour or so, I called Perkin Vonburstig's number, but only managed to develop a relationship with his android for my trouble.

The doorbell rang just as I'd demolished one stack of paper and was ready to start on the next one. The next one of nine. I wondered if this Vonburstig guy had important information about Shayla Greenfree as I walked to the door, ready to do battle with one of the usual Saturday solicitors for a "really good cause."

But the man at the door wasn't a solicitor. He was a good-looking man in a gray wool suit. He smiled widely, dark eyes bright and friendly.

For a moment, at the door, I thought he was Bob Xavier and got ready to yell. Then I realized I was looking at Bob's older brother, Captain Cal Xavier of the Verduras Police Department, and prepared myself to cringe instead. With good reason.

"So have you figured out why Ms. Greenfree shouted out your name yet, Ms. Jasper?" he asked politely, benevolently.

"Um, no," I answered, feeling my throat tighten.

That was just the beginning of his courteous interrogation. I led him into the living room, wondering how much he knew about the missing occupant who had spent the previous night on the now empty futon. There was no way to tell from the captain's smiling face. And Captain Xavier kept smiling for nearly an hour as he asked question upon question. It seemed he knew Wayne and I were talking to other suspects, and wanted to know why. And he wanted to know why we'd been on the scene so often at previous murders. And why . . . And why . . . I almost choked when he asked why we'd gone out to the signing on such a stormy night, anyway. Choking was better than telling him it was because of Ingrid. Because of his brother.

The only high point of the interview was his concession that no one remembered either me or Wayne going near the authors' table the night of the murder. All right! I hadn't thought about that. We had something like—well, maybe something close to—an alibi.

Still, by the time he left, I was ready for fetal-ball bowling again.

Wayne came home minutes after Captain Cal's departure, but he got to hear all about it. Misery shared is misery doubled. He patted my hand, mumbling sympathy, checked once more to see that Ingrid was truly gone, and then baked us a simple focaccia with artichoke hearts, sun-dried tomatoes, and olives, along with a mixture of herbs I couldn't identify but whose aroma and taste mingled with the yeasty pizza bread to cheer me up. For a while anyway. Until it was time to visit Fictional Pleasures. I would have liked to stay with the gustatory pleasures a while longer. A long while longer.

"Captain Cal's going to frame us," I predicted morosely as half an hour later I drove down the now too familiar tree-lined lane to the bookstore for the suspect-think-tank Ivan had promised us.

"Pretty bird, stooo-pid bird," PMP greeted us as we walked in. Was the poor bird having an identity crisis? Or was I projecting? "Anything with cats in it? *Scree.* I understand. Oh, shut up!"

I looked around. Ivan had arranged the teak folding chairs in a lopsided circle eerily like the one set up on the night Shayla had died, but at least the authors' table was gone now. Yvette Cassell was already seated in the circle, along with her husband, Lou, on one side, and Ted Brown on the other. None of them was speaking, not even Yvette. Her little eyes darted here and there from behind her tinted glasses, though, and every once in a while she squinted them as if in thought.

Phyllis and Zoe were talking by the tea urn, too softly to be heard at the door. Zoe slapped the side of her head, whether from amazement or in self-abuse or for some other reason entirely, it was impossible to tell. Phyllis kept on speaking, her large hazel eyes serious and intent as she bent toward Zoe.

"Wayne, Kate," Ivan greeted us, striding around the counter, his arms extended in hugging readiness at odds with the deadpan expression on his bulldog face.

"Who's Perkin Vonburstig?" I demanded quickly before I was enveloped.

Ivan's eyes widened ever so slightly. His arms dropped. He swiveled his head for a quick glance over his shoulder.

"He called me yesterday," Ivan whispered, once he brought his head back around. "A very cooperative man. About the missing books—"

"Who called you?" a voice interrupted sharply. I hopped in place, in sync with my heart. It was Marcia Armeson, her meager features as melancholic as ever under her flamboyant, wavy black hair. How had she snuck up on us like that? Had years of working at Ivan's store made her invisible?

"You just don't understand!" PMP squawked.

Ivan looked at his bird gratefully.

Then Dean Frazier came in the door to join us, and PMP let out another volley of greetings.

"Dean," Ivan said eagerly, hastily disengaging himself from Marcia. "How are you?"

"Better," Dean answered quietly. And he looked better, his weathered face almost serene beneath his gray beard and dark brows.

Wayne and I hurried to take our seats in the circle, putting as much space between ourselves and Marcia as possible. Though of course, we were closer to Yvette now. She tilted her head as she eyed us. But then her interest moved to the odd couple ambling up the aisle from behind the Westerns. Vince Quadrini, as statesmanlike as ever in another pinstriped suit, and Winona Eads, her red hair as disheveled as ever, her youthful eyes still skewed in her oval, freckled face.

And then everyone still outside the circle seated themselves as if by psychic order, and Ivan opened his mouth to welcome us. But Yvette's mouth was in the lead before the starting gun was even fired.

"Okay, listen up, you guys," she declared. "One of you is a murderer." She paused and surveyed us all as Lou looked up at the ceiling, a slight blush staining his beautiful mushroom-brown skin.

"Where were you on the night of February twenty-ninth?" she demanded abruptly, leaning forward to glare at me.

"Huh?" I said, startled, struggling to remember. February twenty-ninth, I realized. The night of the murder.

"Um, here, I guess," I finally answered.

"They were all here, honey," Lou whispered in his wife's ear.

"I know that," she hissed back. "I'm not fu-fuddin' stupid."

I shook my head to clear it. I had my own set of questions to ask. I wanted to know about S.X. Greenfree.

"I know some of you here today knew Shayla Greenfree

better than others," I began. "Maybe if we could each talk a little about our impressions—"

But no one got a chance to talk about their impressions of Shayla or anyone else. Yvette whipped her head around toward Ted Brown, seated conveniently next to her. Conveniently for her, that was.

"Yeah, Ted!" she snapped at her fellow author. "Just how well did *you* know Shayla?"

Ted didn't even have to say "huh?"

"Yvette, perhaps if we acted in the spirit of harmony here," Ivan interjected as Ted blinked his heavy-lidded eyes in his long face, the biggest reaction I'd seen from him since the night of the murder. "We might—"

"And just how the hell far would you go to keep harmony?" Yvette challenged. "Hmm, Ivan?"

Ivan reared back in his chair, mouth open but unspeaking.

Yvette dug in then, lobbing questions from her chair like bricks. But her technique needed work. Ivan and Ted had both remained silent. Marcia did too, smoldering, arms crossed, when asked why she'd run out to the storeroom. And Zoe had punched her own hand and told Yvette to "stop it" when Yvette asked Dean if he was happier now that Shayla was dead. I was glad Zoe had objected to the question. I would have been tempted to punch Yvette herself. And Winona just squirmed and looked at the floor when Yvette demanded to know why she'd tried to run the night of the murder. The only one to actually answer Yvette was Phyllis Oberman, who used Yvette's inquiries about the availability of poisons to acupuncturists to somehow segue into a lecture about the deficiencies of Western medicine.

". . . And the use of shock treatments on disturbed patients," Phyllis expounded, leaning her magnificent body forward. So far, even Yvette hadn't been able to wrest the conversational floor away from her. "Yes, shock treatments.

A so-called treatment that exemplifies the lack of integrity in traditional Western medicine. Can you imagine, being electrocuted repeatedly like that and being unable to move?"

Unfortunately, I could. In fact, I was still shivering with the images the question had brought to my mind, and the feelings to my body, when Vince Quadrini cleared his throat.

Everyone turned his way, even Phyllis. Even Yvette.

"If I may beg to differ," he began politely. "What you are calling Western medicine helped my late wife to live two full years longer than she might have when she was diagnosed with cancer. And with far less pain, I might add—"

"Well, Western medicine has some valid uses," Phyllis conceded and took a breath.

Ivan grabbed the opening.

"Perhaps if we could return to the question of Shayla Greenfree's death," he suggested.

Yvette sat up in her chair, ready to lob another brick, but I cut her off at the mouth before it even opened.

"Dean, could you talk to us a little bit about Shayla?" I asked. "What was she really like?"

"That's not a simple question," Dean answered quietly. He stroked his beard and his eyes went out of focus. "I'd have to think on it to really paint a picture of Shayla. I could say she was a kind woman most of the time, a curious woman. And a bright one—"

And then Vince Quadrini interrupted again, but not so politely.

"How can you be so calm?" he demanded. "S.X. Greenfree wasn't just kind and curious and bright." His voice rose suddenly in pitch. "She was brilliant! Don't you understand? She was brilliant. And now she's dead!"

€IGHT

Then Vincent Quadrini began to cry. The rest of the circle went silent as the formerly statesmanlike Mr. Quadrini wept in great desolate heaves like a child who finally understands that a favorite toy has been irretrievably broken.

Had he been in love with Shayla Greenfree? Or was he really crying about his wife, dead of cancer? Or were we all watching the reaction of a man whose guilt over murder had just overwhelmed him? That guess brought up all the little hairs on the back of my neck.

The Fictional Pleasures heater let out a fiery roar as if expressing its own opinion, then went silent again.

I looked over at Wayne, pulling at my turtleneck. It was too hot in here. Wayne's face was impassive, but there was a tilt to his head that indicated he was doing some wondering about Mr. Quadrini himself.

A high-pitched wail stopped me mid-thought. Whatever the reason, the man in the pinstriped suit was really suffering. Why wasn't anyone attempting to comfort him? Why wasn't I? I rose from my chair at the same time as Phyllis Oberman.

Phyllis got to Mr. Quadrini first, and laid a tentative hand on his shoulder. Her touch looked gentle. At least she wasn't holding any acupuncture needles.

"Perhaps, if you allowed yourself—" she began, her voice less brusque than usual.

"I'm fine!" he shouted through his tears. So much for comfort. Then more quietly, "I really am fine. I'll be all right." And his sobs did begin to wind down. Slowly and painfully.

"I understand," PMP put in helpfully. "I understand."

Phyllis removed her nontraditional hand carefully from Mr. Quadrini's traditional shoulder, straightened her magnificent body and left not only the circle of chairs but Fictional Pleasures entirely, without another word.

The whole circle seemed to deflate, as if Phyllis had taken most of the air with her upon departure.

Winona Eads stood then too, awkwardly, her strangely skewed eyes looking at Phyllis's disappearing back longingly.

The possibility of discovering what had really happened to Shayla Greenfree seemed to be dissolving, for all of Ivan's efforts. And possibly *because* of Yvette's. The group approach wasn't going to work. We'd have to talk to everyone separately. I looked over at Wayne and hoped he'd received my unvoiced message.

Then I jumped up and stepped out of the circle, jogging to a position near the front door to head off Winona.

"Hey there, Winona," I said just as her long legs swept her into my speed trap. "Could I talk to you?"

"Um, I guess so," she mumbled, looking down at her running shoes.

"I mean really talk," I went on. "Maybe at your home . . ." I let my sentence dribble away nonthreateningly. I didn't want to scare her off. And I could already smell an acrid hint of fear emanating from her tall body.

"Um, I don't know," she finally murmured. "I guess so." She angled her head so she could look at me directly. For the first time, I saw the beauty in her perfectly oval face, real beauty. One eye might have been higher than the other, but they were both exquisitely large, almond-shaped, and colored an oceanlike shade of turquoise. Her freckled skin had a milky white undertone and satin texture; her lips were lush. She looked back down at her feet. Was her awkwardness a way of hiding her beauty? But why would she feel the need to hide her beauty?

She wrapped her flannel-covered arms around herself and hooked an ankle around the calf of her other leg.

"I gotta do some stuff, errands, you know," she continued, switching legs. "But I'll be at home later, I guess."

"That'd be great," I began. "How about—"

But before I could name a time, she'd bolted out the door. The cool air floating after her felt good. And I was glad that Ivan's list had included addresses as well as phone numbers. We wouldn't need an appointment to visit Winona. We could just show up.

I surveyed the rest of the group, looking for my next victim. The circle had broken up now. Wayne was with Ted in one corner. They seemed to be shaking hands. That was a good sign. Marcia was gone from sight. Vince Quadrini had calmed down now and was wiping his eyes meticulously with a perfectly pressed handkerchief. But my own eyes stopped at Zoe and Dean, who stood near the chairs, huddled together.

Zoe hit the side of her head as Dean said something I couldn't quite hear. I moved toward them stealthily.

"I wish you wouldn't do that," Dean was saying quietly.

"What?" Zoe asked, her eyes flickering as her head swiveled his way.

"Slap yourself like that," Dean answered. "There's no call to hurt yourself."

"Oh, I'm just slaphappy," Zoe answered and laughed. "Get it, *slap*happy?"

Dean, I thought. If anyone knew who Shayla had been, it had to be Dean. But could I press him in his current state of grief? Should I? Dean's weathered face was more serene than Zoe's. But then Zoe was on steroids, I reminded myself. Still . . .

"Oh, Zoe," Dean murmured. "Please don't be so hard on yourself."

"Dean, you're such a softie," she replied, putting her hand on his arm. "But thanks, my friend. I'll try and cut down on the obligatory self-abuse."

My mind never made itself up. My body did. I walked the last few steps to stand in front of the couple.

"Dean," I announced. "I need to talk to you about Shayla."

"Of course," he agreed, never missing a beat. He must have seen me coming. Zoe hadn't. That much was clear from her little hop and shuffle.

"Lord knows I need to talk more about Shayla," Dean told me. "How about tomorrow?"

It took me a moment to take in Dean's ready assent.

"Thanks," I finally blurted out and turned, leaving Zoe and Dean to talk in relative privacy.

Ivan was back behind his sales counter. And Yvette and Lou Cassell were there with him. Ivan's face didn't show much, but his body was pressed to the wall in the posture of a newly apprehended felon. And Yvette was shaking her little finger in his face while her husband averted his eyes.

"Shut up!" PMP screamed. "Will you shut up, you stooo-pid bird!"

Yvette turned to shake her finger at PMP.

I averted my eyes. This was no time to chortle. And if it

came to a scream-out, I wasn't sure if I'd bet on the bird or Yvette. But I forgot the two of them completely when I saw Wayne walking toward Vince Quadrini, now alone in the circle of teak chairs. Good. Someone needed to speak to the man. But whatever Wayne said, it didn't seem to be what Mr. Quadrini wanted to hear. He shook his head violently and rose from his chair. Then he strode out the door of the Fictional Pleasures bookstore without a goodbye.

Wayne looked at me and shrugged apologetically. I looked back at him across the room and suddenly my mouth felt dry. Wayne hadn't argued with me since this whole thing had begun. He hadn't sighed his martyr's sigh. He hadn't tried to order me to keep out of the action. He hadn't told me how dangerous investigating was. What was wrong with him?

An inner voice of doom provided the answers to all of my questions. And gave my dry mouth a taste of bile to go along with the information. Wayne must have thought we were in trouble if he was going along with this. Really bad trouble.

Wayne didn't say anything to refute the voice of doom on our way out of the store to the Toyota.

All he said was, "Let's go see Ted."

Once we were in the car, I turned the key in the ignition with chilled fingers. Really, really bad trouble?

"Ted agreed to talk to us," Wayne growled as I pulled out onto the street. "He'll meet us at his house."

"Right," I said, resisting the urge to salute. "He lives in San Ricardo, doesn't he?"

Wayne nodded and we rode in silence for a while.

"Wayne?" I finally asked quietly. "Do you think we're . . . we're in trouble?"

"She called out your name, Kate," he answered, his voice soft, but agitated. "I'd like to be able to handle this on my own," he added, his voice growing louder. "But I know there

is no way, damn it, no way, I can stop you. There never is.
I—"

He stopped suddenly, as if shocked by his own vehe-
mence. I could imagine why. His voice was closer to a shout
than I'd heard for a very long time. I wanted to tell him to
yell some more, to get it out of his system, but one glance at
his burning red face told me he was already ashamed of his
display. Then I felt like wailing, the way Vince Quadrini
had. I wasn't sure why. Maybe for all the pain and anger and
hurt that Wayne kept stored inside. But I didn't do any of
that.

"Right," I said instead, controlling my own voice, and
took the on-ramp to the highway that would lead us to Ted
Brown's house.

Actually, Ted Brown's house was half a duplex, a very
rundown duplex, at least on his side. Ted was already parked
in front, just climbing out of an ancient VW bus when we
got there.

My heart hiccupped at the sight. Was he the one who'd
been following us? I shook my head. Impossible. His bus
was a dirty blue-gray, not red. And it certainly hadn't been
repainted recently. It probably hadn't even been washed in
years.

Ted Brown shot his hand out in front of him, in an abrupt
pantomime of welcome. There were no flowers along the
path to his door, just dirt and encroaching weeds. But I
stepped up quickly, afraid his welcome might dry up as
completely as the patch where his lawn must have once
been. As Wayne and I hurried toward Ted's peeling front
door, I wondered what the occupant of the other side of the
duplex thought of Ted's yard. A ruler could have marked the
line between the two halves of property, the neighbor's
green and growing lawn shorn to a perfect inch and bor-
dered by flowering shrubs.

"Wasn't expecting company," Ted mumbled morosely as

he opened his door. Smells of old cooking and old dust drifted into my nostrils. I stifled a sneeze and stepped in, adjusting my eyes to the relative darkness inside.

Ted flipped a switch, drizzling the room in a 25-watt glow. He might as well have left it off. The inside of his home was a lot like his yard, only the dirt inside was littered with paper instead of weeds. Mounds and mounds of paper. I could just make out the lone chair, table, and word processor buried underneath. The only decoration was on the mantelpiece, along with a dead spider and an accumulation of dust that threatened to incite my nose to another sneeze. The decoration was a framed photo of a former Ted, his long face and heavily lidded eyes looking cheery as he wrapped his arm around a short, plump blond woman and a brown-haired little boy.

I walked toward the photo without thinking, holding my breath to keep from inhaling the musty air.

"Can't offer you a seat," Ted told us. He jerked out a laugh. "Unless you'd like to stack up some rejected manuscripts. They oughta be good for something."

I picked up the photo from the mantelpiece and stared. The photo seemed to be the one thing in the room that wasn't dusty. I wondered how long ago it'd been taken. Ted had changed—

"My former family," he barked. My hand jumped. I replaced the photo before I dropped it. "Dead son. Ex-wife. Any more questions?"

Oh God, now I remembered what Lou had said. The son who'd died young like Lou's brother. I didn't have any more questions. And I probably couldn't have asked them anyway. My larynx was paralyzed. And not by dust, by chagrin. Why had I picked up the picture? I would have slapped my head like Zoe, if I could have moved.

"Wanted to ask about Shayla Greenfree, actually," Wayne

put in quietly, stepping my way crabwise and reaching for my hand.

I grasped it gratefully, wondering who was comforted more by the loving touch in this arid landscape.

Ted threw back his head, almost dislodging the cowboy hat he wore over his long ponytail. He jerked out another laugh and grimaced.

"Shayla, so you want to know about Shayla?" He paused, and the departing grimace left his face somber. And thoughtful. "In a word—no, make that two words—she was a ruthless bitch. I suppose I should be able to characterize her more eloquently, especially since the witch is dead—ding-dong, et cetera—but that's all that comes to mind at the moment."

"Why 'ruthless'?" Wayne prodded.

"You didn't ask why 'bitch,'" Ted commented. "Someone else must have been talking about the woman, right? Ruthless? Is it ruthless to steal someone else's idea and rewrite it from a 'woman's perspective'? Is it ruthless to promote the idea as your own?"

"The alien left on earth who uses his psychic skills to track down—" I began, my larynx working again.

"Or hers," Ted broke in. "Don't forget her psychic skills. Shayla certainly didn't. She took my idea and ran with it."

"And made a fortune," Wayne added.

Ted looked up as if surprised to be joined in his complaint.

"Ever ask her if she'd copied you?" Wayne inquired.

"Once," Ted replied, his long face split by that bitter grimace again. "She claimed she'd never read my lousy stuff. Only she didn't actually say 'lousy'. She just ever-so-politely implied it. She was a survivor, that one. Somehow, everything she touched turned to gold. Everything I touched turned to mold."

I sniffed the air. The mold wasn't just rhetorical. I took a careful breath. At least it didn't smell like skunk.

"Did you hate Shayla?" I asked. I felt Wayne's warm hand tighten around mine and realized it was cold in this room as well as dark. Hospitality by the Addams Family. There were probably headless roses in the next room.

"Huh!" Ted snorted. " 'Did you hate her enough to kill her?' " he mimicked in a falsetto. "You sound just like Yvette Cassell, our nosy little leprechaun lady."

"Yvette!" I objected. Then I really felt Wayne's hand tighten. I simmered silently. How could this man compare me to Yvette?

"Who do you think killed Shayla?" Wayne asked quietly.

And as he asked, I realized Ted hadn't answered my question. Or probably Yvette's either. His derision had its uses.

"Well," he answered, rolling his eyes upward. "Yvette's nuts . . ."

I opened my mouth to object, then closed it again. Why did I want to defend Yvette? Just because Ted had compared the two of us?

"And that woman who works for Ivan, Marcia something-or-other, she's mean and nasty," he went on. "But if I were writing it, I wouldn't use either of them as the murderer. Too obvious. Yvette, jealous and nutty as a health food casserole. Marcia, mean and hiding something. Now, Quadrini, though, he'd make a good murderer. The perfect elderly gentleman. Wealthy, one of the privileged few. So what's he hiding beneath his pinstriped veneer? And Dean, so sincere, so eager to please . . ."

Ted took a pen out of his pocket, picked up a sheet of paper at random, and started making notes on the back as he ripped the cast of Fictional Pleasures to pieces with his sharp tongue. Was he going to make a book out of this? If he did, I just hoped it would sell better than his earlier ones.

By the time we'd left Ted Brown's duplex, I felt raw from

the acid of his words. And my head ached from the combination of paper, dust, dirt, and mold. Did brilliance go hand in hand with cruelty? I shook my head. I knew other writers, other artists, who weren't cruel. Who were in fact, unusually kind and compassionate. But Ted had a mean mouth on him, that was for sure. And he hadn't included himself in his scathing appraisal of the suspects. Though he'd certainly included me. And Wayne. He hadn't given us any really useful information either, for that matter. At least as far as I could tell. I was still sorting out the fact from the vitriol as we got in the Toyota and drove away.

I was on the highway, halfway back to Tam Valley, before I could even talk again. Somehow the drive away from Ted's duplex had felt more like an escape. I could smell the scent of his dark house on my clothing.

"Do you think that's what a visit with Oscar Wilde would have been like?" I asked Wayne. "Or Dorothy Parker?"

"No," Wayne concluded after a couple more miles. "There's a difference between true wit and plain viciousness."

He paused again and added, "Not that I'd like to give the theory a test, for all of my love of Oscar Wilde's words."

I settled back in my seat as I drove, cherished beliefs about Oscar Wilde in place. A man like Ted Brown couldn't have written *The Ballad of Reading Gaol.* That I was sure of. Or, I suddenly realized, Shayla Greenfree's Beth Questra series. Maybe that was the real source of Ted's bitterness. She had taken his idea, yes. But worse, she'd improved on it.

"So, what did we get out of— " I began.

"Pull off the road, Kate," Wayne ordered suddenly.

"Whuh?" I said, but an instant later I pulled over into an emergency lane as ordered.

Wayne leapt from the Toyota and ran back toward the car that pulled over behind us. It was a kelly-green Volkswagen bug.

ᛈINE

But the person who emerged from the Volkswagen bug was not the trench-coated, bulky figure I'd expected.

This person was tiny, no bigger than a child, with curly red, Little Orphan Annie hair. Was it Little Orphan Annie in the flesh? My mind was still fuddled by the sudden order to pull off the road. But Wayne's wasn't.

"Take off the wig," he commanded the small figure, as a truck roared by us in a noxious cloud of exhaust.

Our follower nonchalantly complied with Wayne's command, pulling the red curls from her head and throwing them into the still open door of her VW bug with an easy toss.

"Ah, shi-shick," she said, putting her little hands on her little hips. "I thought you guys wouldn't notice . . ."

The tiny person under the wig was, of course, Yvette Cassell. The air whooshed out of my lungs with the realization. I wondered why I hadn't recognized her immediately, wig and all. Who else would drive a kelly-green Volkswagen bug but a leprechaun?

What was it that Ted had said? "Nutty as a health food casserole." Maybe Ted was more observant than I'd given him credit for. Because it was nutty to follow us around. Especially to pull off the road after us, when she could have sped away, with us none the wiser.

"So, what'd you find out from Ted, huh?" Yvette went on, raising her voice to compete with a motorcycle whizzing past. "Some fuddin' character, huh?"

"Forget Ted!" I told her, glad that the noisy, not to mention smelly, vehicles passing by gave me an excuse to raise my voice too. "Why were you—"

But as usual, Yvette interrupted without answering.

"I'm having a meeting at my house tomorrow—brunch, eleven," she shouted. "Bring something if you want to."

"You followed us from Ted's to invite us to brunch?" I shouted back angrily. "Come on—"

But Yvette was already back in her Volkswagen before I could finish my sentence, and back into traffic before I could close my mouth.

"Holy shick, Batman," I mimicked, once Wayne and I were safe inside the Toyota again.

But Wayne wasn't laughing. And neither was I, really. For all her silliness, Yvette was as elusive as the Loch Ness monster. And her interruptions were as effective a deterrent to interrogation as Ted's derision. She was strange, that was for sure. But strange enough to commit murder?

At least Ingrid was missing when Wayne and I ventured into our home, though her belongings were still scattered around our living room. And my answering machine was blinking at me.

Oddly enough, the first message was from Winona Eads.

"Um," she mumbled as the tape ran. "I guess you could come over this evening, if that's okay. I guess."

Wayne and I looked at each other. Was this important? Did Winona know something?

I played the second message impatiently, expecting a Jest Gifts blast. But the voice wasn't from Jest Gifts.

"Perkin Vonburstig here again," it said. "I will try to reach you again later."

Damn, I never had found out who Vonburstig was. In fact, I'd totally forgotten about him. I tried his number as Wayne waited patiently by my side. But all I got was his android answering machine. I banged the receiver down mid-syllable.

"I'm calling Ivan!" I announced angrily. "It's time to find out who this Vonburstig guy is."

"Wait," Wayne put in, his hand out and blocking the phone.

"Wait?" I shot back. "Wait for what?"

Then it dawned on me. Wayne didn't trust Ivan. Ivan, his own friend. That was the other reason he was going along with this investigation. That was part of the really bad trouble for him.

"Oh, sweetie," I murmured and opened my arms. He hesitated, then allowed himself to be comforted. For a time, I felt I was larger than this six-foot-plus man as I held him as close to me as I could, stroking his bent back as I did.

"Not very macho," he growled a while later, straightening up out of my arms.

"I know," I told him. "I never liked macho."

So we decided to deal with Vonburstig without Ivan as an intermediary, whatever it was that Vonburstig wanted. And we decided to visit Winona. As soon as possible. Wayne had to call La Fête à L'Oiel to arrange his own replacement for the evening again. And I shot the stacks of Jest Gifts paperwork on my desk a glance. A very short glance. Then I returned Winona's call.

"Would you like us to bring some food?" I asked her once

I got her on the phone. It was close to dinnertime, and I for one was hungry.

"Um, I guess so," she murmured, but I heard a hint of eagerness in that murmur. "Maybe enough for Johnny too?"

"Johnny?" I asked, surprised. Was that her boyfriend? Somehow I hadn't imagined her with a boyfriend.

"My son," she answered, no longer murmuring. In fact, her voice had an edge now. Of hostility? Defiance? I had difficulty with nuances on the phone. Or face to face, for that matter.

"Oh sure," I came back, hoping she hadn't noticed my moment of internal ping-pong. I erased the curiosity from my voice. "What would you guys like?"

"Oh, whatever you think, I guess," she told me, her voice soft again, wistful. That nuance I could hear. "I've heard Japanese is good," she finally added.

So we stopped and got Japanese take-out: miso soup, udon noodles, veggie tempura, California avocado sushi and agedashi tofu. For starters. I didn't know how old her son was or how much he could eat. And I wanted plenty of food to ply his mother's tongue.

Winona had an apartment in the cheap end of Morris. Morris was the cheap end of Marin County in the first place, not as poor as the Tenderloin of San Francisco by any means, but still not a place you'd want to be alone at night either.

When Winona peeked out the door of her apartment, chain lock in place, I didn't fault her for paranoia. And when we walked in and saw her son, I realized the reason for the earlier edge in her voice. Winona couldn't have been much more than twenty. And her son looked around six or seven, as he stared up at us with those familiar turquoise eyes in his freckled face. Winona must have given birth to Johnny while she was in high school. No wonder she felt the need to hide her beauty.

"We brought Japanese food," I said cheerily, holding out the white cardboard boxes.

Winona smiled. It was a brief but lovely sight.

"For us?" her son asked. "For us?"

I nodded and looked around Winona's apartment as Johnny began jumping up and down in place and chanting, "Let's eat, let's eat."

Winona and Johnny's home was a studio apartment, with one bed in each corner neatly made up under its own bright plaid spread, and a table with two chairs in the center. Bookcases made of bricks and boards held paperbacks and what looked like textbooks on either side of the table. A few toys were arranged neatly on one of the beds and in a box beside it.

"I suppose we could eat in the kitchen," Winona suggested, interrupting my survey. And Johnny's chants.

"The kitchen sounds great," I answered hastily, ashamed to be caught staring.

The kitchen was neat and small. We all sat around the homemade pressboard table eating Japanese take-out on mismatched plates.

Johnny laughed with delight at the unaccustomed mixture of foods. And dissected them all, with scientific comments. And jokes. I laughed with him, realizing there was something intrinsically funny about avocado sushi.

"I called you because S.X. Greenfree was important," Winona announced suddenly as I was slurping up some udon noodles and Johnny was carving seaweed.

"Important?" Wayne prodded, his mouth apparently empty and ready, unlike my own.

"To me, to my life," she explained. She hesitated, looking at the ceiling, but only for a moment. "See, I'm working at a drugstore and going to school to be a dental hygienist. I'd love to be a writer . . ." She sighed, then went on. "But no way I'm any good like S.X. Greenfree. Still, when I read her stuff, I'm, like, more proud of myself, I guess you'd say. And I think maybe I will be a writer someday . . . maybe. She gave me that. So I owe her something."

Then she looked straight into my face without squirming.

"I don't want someone to just murder her and get away with it. No way. So I want to help. I'm not running away or anything, anymore."

I felt like applauding, but asked instead, "So what do you think happened?"

"Um, I don't know," she answered, looking back down at the table.

And it seemed that she really didn't. Winona had been in one of the back aisles of Fictional Pleasures that night, she told us, blushing. She'd almost finished the book she'd been reading there off and on. So she hadn't really seen much. Only her idol, S.X. Greenfree, as the author had walked in and sat down at the table. And then collapsed. And even then, Winona's view of her idol from the back aisle hadn't been very good. And then she'd run, or tried to. Just because she was scared. That was all she could remember.

And apparently, that really was all. Despite her good intentions, it didn't seem that Winona had much to offer in terms of observations. According to her, that night was the first and only time she'd seen S.X. Greenfree. And she hadn't noticed anything she thought was important. End of story.

"Wanna play table croquet?" Johnny asked, pointing to the miniature croquet set that sat between the salt and pepper shakers on the kitchen table.

"No, Johnny," Winona told him firmly. "They have stuff to do, you know. Adult stuff."

I wanted to object. Maybe spend the evening playing table croquet with Johnny and encouraging Winona to write.

But Wayne nudged me before I offered any of that. He was right. It was up to Winona to decide how long we stayed. So we stood up from the small table to leave. I thanked Winona for talking to us. I knew that her speaking up had been an act of bravery in and of itself. Maybe, when I knew her better, I'd have an opportunity to play table croquet and encourage her writing. Once we were sure she wasn't a murderer.

She had one last thing to say as we left.

"That little woman with the tinted glasses?" she muttered once we were outside her door.

"Yeah?" I prompted eagerly.

"I don't like her," she whispered. "No way."

Then the door shut behind us and the chain lock slid into place.

Unfortunately, Ingrid was sitting in our living room when Wayne and I got home. There were worse people in the world than Yvette Cassell, I decided as our guest began to speak. And Apollo began to yip.

Wayne and I skipped the evening discussion of Whol-ios and our other hospitality inadequacies and went straight to bed, snuggling quietly in skunky togetherness.

Syringes, I thought, just as my mind reached toward sleep. Dental hygienists have access to syringes. And then I was out.

I woke on Sunday and stared up for a while at the morning sun that poured in through the skylights. Finally, I turned toward Wayne. He was staring at me, a soft smile on his rough face.

"We gotta find out who killed her," I declared. And watched that sweet smile fade. I damned my timing. But it was too late to take it back. "How many other women did S.X. Greenfree inspire to feel proud?" I asked more quietly.

"And how many more Zoes and Teds did she hurt with her ruthlessness?" Wayne countered.

"Oh," I murmured, deflated.

"Sorry," Wayne whispered. "You're right. The woman didn't deserve to die."

We shared some Whol-ios with Ingrid for breakfast. And then both went to work in our respective offices. Wayne was lucky. He couldn't hear Ingrid's made-for-melodrama sighs from his back room.

By ten-thirty, Yvette's suspects brunch was sounding good to me. At least, compared to lunch with Ingrid. We'd pick up something besides Whol-ios on the way to Yvette's. I played with the idea of deducting all the takeout food from my taxes. But I didn't think there was a column for unwanted-guest avoidance.

We arrived at Yvette's a little after eleven o'clock, a bag of whole-grain goodies in my hand and a six-pack of herbal iced tea in Wayne's.

I hate to be late, even to a gathering of murder suspects. So I zipped up to the curb, jumped out, opened the gate, and rushed into the Cassells' yard, Wayne in my wake, without even looking around me. But then I noticed the yard and paused for a gasp.

The Cassells' house was predictably green with white shutters, but the yard was greener yet, and filled not only with green and living things, but with green and non-living things. Green and non-living sculptures, actually. Of elves, harps, leprechauns, and castles, to name a few, all coyly peeking out from behind bushes and tree trunks and neat clusters of primroses. Wayne came up beside me and stared, too. Lou couldn't have designed this, could he? It had to be Yvette—

"Wow," someone murmured from my other side.

My shoulders jerked up and settled back down onto my body. I hadn't heard any footsteps, too lost in the garden of Irish delights.

I swerved around and saw Winona, her lovely freckled face wide with wonder.

"No way," she murmured, shaking her head. "No way."

No way, precisely. I laughed as I threw my arms around her and squeezed.

There was a blush beneath Winona's freckles when I released her from my hug, but she didn't look displeased by the gesture either. I wondered about her parents. Did she have parents? If she did, they certainly weren't helping her financially. Or emotionally either, I would have bet.

I opened my mouth to ask her, but thought better of it and turned back toward Yvette's open front door instead. Wayne was already on the doorstep. The three of us entered the house cautiously, single file. I was last in line and the decor stopped me at the threshold, smack behind Winona's stalled body. I peered around her in awe. Yvette's home was as full as Winona's had been bare.

I should have expected the Irish knickknacks: porcelain figurines, needlepoint, teacups, posters. But there wasn't just one theme in this house. There was a bunch of cat bric-a-brac too, for starters. And real cats. And dogs. An English bulldog sniffed my ankles as a taller Labrador retriever checked out the middle portions of Winona's anatomy. The room also housed an extensive collection of implements of murder: daggers nestled with bone teacups, swords hanging alongside poster-size blow-ups of Yvette's book covers, a shillelagh resting conveniently next to the door in the shamrock umbrella stand. And then there were the African masks staring at us. And all the *Star Trek* stuff. The *Enterprise* hovered over a granite bust of Sherlock Holmes. A cardboard cutout of Mr. Spock stood guard by a wall-to-wall bookshelf. With a live Siamese cat rubbing up against the Vulcan. Still, there was a sense of organization to the chaos. Everything seemed grouped by size or color. Or by something that matched. Even the cats took their places at aesthetically appropriate positions.

Yvette must have noticed my mouth hanging open. That or Winona's stalled body. But it was me she spoke to.

"Lou's *Star Trek* collection is a fu-figgin' trip, huh?" she prompted cheerfully.

The *Star Trek* stuff was the least of it. But I didn't say that.

"Well, I guess you're of Irish ancestry," I commented finally.

"Lou too," she told me.

My mouth fell open again. But I hastily closed it, hoping she hadn't noticed my surprise.

"Yeah, Lou has as much green in his blood as I do," Yvette went on with a smile. "Shi-phooey, maybe more. On his mother's side. We met at a Remember Ireland Festival."

I nodded, embarrassed.

"And don't worry," she assured me. "Damn-darn few people ever stop to think that African-Americans have any blood but African in their veins."

I gulped and attempted a smile. She had noticed my reaction.

"So, come the hell on in," she invited.

Winona finally began to move in front of me. I followed her into the Cassells' living room.

It was then that I took in the other occupants of the room, mixed in with the cardboard cutouts and animals and weapons.

Wayne was already talking to Lou Cassell near another bookshelf, this one guarded by a couple of Persian cats. Zoe Ingersoll and Ivan Nakagawa were there too, chatting behind a giant revolving blow-up of *A Small Detection,* Yvette's most recent book.

Vince Quadrini was seated in a green velvet armchair, looking something like a more gentlemanly Godfather in navy blue pinstripes today. Dean Frazier bent over him, handing him a cup of tea. I just hoped it wasn't poisoned.

I walked up next to Winona, who now stood in the center of the incredible room looking as awkward as ever.

"Who isn't here?" I whispered in her ear encouragingly.

"That lady from the bookstore," she whispered back.

I nodded. "Marcia Armeson."

"And the tall woman, the acupuncturist . . ."

"Phyllis Oberman . . ."

"And Ted Brown." Winona bent her long body down closer to mine. "I don't really like his writing much," she confided.

"Me neither, though he's good with suspense," a voice from behind us put in.

Winona and I jumped together, then accepted cups of tea from Yvette. I handed our hostess my bag of whole-wheat goodies.

Then Yvette disappeared in a whirl of green velour, only to reappear minutes later to distribute small china plates and napkins, and to direct everyone to a table where little sandwiches, sushi rolls, muffins, sliced fruit, and my own contribution of whole-wheat pastries were spread out on trays. Along with the herbal iced tea that Wayne had brought. And glasses. Yvette was fast.

And even faster, once we'd all taken our seats on plush green upholstery, balancing our respective plates, napkins, glasses, and cups on our knees. She grabbed the oak shillelagh from the umbrella stand before sitting down in a smaller version of Vince Quadrini's easy chair to call the meeting to order.

I was biting into a muffin and staring at the intricate carving on her oak cudgel when our hostess spoke.

"So we're going to get to the fuddin' bloody bottom of this thing today, okay?" she began.

Obedient nods answered her. Even the dogs nodded. The cats just looked bored.

"Anyone want to confess?" she threw out.

No one nodded this time. Except the dogs. The cats continued to look bored.

"You, Ivan," she went on, pointing her shillelagh in his direction. "You had the best opportunity . . ."

And so it went. The scene could have been a remake of the one at Fictional Pleasures, though Yvette was a wee bit more subtle with her interrogation this time. As if an edited version of the same script was being used. No "Where were you on the night of the twenty-ninth," but a lot of accusations and requests for unavailable information, while Lou looked increasingly embarrassed.

When she got to Vince Quadrini and questioned him about his "obsession with S.X. Greenfree," the pinstriped Godfather merely stood, nodded, and left.

I took Mr. Quadrini's exit as an excuse to go to the bathroom. Herbal iced tea does have a tendency to race through a body. Especially mine. And, anyway, I wanted to see Yvette's bathroom. You can tell a lot about a person from their bathroom.

Yvette's bathroom was wallpapered in shamrocks. So much for anything new.

My iced tea recycled, I washed my hands, dried them, and crumpled up the paper towel to toss it in the wastebasket. Then I saw the syringes.

TEN

꙳

I looked closer into the green wastebasket, inhaling the scent of rubbing alcohol as I did. Sure enough, there were a good half-dozen syringes deposited there, small plastic ones, but syringes all the same, lying underneath a scattering of paper towels.

I grabbed a clean paper towel and cautiously pulled one of the syringes from its nest, plunger-end first, avoiding the wicked-looking metal needle at the other end. My hands shook with the effort. And once I held my prize, I had to resist the urge to run from the bathroom to the living room, waving it in front of me.

But when I got back to the living room, walking as coolly and sedately as possible, the suspicious syringe wrapped in paper toweling in my hand, I saw that Vince Quadrini's departure had created more than an excuse for my trip to the bathroom. Half of our group seemed to have left. Zoe, Ivan, and Winona were nowhere to be seen. But Dean was still there, talking to—no—*listening* to Yvette as they stood near her oversized hanging book cover, Dean stroking his gray beard thoughtfully.

"This dam-dang case is shaping up," she announced triumphantly. "I've almost got it . . ."

Should I challenge Yvette directly with the syringe? The ever elusive Yvette. A prickle at the base of my spine turned me away from her like a divining rod. Lou? I looked around. Lou and Wayne were talking over by Mr. Spock, too softly to be overheard.

It was time for some shock treatment I decided as I walked toward the two men. I unwrapped the syringe, still holding the plunger end by the paper towel and held it up between them. Wayne looked shocked all right. He came as close to jumping back in surprise as a man with a karate blackbelt is about to. But unfortunately, Lou looked unperturbed.

"Oh, sorry," he said pleasantly. "Did I leave one of those out again? We have to give the Siamese shots and . . ."

Finally, his voice withered away. The meaning of my holding the syringe hit him.

His body tensed visibly, changing as suddenly as his feline features to an attitude of intensity, even ferocity.

"Now look here," he commanded, his tone even and cold, his brown face jutting forward. "Yvette is a completely ethical and honest woman. Those syringes have nothing to do with Shayla Greenfree's death. You can call our veterinarian if you'd like. I'll give you her phone number. She'll tell you that we have a sick cat."

"All right, fine," I conceded, chilled by Lou's abrupt change of mood and physique. Was his instant transition from pussy cat to tiger a Jekyll and Hyde phenomenon? Wayne moved closer to my side.

Lou must have noticed my nervousness. And Wayne's move.

"Listen," he sighed, softening his tone and his body as he

pulled his head back. "You have to understand my Yvette. Her imagination takes her too far sometimes. And she's not always so good with live people. Fictional characters are much easier for her to deal with." He chuckled, and I saw the affection in his big brown eyes now. "But Yvette has integrity. Too much, probably. And I can assure you, she's no murderer."

That seemed like a pretty good parting line, so Wayne and I made goodbye sounds to Lou and then turned to go.

That's when I saw Yvette, standing still and silent less than a foot behind me. A siren went off in my head. I just hoped she couldn't hear it or see the accompanying adrenaline hit my body. Damn, that woman could be quiet when she wanted to. I wondered how long she'd been listening.

I handed her the syringe carefully and thanked her for brunch before walking out the door.

We caught Dean in the front yard. He was smiling down at a green statue of a leprechaun, complete with pipe and shamrocks. There was a slight resemblance between man and statue, in the beard and the weathered face.

"You serious about talking to us today?" Wayne asked him.

"Surely," Dean replied. "Would tonight suit? I have to warn you, I don't cook—"

"We'll bring take-out," Wayne and I offered simultaneously.

"No, no," he objected graciously. "I'll provide take-out. Lord knows, I ought to be able to do that at least."

After a lot of polite to-ing and fro-ing, we agreed that we'd provide the apple juice and dessert, and Dean would provide some kind of entree.

"So," I asked eagerly once we were in the Toyota and rolling toward home. "Do you believe what Lou said about Yvette?"

"Maybe," Wayne answered, shrugging. "But notice he didn't assure us *he* wasn't a murderer."

We chewed on that one all the way home. Would Lou kill to protect Yvette? But why would he have to? And then there was his dead brother . . .

We were still talking on the way into the living room. Neither of us even registered Ingrid's presence. Or the presence of the man sitting next to her on the futon. Our futon.

"Well, howdy-hi, you guys," her companion greeted us, on his feet instantly. He was a small and slender man with a luxurious mustache and dark soulful eyes. "Holding out on me again, huh? Lucky your new roommate gave me the poop on your little ol' murder."

Roommate? Ugh. My whole body cried out for release. Because the man with our *roommate* was Felix, my friend Barbara Cha's boyfriend. And more importantly, it was Felix Byrne, pit bull reporter for the *Marin Mind* and a correspondent for the Philadelphia *Globe*. I wanted to run away. My legs were twitching with the urge. But it's hard to run when you're in your own house. Felix strode our way, shark's smile in place.

"So, you find another friggin' corpse—"

"We didn't find a—" I objected.

"No, you actually witnessed the whole tripping thing, man," he ground on inexorably, "and didn't bother to call your friend, your compadre, nooooo—"

"Time to go," Wayne interrupted Felix.

Felix's soulful eyes took on that hurt look he was so good at. He opened his mouth to argue some more. As much as he was scared of Wayne, I knew Felix would get us sooner or later. He'd wear us down as piteously as a cat torturing a mouse.

"Listen, Felix, here's the deal," I said, deepening my voice, trying to sound as scary as Wayne. "I'll fill you in on exactly what happened—"

"Briefly," Wayne put in.

"Briefly," I agreed. "And then I'll refer you to an even better source."

Felix leaned forward. "Yeah?" he shot back. "Who?"

"Yvette Cassell," I told him. "She's a famous writer; she was there; she knew the victim, and she's got a mouth the span of the Golden Gate Bridge." I waited a count of two for that information to sink in before finishing up. "And in return, you'll give us back any information you pick up from your sources."

"Holy moly," he breathed. "Yvette Cassell." Damn. Maybe Yvette really was famous. "Will this Cassell woman talk to me?"

"I'll give you her phone number and address," I replied. "And when you talk to her, tell her I sent you."

He fondled his mustache for a moment, then put out his hand.

"Deal," he agreed, slapping his palm against mine. "Now speak."

I spoke, briefly. And then Felix ran out of our house to find Yvette Cassell.

"A match made in heaven," I said to Wayne as the sound of Felix's footsteps disappeared down the gravel path.

Wayne just smiled and shook my hand.

Then I realized that Felix had never given *us* any information.

"Poison," I began, suddenly realizing we didn't really know anything about the poison that had been used to kill Shayla Greenfree. All I'd been thinking about was syringes. Access to poison was a much more interesting question. "Do you think Felix knows—"

"So are you guys really, like, part of a murder?" Ingrid asked from the futon, her voice a mixture of excitement and fear.

Wayne's smile disappeared. I thought about the fear in our houseguest's voice.

"Yeah," I told her. "And being around us could be really dangerous. Whol-ios does that to a person."

"What?" she squeaked, jumping up. "Are you making fun of me?"

"No, Ingrid," Wayne chimed in, his homely face solemn and menacing at the same time. "This could be very dangerous for you."

"But I don't have anything to do with it!" she objected. Apollo let out a little yip in agreement, hiding behind his mistress's muscular calves.

Wayne and I retreated to our bedroom for a continued discussion of the situation. Actually, to giggle together hysterically, but quietly. Not easy, but we did it. Then we decided to get some work done before our dinner with Dean. Unfortunately, Ingrid was still there when we came out. I went back to work on my stacks of Jest Gifts paper as she pelted me with questions and objections and arguments.

"So are you guys jiving me?" she demanded as I checked off order forms.

I borrowed Wayne's grunt for a reply.

"Do you really think it's dangerous?" she continued as I calculated payroll deposits for the week.

I shrugged. Another Wayne adaptation.

"Why me?" she asked piteously. "Why do these things always happen to me?"

I just shook my head and sighed. Poor thing. I just hoped it wouldn't take her long to find a new home.

After a few hours, I'd actually managed to get a fair amount of work done. Maybe I ought to tape Ingrid's voice, I decided. She certainly was a spur to work.

"Hey, Ingrid," I began.

But by this time, she'd miraculously run out of words for me, and retreated to the living room to talk to her dog. I didn't interrupt. I gathered from Apollo's yips and groans that he had more of an understanding of her unique sensibilities than I did.

And, anyway, it was time to visit Dean.

"Poisons," I mused, as Wayne drove. Tonight, he'd insisted on driving his Jaguar. I sank deeper into the decadence of real leather, reminding myself that leather was only a by-product of the meat process. It was a great anti-guilt mantra, especially when buying running shoes. Whether or not it was true. "Who would have the best access to poisons?"

"Depends what poison," Wayne threw in. "Acupuncturists use herbs."

"Vince Quadrini's wife died of cancer," I countered. "I wonder if he gave her morphine injections?"

"And Dean Frazier is an anesthesiologist," Wayne reminded me as he pulled into Dean's driveway.

Timing is everything. So they tell me.

Dean's clean, white living room bore a slight similarity to Yvette's. Because Dean was a collector, too. He collected chess sets, rocks, fish-filled aquariums, books, watercolors, and carved Buddhas. But Dean's collections were all neatly segregated and orderly under carefully arranged track lighting. Chaos was expelled from this realm. His books were alphabetized. I didn't have the nerve to ask if his rocks were too.

After a brief hand-shaking ritual, we followed him into the kitchen carrying the berry cobbler and the two bottles of Martinelli's sparkling cider we'd brought as offerings. As we entered, I saw that he collected food too. Provisions for at least twenty years or so were stored on spotless shelves spanning one wall, all the way to the ceiling. Identical glass jars of beans, dried fruit, lentils, nuts, rice, grains, and about everything else that could be dried were arranged in perfect symmetry. I wondered where the water collection was. I hoped there *was* a water collection. And I hoped Dean learned to cook before the apocalypse.

I sniffed. He certainly hadn't been cooking today. The faint smell of garlic that scented the room was as subtle as the classical music that floated gently from hidden speakers. I pulled my eyes from his apocalypse shelf and looked at his precisely set table. A familiar set of white cartons sat in the center. Only this time it wasn't Japanese take-out. It was Italian.

"Shayla's husband is a man named Scott Green," Dean told us placidly once we were finally seated and digging into pasta primavera smothered with garlic, chard, and mushrooms. "And Scott Green is my lover."

I choked on my pasta, surprised more by Dean's directness, if not his information. I tried to choke unobtrusively and took a swig of Martinelli's to wash it down. Luckily, Dean hadn't noticed my reaction. His eyes were fixed on the shelves of glass jars behind us.

"But Shayla was my friend too," he went on as I began breathing again, in and out of my nose as noiselessly as I could, trying not to break his flow of words. "My best friend, next to Scott. Lord, it must be at least fifteen years I've known them. The three of us had a friendship not many people might understand, I expect. But it suited us."

A magic circle, I thought, remembering Zoe's words.

"But why did it suit Shayla?" Wayne asked quietly. There was a real need for understanding on his face. Though I wasn't sure that Dean saw it. I don't think he was really seeing either of us.

"Ah, Shayla," Dean sighed. His eyes moistened. He pulled on the chain around his neck, freeing the jade stone from beneath his shirt, then laid his palm on its smooth surface ever so gently. Had Shayla given him the green stone? "Shayla was a complicated woman. She was originally a professor of anthropology, you know, not that she used the name Shayla then. But she wanted to write. With a vengeance. And she did. But it wasn't until the Beth Questra series that her career really took off."

Dean lowered his shaggy head to actually look at us.

"Scott supported Shayla in her writing," he told us. "Cheered her on, kept on telling her she'd do it eventually. And she did. They were a real love match—"

"Really?" I asked, not knowing I'd spoken till the word left my mouth. I wanted to understand as much as Wayne did.

Dean peered into my face.

"Really," he assured me. "You have to think on it awhile to comprehend, I expect." His eyes wandered upwards again. "Everyone assumes love has to mean sex. But there are all kinds of love. And their love was true. As unshakable as . . . as the earth. How can I explain?"

I wasn't sure if we were supposed to answer his question in the ensuing silence. After a few peaceful bars of Vivaldi, I was about to prompt him. But he spoke first.

"Let me tell you a story," he said, slipping the jade amulet back beneath his shirt and stroking his gray beard instead. "Some years back, Shayla had an affair with a man she met at an anthropology conference."

He took a big breath.

"Oh, yes, Shayla had her affairs," Dean apprised me as if I'd asked. Or maybe he was reminding himself. "But her affairs were never serious. Because she loved Scott. With her heart, you see. She knew Scott was gay when she married him, right out of college. The truth be told, that was a big reason *why* she married him. She wanted a life other than that of a typical wife and mother. And in those years, it just wasn't done, you see. But she hoped it might be possible with Scott."

Now I began to understand. Shayla had to have been older than I was. A good ten years older, probably. Was she in college before Betty Friedan had even published *The Feminine Mystique*?

"So they both had affairs," Dean went on. "But Scott's were more enduring." He smiled. "I guess fifteen years

counts as enduring. But Shayla kept hers brief. Then she met
this man at the anthropology conference. And I do believe
she fell in love with him. She came to me. She couldn't tell
Scott, you see. Because the man wanted her to divorce Scott,
to marry him. She came to me and said she loved Scott
more. I didn't know what to tell her. Lord, I've wondered if
I should have said something, anything. But finally, she just
stood up and announced she loved Scott too dearly to
change. She never saw the man from the conference again.
Dear God, she could be a wonderful woman."

If loyalty was love, he was beginning to convince me that
Shayla had loved Scott dearly indeed.

"Romantic love," Wayne murmured.

Dean smiled. It looked good on his weathered face.

"It was romantic," Dean replied, his voice a little louder
now. "And real. Scott and I met doing hospice work. He was
volunteering . . ."

As Dean spoke about his relationship with Scott, I
thought about hospices. Syringes for two? And talk about
your poisons.

". . . I don't believe Scott really accepts his gayness entirely, even to this day," Dean was saying.

Would the two men become more of a couple now? Now
that Shayla was gone? I peered at Dean suspiciously. And
saw the loss in his reddened eyes. On the other hand, maybe
the magic would be gone in Shayla's absence. Maybe three
were necessary to the relationship. I hoped not for Dean's
sake. I reached out a hand to pat his. But Wayne spoke before our hands touched.

"Possible to talk to Scott?" Wayne asked.

"Bet it would be," Dean answered, rising from the table
and leaving the kitchen in an instant.

Wayne and I looked at each other, confused by his sudden
departure. Where had Dean gone? Did he have Scott stashed
somewhere? Or maybe a weapon? I took a bite of garlic bread.

It was too good to waste. And another bite of pasta. A few bites later, Dean returned with a portable phone in his hand.

"Scott," he whispered, pointing at the phone.

"Huh?" I said.

But Wayne was quicker. Within seconds he had the phone, and within minutes he'd arranged a lunch date with Scott for the next day. At the house where he and Shayla had lived together. Damn.

In the Jaguar heading home, though, Wayne didn't seem triumphant. His brows were pulled over his eyes like shields as he steered silently.

"More take-out for tomorrow?" I asked him lightly.

"They loved each other, Kate," he growled. "A true marriage."

My heart fell to my shoes. And it hurt down there. Wayne's need to marry was so intense, it had to hurt. I'd stopped trying to argue its logic long ago, only acknowledged the need. But I still hadn't filled it. Stopped by my own illogical resistance. I shook my head. Scott and Shayla had possessed love and marriage, but not sex. Wayne and I had love and sex, but not marriage.

"Ours will be a true marriage, too," I told him.

"Really?" he asked softly, like a child listening to a well-worn story but still hoping the make-believe was true.

"With sex and everything," I added.

He laughed and pushed down on the pedal of the Jaguar.

"In fact . . ." I whispered tantalizingly.

We were home in minutes. And holding each other as we walked up our front stairs. He was such a solid man, it was like holding a rock.

It was a good thing we were holding each other so tightly or the body hurtling down the redwood stairs would have knocked both of us over, solid or not.

€LEVEN

⚼

The hurtling body fell backwards against the stairs, arms
flailing frantically, as backside met redwood.

"Ow-ooh!" he howled. "Goddamn, splinters too. This
house is a goddamn minefield!"

The man on the stairs was Raoul Raymond, our tango
teacher, but he wasn't slithering gracefully tonight. And he
seemed to have lost his accent too. And gained something in
return.

"Raoul," I informed him, backing down a stair, in step
with Wayne. "You smell terrible."

And he did. His pungent scent was nauseatingly familiar,
but strong. Really strong.

"No shit!" he shouted again. "Lady, you've got skunks!
How do you stand it? The little creep sprayed me. Me—"

"What are you doing here?" Wayne interrupted.

Wayne and I moved back down another step in unison as
we waited for Raoul's answer. I pulled my shirt over my

face. I wondered how the tango class was going to take to Raoul's new fragrance.

"Visiting," he muttered, averting his face from mine as he rose from the stairs. "Ingrid."

"Oh, good," I told him through my shirt. "Maybe she could stay with you."

"The skunk?" Raoul demanded, affronted. And clearly still addled by his encounter.

"No, Ingrid," I explained.

"Oh." Raoul seemed to gain back some composure. He brushed himself off, as if he could brush off the smell. But he still stank.

"Of course, if the lovely Ms. Regnary could be convinced," he offered, his accent back in place.

"You can always try," I said encouragingly.

"Thank you, Ms. Jasper," he replied. "You are truly a lady of much graciousness."

And then he sidled by us. We gave him plenty of space.

We gave Ingrid plenty of space too as we walked past the living room. Unfortunately, no skunk had sprayed her. Apparently the incident had occurred outdoors.

"Is Raoul okay?" she whispered.

"He's great," I told her. "And he might be rich."

"Rich?" she said, interest perking her voice.

"And he'll only smell for a little while," I added.

I was glad she didn't ask me how long "a little while" might be, because frankly, I didn't know.

The next morning was Monday. And I was on the phone. To Jest Gifts. To the temporarily (I hoped) artistically impaired manufacturers of my shark cups. To the temporarily (I hoped) number-challenged bank I did business with. To our box suppliers. To my accountant. To an unhappy customer. Back to Jest Gifts. And finally, to an individual they called "the skunk broker."

The skunk broker had been a stockbroker until he had undergone an "absolutely inspired lifestyle transformation" some years back and begun working with animals instead of money at the local animal shelter. And helping people get rid of unwanted fauna in the evenings. I wondered if his lifestyle change had been inspired by the stock market crash. In any case, his earlier offer to trap our skunks and release them in the wild for fifty dollars was beginning to sound good to me now. I just wished he could find a box for Ingrid, Bob Xavier, Raoul Raymond, and whoever had killed Shayla Greenfree.

Finally, it was time to drive to Scott Green's. Green, Greenfree. As I pulled out of the driveway, I wondered when Shayla had changed her name. But that question could wait. I started to tell Wayne about my talk with the skunk broker as I pulled out onto Shoreline.

"What evidence do we have that he actually releases them in the wild?" Wayne asked reasonably once I had finished my report.

"Evidence?" I said, as quick on the uptake as usual.

"How do we know he doesn't just take them a block over and release them under someone else's house?" Wayne pressed.

Damn. It would make good business sense. Multiply fifty dollars a head times a few skunks every few days. And then there were the skunks multiplying themselves. Not bad for a moonlighting job. Skunk recycling for fun and profit.

By the time I was driving my Toyota over the Golden Gate Bridge toward Scott Green's house in San Francisco, I was too entranced by the view to care about skunks anymore. The air was crisp and coolly clear. We could see the suspension cables of the Bay Bridge, the green of the Presidio, even the pointy Transamerica pyramid building, shimmering in the distance. Not to mention the tourists right up close, hiking in short-shorts over the bridge. You can always tell the tourists. They're color-coded blue from the unexpected chill of sunny California. Especially on the windy bridge. And it is windy. As if in proof, a gust unceremoniously ripped a sun hat off a tall woman and dumped it into the churning waters some two or three hundred feet below. I imagined a piscine bookkeeper adding another digit to the score somewhere beneath the burbling blue water.

Scott lived in the Noe Valley district of San Francisco. Even on a Monday, the residential district was bustling with people: Birkenstock-shod mothers (and fathers) pushing baby strollers, couples of all mixes walking hand in hand, dogs dragging their owners, and a few folks who knew it was Monday, dressed for success with their trademark furrows between their brows as they strode purposefully toward something seen only by them.

After the requisite ten minutes spent cursing while looking for a parking space, we finally beat out a four-by-four and screeched up next to the curb, then hiked some six or seven blocks to Scott's house. Shayla's too, I reminded myself as we opened the gate and walked up the short path to the unprepossessing gray-blue two-story wooden structure before us. Or maybe not so unprepossessing, I thought, as I noticed the immaculate white trim, the intricately carved woodwork, the brightly flowering window boxes, curved stairway, and oval windows.

"Wow, this is really—" I began.

The front door swung open and a familiar small woman popped out, turning at the doorstep to say goodbye.

"Well, thank you for the interview, Mr. Green," she said. "The *Architectural Review* will be sure to want the fu—article."

"Well, thank you for your interest, Miss Poirot," a deep and soothing voice replied from the house. "It was a pleasure."

And then Yvette turned and saw us.

Her head jerked back for one satisfying moment. But only one moment. Then she grinned.

"Just call me fuddin' Hercule P.," she whispered with a wink and pushed past us, a blur in green.

"All right, Fuddin' Head," I whispered after her.

She swiveled that head around to glare, mid-escape, but then her glare became a pleasant smile. I cut my laugh down to a snort and turned my own head back to the doorway. Our host was peering out at us.

Scott Green looked like a white lab rat equipped with aviator glasses. He was a tall, slender man with silky, white blond hair and close-set eyes under his glasses. His nose was long and sharp. I waited for it to twitch, fascinated.

"GRAAARFFF!" exploded from his side. In stereo.

"Down, Baroque," he admonished, looking at the two panting grenades I'd never even noticed. "Down, Rococo."

And then the furry monsters with the saliva-dripping teeth turned back into friendly-looking collies. I wish my heart could have reverted back to normal as quickly. The successor to rap music was playing a tune on my aorta that would never be replicated.

"Wayne Caruso, Kate Jasper," Wayne put in from my side, sticking out his hand.

I pasted a smile on quickly. I wondered if I had any color left in my face at all.

"Cute . . . puppies," I squeaked.

Scott Green laughed. It was an amazingly deep laugh, coming from that slender body.

"That's the nicest description anyone's given these two hellhounds after that bark," he told me. "But let me thank you on their behalf."

"Uh, Mr. Green," I said after a minute, feeling I owed the man something. "Do you believe that the woman who just left really interviewed you for a magazine?"

He laughed again. "No, that's Yvette Cassell. I just wanted to see what she was up to."

But then the light went out of his eyes and his whole face locked in anger.

"I want to know who killed Shayla," he growled. "She was a beautiful spirit, a marvelous woman. She didn't deserve to die. And once I find out who killed her, I'll kill them myself. Do you understand?"

I nodded quickly, suddenly cold. This man didn't look like a lab rat anymore. And I promised myself that if we ever figured out who killed Shayla, I wouldn't let Scott know before I told the police. Because this man was serious. I saw it in his posture and heard it in the pitch of his voice. I could even smell the intention emanating angrily from his body. He was wounded and ready to fight back. No more lab rat. Now he looked like a hunting dog. With teeth.

"I wanted to talk to you because I know you're looking into Shayla's death," he went on. "Dean keeps me informed. And the police are useless." His hands bunched into fists. "The captain acts more like he's running for office than investigating.

"I want . . . I want . . ." Tears appeared in his eyes. He shook them away.

"Sorry," he said after an obvious effort to bring himself under control. I would have liked to put my arms around him, to comfort him. But I had a feeling nothing was really going to comfort him, not for a long while anyway.

"Come on in," he finally offered brusquely.

And we followed him into his house. The first thing I saw as we entered was a pair of Zoe's hangings. They seemed to mark the entrance to an enchanted kingdom, rich with swirling colors in dye and stitch that hinted at a hidden castle in the clouds. Or maybe that was just what I saw in the swirls.

"Zoe Ingersoll?" I breathed.

"Yes, these are Zoe's," he answered, his deep voice softening. "God, she's a genius."

Zoe wasn't the only genius represented here, I decided as Scott led us into a room with sunlight pouring through skylights and oval windows to shine in exactly the right places, theatrically illuminating curved ceilings and four floor-to-ceiling spiral columns. The furnishings were spare: a wooden armoire, bookcases, one painting. And a mantelpiece with seven handblown glass cylinders of varying but complementary shapes and colors holding seven yellow candles, all lit. A photograph of Shayla stood in the center of the candles.

"Did you design this house?" I asked.

"Oh, yeah," Scott answered, tilting his head away as if embarrassed. "I'm no Frank Lloyd Wright, though—"

"But," I objected, "it's beautiful, magical."

"No," he insisted. "Shayla was the genius in the family. I built this house for her. I'm just a mediocre architect, lucky enough to have family money behind me."

"But—" I began again.

Wayne gave me an unsubtle nudge. And I stopped arguing. This was not the time to dispute Scott's genius relative to his late wife's.

The dining room we ended up in was simple. A wooden table with triangularly shaped legs and six linen-shrouded seats. And a sideboard in a recessed window. A feast was laid out on the sideboard, no take-out in sight. It smelled wonderful. Of onion and lemon and ginger. And chocolate.

"Eat," he ordered, pointing. "I have no one left to cook for now."

"Except Dean," I reminded him gently.

His face relaxed then, enough to see the charm again, the humor. The gentleness beneath the anger. His whole body seemed to lighten.

"Except Dean," he repeated in a whisper. "Dean understood my love for Shayla, even shared it. He understands and shares my grief too. She was a glorious woman. And Dean knew it. I'd go crazy without him."

I stood still for a moment, unable to move.

"Eat," Scott repeated finally. He extended his arms as if to embrace the universe. "Eat!"

The dogs, who'd stayed silent by his side up till now, exploded in a new fit of barking.

"Not you, you little fools," he told them, patting each on the flank with affection. The dogs looked up at us as if to ask why we weren't taking Scott up on his offer. So we did.

The food on the sideboard looked good. And vegetarian. Dean must have kept Scott very well informed. Even Wayne looked impressed as we picked up our plates. Crusty bread, four kinds of vegetable pâté, avocado soup, gingered eggplant salad, and a glass tray of rum and chocolate fruitcakes. Along with teas and juices.

"Did you do this all yourself?" I asked in wonder.

He answered with a shrug reminiscent of Wayne's. I just hoped the food was as good as Wayne's too.

I filled my china plate and bowl and sat down at the formally set dining table to eat.

I slurped a spoonful of the avocado soup. Ah, that was where the scent of lemon had come from. The avocado and lemon were in perfect balance. And the gingered eggplant was sweet and sour and spicy, the pâtés all herbed but with distinct flavors and perfect on the crusty bread. I had succumbed to the pleasures of the palate and almost forgotten why we were here when Scott interrupted my feasting.

"Dean said he told you a little," he commented, laying down his fork. His voice deepened. "But maybe not the whole story. I want you to understand Shayla. You see, from the beginning, Shayla's parents tried to stomp on her dreams. But it just made her more determined. She was like that. Nothing stopped her. She wanted to be more than a housewife. And by God, she was. So much more." Tears came to his eyes again.

"Are her parents still alive?" Wayne asked quickly.

"No," he answered. "They both passed away within months of each other some ten years ago. Shayla was an only child."

Scott pushed his plate away and took a sip of tea.

"We met in college," he told us, his voice softening in recollection, "We talked and talked, and stayed up talking some more. We played with ideas, with words, with puns. Then I waited for the inevitable, for her to ask why I wasn't interested in her sexually. I'd tried with various women but it just didn't work. I couldn't stop thinking of men in a time when that just wasn't allowed. But Shayla was one in a million. She said, 'You're not interested in women sexually. That's okay.' And suddenly, it was okay.

"I think that's when I fell in love with her. She said the unsayable aloud, and really didn't mind. We were best friends for three years. She had a couple of love affairs, one with a professor, but I was her friend. Her best friend. She was the one who proposed marriage. I reminded her that I was not interested in women beyond a certain point. I couldn't even say 'homosexual' then. I can barely say it now. But she just said, 'Exactly. And I don't want to be a housewife.'

"We made a deal then, a marriage of convenience, but of real affection. She could pursue her ambitions, and I could stop being afraid that someone would notice I wasn't sexually normal. Shirl—Shayla came to terms with my sexuality far more easily than I ever could. She was the one who allowed me to accept myself." Tears began in his eyes and poured down his cheeks. He went on without seeming to even notice.

"I loved her. She loved me. Shayla was an absolutely glorious woman. We were husband and wife, maybe not traditionally, but lovers in the sense of truly loving. And God, the love of the mind. We could talk for hours. Her thoughts darted everywhere. She could talk on any subject. And with an enthusiasm that was unstoppable."

Rococo sighed and Scott leaned over to stroke the animal. He'd wiped the tears from his face by the time he resurfaced.

"Be sure to try the rum and chocolate fruitcakes," he ordered briskly. "Shayla loved them."

Then he rose and placed one of each on two small plates and delivered them to the table.

Neither Wayne nor I said a word, hoping Scott would continue once we were eating again. I bit into the chocolate cake. The flavor of a basketful of fruits and spices and chocolate filled my mouth. And Scott went on talking. It was hard to enjoy the extraordinary flavors while listening to Scott's pain. But Shayla had loved these fruitcakes. So I ate them, for her.

"Shayla had affairs," Scott announced, a challenge in his voice. Neither of us responded. He sighed and Rococo echoed his sigh. "She had to, really. We even talked about them. They were each of short duration. And she was so busy with her writing and publicity the last few years, I don't think she even had the time. Or the energy."

I thought of the man she had met at the anthropology convention. Had she ever told Scott? I shook off the thought and took another bite.

"There was a time when Shayla collected friends like baseball cards. Everyone was interesting to her. But she couldn't keep up with everyone she knew. In the last few years, she'd become far more reclusive. There were so many people interested in her as a famous author rather than as a person. She would start up friendships, then drop them."

He shook his head. "She loved meeting new people, but tired fast. I was her friend, her best friend." His eyes moistened again. "Our love was true."

"What about Zoe?" Wayne asked.

Scott's light skin pinkened. Was he embarrassed by his wondrous wife's insensitive behavior?

"Zoe was her friend, but I think that was ending." He gave his head a quick shake as if ridding it of some thought. I would have liked to know what thought. "And of course Dean was her friend, and Sadie, the elderly woman next door."

He stopped and sipped his tea again. His eyes were troubled. And his voice was distant as he went on.

"And of course, Shayla had a sort of friendship with her agent and editor." He frowned. "But all the public friendships, those associations, wore her down. There were so many. Writers' clubs, women's groups, fan clubs. That man, Quadrini, hosted a fan club for her every month. She attended on sufferance."

I wondered if my reaction was reflected in my face. Shayla sounded unappreciative at the least, cold and aloof. Was this the glorious woman he loved?

"She wasn't always kind to a fault, my Shayla," Scott admitted quietly. "But it was hard for her, you see. Every step of the way. She began as a feminist before there were feminists. She did what was necessary to have the kind of intellectual life she thrived on. She was fascinated by ideas, by power. Certainly, some people saw her as ruthless. But for a woman in academia, ruthlessness was necessary. It was her only way in. And people were hard for her up close. She was a good observer, but detachment was really her strong suit." He smiled softly. "When she was in love with an idea, though, a project, her whole being lit up."

"How'd she start the Beth Questra series?" Wayne asked.

"She was always writing, but never quite making it. Then she discovered the perfect vehicle, an alien with psychic abilities, a superwoman in a way. With dignity and power."

"Did she . . . get the idea from Ted Brown?" I asked. I almost said "steal," but caught myself at the last instant.

Scott looked down at his tea, frowning again. This wasn't as easy as explaining his true love. I wanted to tell him it was all right to love someone with imperfections. But I was here to prompt and listen. Not to lecture.

"Not consciously," he answered finally. "But unconsciously . . ." He shrugged again. "I remember her reading Ted Brown's book and being excited—she loved the alien idea—but just remember, Brown wasn't the first either. There were Adams and Smith before him. And you see, she knew she could write it better. Better than any of them. And she did.

"And it wasn't just the writing. She groomed herself, changed her whole appearance. She went at publicity with a military sense of strategy. She even took diction training. And she made it."

Scott stopped speaking for a while and we finished our fruitcakes, savoring the flavors, Shayla's favorite flavors.

"Will there be a funeral?" Wayne finally asked, gently, softly.

Scott shook his head.

"Shayla was adamant on that," he told us. "No more publicity after she was dead." Scott smiled, his eyes defocusing. "Shayla hated the publicity after a while. She did it because she had to. Shayla once said that Salman Rushdie was lucky on one point. At least he didn't have to do any more publicity events."

He laughed, but there were tears in his eyes.

When Scott's smile dimmed and Rococo began to whine, we rose to leave.

"Find the killer," Scott told us at the door. And then he and his dogs were gone.

I took one last look back at the lovely house Scott had

built for his wife, the woman he loved, and tears sprang up in my own eyes. For Scott. Not for Shayla.

"Psst!" a voice said at my shoulder.

I turned, expecting to see Yvette, but the woman at my side had to be twice her age, wrinkled, with bright raisin-black eyes and sparse white curls brushed over her pink scalp. She leaned on an aluminum walker.

"Please find out who killed her," the old woman whispered. "It pains Scott so."

And then the woman turned and hobbled away on her walker just as abruptly as she had appeared.

"Sadie?" I shouted out.

She turned.

"We'll try," I told her.

She smiled and then made her way back onto the sidewalk and into her own house next door.

Wayne and I made our own way to the sidewalk carefully and cautiously. I wondered if he felt as fragile as I did. As fragile as Sadie. As fragile as Scott.

At the gate, we looked at each other and shared a quick, tight embrace.

As we broke apart, I saw Scott's next visitor coming up the sidewalk. It was Felix Byrne, our own pit bull of a reporter.

I shook my head. It was useless to try to head him off.

But it wasn't until we stepped onto the sidewalk ourselves that I saw Yvette Cassell, crouched behind a bush, ready to spring.

TWELVE

As I watched Yvette skulking in the bushes, I wondered if Felix had contacted her yet. I didn't have long to wonder. Felix was only a yard away from us now.

"Hey, Felix!" I greeted him with a shout.

Only a blink showed his surprise at seeing us. I'd hoped for more. I was tempted to slap him on the back. Years of tai chi practice had given me a backslapping technique that could be extremely dangerous for the slappee, and extremely satisfying for the slapper. I reminded myself of the principles of tai chi. Ethics can sure ruin a lot of fun.

"Yvette Cassell," I told him instead. "She's—"

"Hey, were you just putting me on about that friggin' woman?" he demanded. "She's as hard to find as the Bill of Rights at a political convention, man. I've searched everywhere in the known universe and—"

"She's right over there," I whispered, pointing behind the bush.

"That gremlin's her?" he breathed. "Holy socks! Why's she hiding behind the friggin' foliage?"

"You're a reporter," I told him. "Why don't you find out?"

He looked at Yvette. Then he looked toward Scott Green's door. He pulled on his mustache, meditating. I could imagine his dilemma. Who to harry first? So many victims, so little time.

"Bye, Felix," I said. And Wayne and I took off down the street. It's painful to watch a pit bull in a state of ambivalence.

"Fu-fuddin' right . . ." rang down the street after us a few moments later.

Then, ". . . but that's friggin' insane," in a deeper tone. Felix had picked Yvette. I was right. They were a match made in heaven. Well, maybe not *heaven,* actually.

When Wayne and I got home, there was a strange beige Honda parked in our driveway. And a man sitting in the car.

I pulled my Toyota past the Honda carefully. There was just enough room in the gravel driveway to park two cars side by side. And if I was lucky, this time I wouldn't knock down the little path-light I'd spent almost two hours setting back up the last time I'd knocked it over. When I got close enough, I saw that the man in the car was Dean Frazier.

Dean got out of his car slowly, his face looking strained as well as weathered beneath his gray beard.

"Was Scott okay?" he asked urgently but quietly, once we'd exited our own car.

"Why don't you come in?" I countered. How could I answer a question like that? Of course Scott wasn't "okay."

"No, no," Dean insisted, holding up his hands. "Don't want to be a nuisance. Matter of fact, I was just now wondering if I should bother you folks at all—"

"Fine." Wayne cut his apology short. "No problem."

I was grateful for Wayne's brusque delivery. At this rate

we were going to spend a lot of time in the driveway talking to a man too polite to come into our house, while pinned uncomfortably between two very closely parked cars.

"I was just concerned about Scott," Dean told us in a whisper. "He's been so . . ."

"Angry," I filled in helpfully. Anything to speed things up.

"Yes," Dean agreed, nodding emphatically. "Angry. Scott's usually an incredibly gentle human being. Lord, he treats those dogs of his like they're children, but now he . . . he almost frightens me."

I nodded. And a dozen questions I should have asked myself earlier filled my mind. Like, why wasn't Dean talking to Scott directly? Had Shayla been their verbal link in emotional times? Or—

"I cared for Shayla too, but not like Scott did," Dean went on. "I'm afraid for him . . ."

As a matter of fact, I thought, I had some questions about Scott too. Why hadn't he told us less and asked us more? If he really wanted to find out who murdered his wife and kill the perpetrator himself, then why hadn't he interrogated us? Dean must have told him that Shayla had called out my name.

"What was it that was so inherently lovable about Shayla?" Wayne asked Dean, and I came back to earth, or to gravel, anyway. It felt warm here between the two cars, too warm. Too intimate.

Dean pulled his head back as if surprised by the question.

"Why, Shayla, she was . . ." He paused to think for a moment. "She was witty and full of ideas. They came rolling out of her so fast, you had to run to keep up with her. I'm a little slower. And she loved Scott so."

"Weren't you ever jealous?" I asked, tired of the endless recital of Shayla's virtues by these two men.

"I expect so, if I'm honest with myself," he murmured. "I always knew Scott loved her more than he loved me. But then, I cared a great deal for her too, so it worked out pretty well, all things considered. It was like a triangle, the bonds went all ways."

I was searching my mind for a segue into the question of access to poisons and syringes at the hospice where Dean and Scott had met. But Dean wasn't finished talking yet.

"I just worry, though, that . . . that . . ." Dean paused, then took a great breath in, and let out something close to a shout, as much as a man like Dean Frazier could shout. "I do believe Scott suspects me!"

"You?"

Of course, I realized. It would be awful if Scott did suspect Dean. But it wouldn't necessarily be illogical. Still, I was surprised that Dean would voice his concern aloud.

"I've offered to stay with Scott, but he won't have it. He talks to me on the phone, but he won't accept my comfort. It's as if he's alone. Good God, I'm grieving too. And he doesn't seem to comprehend that. I just—"

Dean stopped mid-sentence. From between the two cars I could hear a crow cawing and kids shouting as they skateboarded past.

"I must apologize," he told us, staring at the gravel. "I don't know why I'm burdening you with this. I didn't kill Shayla, you know. I expect it looks bad, me being an anesthesiologist and all, but I most certainly did not kill her."

And damn if I didn't believe him.

"You know, Scott still cares for you," I told him gently. "He's just hurt."

"I expect it's possible," Dean replied, unconvinced. "I'll just have to think on it."

"He smiled when I said your name," I added.

"Really?" he whispered, face coming up.

"He said he'd go crazy if it weren't for you." I piled it on. I was pretty sure that Scott had said something like that.

"Oh, thank you," Dean breathed, his weathered face

beaming. He grabbed my hand in his and held it for a moment. "I'll go straight to Scott's. He might be needing me terribly."

Wayne and I got out of the way as Dean pulled his Honda from our driveway.

Once he was gone, I turned to Wayne.

"Did I just cheer up a murderer?" I asked.

But before Wayne could answer my question, another car drove up. At least this one parked on the street.

An elegant, brown-skinned woman in a mauve suit climbed out. It was my friend Ann Rivera.

"Hey, you guys," she greeted us and grinned.

That toothy grin always looked so funny on her ever-so-professional face that I couldn't help smiling back.

She walked up the driveway and gave us both hugs.

"Barbara told me I oughta check in with you two," she said once she was finished. The hug felt good. That was one Marin ritual I endorsed. At least from a real friend.

"Barbara?" I said, suddenly surprised that my psychic friend, Barbara Chu, hadn't checked in with me herself by now.

"Yeah," Ann replied. "About the murder you're involved in. Sometimes I wonder, Kate, what it is that gets you into these . . ." She stared at me for a moment before shaking her head and going on. "Anyway, she thought I might be able to help you with at least one of the smaller mysteries."

"But how does Barbara know—"

I stopped myself mid-question. My friend Barbara was psychic, or at least sporadically psychic. Or something. She always knew everything, everything except little things like the identities of murderers. But still, I needed to talk to her soon.

"What smaller mystery?" I asked instead as we walked up the stairs.

"Wayne, you gonna cook me an early dinner?" Ann asked, turning to my sweetie. She hadn't become a hospital administrator on her dressed-for-success looks alone. She was one smart woman.

"Sure," he began. "At your—"

Then we both remembered Ingrid.

"Wait a sec," I ordered and ran up the front stairs, opened the door, and peeked in the living room.

The living room was empty, though Ingrid's luggage was still present. I took in a happy breath and gave Wayne a thumbs-up signal.

"Be glad to cook you dinner, anytime," he told Ann. He even treated her to a graceful waiter's bow.

"What smaller mystery?" I repeated as we all walked into the house and settled down in the kitchen, Ann and I at the table, Wayne bustling around from refrigerator to counter to stove. Damn, it felt good to have our house back, for however short a respite. The sun was filtering in through the window over the sink; the neighborhood sounds drifted in too, sans Ingrid's voice, and my ancient kitchen chair felt warm and comfortable—

"Remember the professional-women's success seminar we went to about ten years ago?" Ann asked as a bunch of scallions flew by in Wayne's hands, followed by some fresh basil. I knew it would be a good dinner. Wayne had to be as starved to cook as to eat after all the Whol-ios we'd shared with Ingrid. He lived to cook. And Scott's excellent meal had probably just whetted his appetite.

I brought my mind back to Ann and away from salivary meal-anticipation. Though it was hard to ignore the fragrance of sizzling garlic and ginger that floated enticingly from the stove.

"You mean that seminar in the city, where we all learned techniques to make ourselves Rich and Powerful?" I asked. I tried not to sneer. Ann might be close to rich and powerful, but I was still in gag-gifts and dressed for recess.

"Yeah," Ann prompted, grinning again. "And remember who was in it?"

Wayne was chopping eggplant now. How had he hidden fresh eggplant from Ingrid? And from me?

I yanked my mind back once more. Who had been in the seminar? I was having a hard time remembering. It'd been so long ago.

"You," I said. It was a start. "Me . . ."

"And Shirley Green," Ann finished for me just as Wayne produced mushrooms and onions. And marinated seitan. Did the refrigerator have a secret compartment I didn't know about?

Suddenly, the name clicked.

"Shirley Green!" I shouted, food forgotten. I stood up from my chair. "S.X. Greenfree, Shayla Greenfree, Shirley Green. Dean told me she'd changed her name, but . . ."

"But what?" Ann asked.

"But S.X. Greenfree was majestic, sleek—"

"A swan, not a duckling," Ann suggested.

That was it, all right. Shirley Green had been tall and slender, it was true. But she had worn heavy glasses, had a frizzy perm, and her shoulders slumped. When had she transformed herself? When had she straightened those shoulders and switched to contact lenses? When had she switched to a better hairdresser, for that matter? My mind's eye held a photo of the old Shirley over a photo of the new Shayla and sure enough, they matched. If you put on enough makeup.

"How'd you make the connection?" I asked Ann in awe.

"She was in my primary group, remember?" Ann answered. I nodded, though actually, I could barely remember the seminar at all. "She was calling herself Shirley Green then, but she told me her pen name was S.X. Greenfree and she was thinking of changing Shirley to Shayla, so I knew who she was when her first book came out."

"Wow," I murmured. "What a relief. Now I know why—"

But I stopped myself. So I had known Shirley Green ten years ago. So what?

"But why did she call out my name?" I demanded, still not satisfied.

"I've got that figured out too," Ann told me, grinning even more widely. "Remember the name-recognition exercises?"

It was coming back, in nauseating detail. A weekend designed to produce successful women on the move up the career path. Lots of rah-rah and endless exercises.

"Georgette Junge," I answered automatically. She'd been the one whose name I'd been assigned to memorize. "I remembered her by thinking of Georgette of the Jungle, since she was so athletic."

"Maybe you were hers," Ann suggested. "Maybe you were Shirley's."

"You're right," I breathed. I hit my fist on the table. That hurt. I told myself not to do that again. And it wouldn't take a memory trick to remind me. The pain radiating from the side of my hand was enough. "It was Shirley Green. Now I've got it. She memorized my name by thinking of 'communi-Kate,' 'cause I talked so much—"

I heard Wayne snort down a laugh behind me.

"See, Wayne," Ann put in quickly, before I could even think of objecting to his snort, much less retaliating. "The idea was that if you used the proper mnemonics, you could remember your assigned person's name for the rest of your life."

"So Shayla did," Wayne commented somberly. "She did, with her dying breath."

That was good for a few minutes silence. But not too many minutes.

Pretty soon, Wayne and Ann were busy convincing me to wait to tell Captain Xavier why S.X. Greenfree had called out my name until he asked me again. The game plan was nonchalance, backed up by Ann's testimony.

It was a good plan. I had a second appetite, a real appetite finally, no matter how recent lunch had been, when Wayne's meal came sizzling onto our plates, vegetables and seitan full of ginger and lemon grass and chilies over soba noodles.

I let the flavors linger on my taste buds as I interrogated Ann about poisons and syringes. She didn't know much personally, but she gave me the name of an emergency room nurse who might know more. And suggested I call the poison-control center. I was just hugging her again and telling her what a good friend she was when the phone rang.

I looked at my watch. It was getting close to six, time for my tai chi class. And time for Wayne to head into the city to oversee his neglected restaurant.

Wayne gave me a quick shrug and tilted his head as if asking for permission to leave.

I nodded and took the phone call as Ann and Wayne walked out the door together.

Vince Quadrini was on the other end of the line. He had some information to share, he told me, his formal, elderly voice steady now. He asked that we come by his place of work the next day. I agreed, exchanged some polite words about looking forward to our meeting, and hung up.

Then I grabbed my purse and ran out the door to make my tai chi class. Smack into Yvette Cassell.

The impact was enough to stop me in my tracks, but it sent Yvette sprawling onto the redwood deck.

"Fu-figgin' way to go—" she began, angrily.

"What were you doing here, anyway?" I shot back.

"Well, Holy moly and howdy-hi," came a new voice into the medley. A bass to our sopranos. Felix rubbed his hands together happily as he came up the stairs. "Finally, I've got you two gonzo brains together. Now we can friggin' talk."

Yvette didn't utter a word for once. She just picked herself up off the deck and ran.

I just wished I could have run with her.

THIRTEEN

✦

Uh-oh, Felix and Yvette weren't a match made in heaven. Or even in hell, it would seem. I wondered briefly what he'd done to her. Whatever it was, I could understand Yvette's desire to run. Felix had that effect on a lot of people he interrogated, including myself. But right then, I wanted the information Felix had never given me at our last meeting. A deal is a deal.

So I gave up on my tai chi class and invited Felix in, telling myself the verbal sparring with Felix that was sure to ensue might be considered a form of tai chi. Mental tai chi. But then my mind bounced back to Felix's sweetie, my friend Barbara Chu.

"How come Barbara hasn't called me yet?" I demanded.

"Barbara?" he repeated, stepping back on the deck. Apparently, this wasn't a question he'd expected. "Her cousin's in the hospital, man," he answered sadly, suddenly looking less like a pit bull and more like a human being. "Dude's really sick. Cancer. He's been in and out of consciousness like a friggin' light bulb since last week. And they've got him baked on some pretty potent chemicals, so he's not even logged on when he's logged on, if you know what I mean."

I did know what he meant.

"I'm sorry," I said softly.

"No biggie for me," Felix murmured, but just the lowering of his voice was enough to tell me it was. Felix was human. And upset. "Jeez, the guy's barely old enough to vote, you know." He sighed, not his melodramatic sigh manufactured for manipulation, but a real one. He probably didn't even know he'd let it out. "So Barbara's been going to the hospital whenever she's not working. She's reading to him from Tibetan books, breathing with him, trying to guide him to the light, all that woo-woo stuff."

"Come on inside," I offered and almost reached out a hand. But even if this being was human for the instant, it was still Felix. So I just walked in and let him follow me.

He plopped into one of the hanging chairs in the living room, then looked around appraisingly.

"Hey, where's the aerobics bimbette?" he asked.

I was glad I hadn't held my hand out to him.

I lowered myself into the other hanging chair and asked my own question.

"If Barbara's been in the hospital all this time, how'd she know about Shayla Greenfree and Ann and the seminar—"

"Hey, hold it a friggin' nanosecond," Felix interrupted, throwing his hand up like a stop sign. "What seminar? What Ann? What's the scoop here?"

Damn. He hadn't known about any of it. My mistake. I shouldn't have assumed Barbara had told him. So I talked. I wouldn't resist. There was no use in resisting the inevitable. Tai chi in action. At least I made it brief. In less than three minutes, I had explained about Ann, the seminar, the mnemonic name exercise, and Shayla's last words.

I was surprised when Felix didn't jump on me immediately with more questions. He seemed to be holding his breath. His face was certainly getting red. And then he finally exploded like an overblown hot air balloon.

"Jeez-friggin'-Louise!" he shouted, leaping from the swinging chair. It swung back and forth wildly, the wooden bar on the bottom slapping the back of his legs on the rebound. He didn't seem to notice. "I never said diddly to Barbara about this Greenfree stiff, man. But Barbara's in another time continuum altogether. She just went presto-bango-woo woo and knew somehow. And then who does she call? Huh? Huh?"

"Ann," I suggested quietly.

"Damn-straight, Ann," he yelped. "Not me, not her ever-loving sweetie, noooo—"

It was time for crisis intervention.

"But you love her anyway," I put in gently.

"Well, yeah," he muttered, throwing himself back in the swinging chair. Now his face was red again. But I knew Felix. Now he was embarrassed. "But still—"

"So what was the poison in the bracelet, Felix?" I demanded.

It took him a moment to reconnoiter. Then his soulful eyes took on a familiar gleam.

"Curare," he whispered. "Do you believe that, man? What a tripping story this is gonna make. And there's more. When that Greenfree woman put the bracelet on her wrist, she was okay. But when she closed the clasp, ten little whiz-bang syringes simultaneously pierced her skin. Kablooey, exit stage left for the writer. Like some friggin' James Bond gizmo-deluxe."

"But how'd the syringes hit the veins?" I muttered, squirming in my own chair, feeling the syringes piercing my own skin in spite of myself.

"That's the beauty part," he replied. "Curare doesn't have to hit the vein. Subcutaneous is plenty, honey. Man, the stuff is powerful. Paralyzes the lungs, then whammo-kaboomo, respiratory failure."

Felix was shaking his head admiringly now. I was feeling sick, thinking of Shayla's respiratory failure in front of us all. Suddenly, I couldn't breathe either. Because none of us had helped Shayla when she'd stopped breathing. My cat, C.C., jumped into my lap and dug a tentative claw into my thigh. My thigh popped upwards without permission. Was C.C. offering comfort or a curare-dipped nail? Whatever she was offering, the sting of feline reality jump-started my breathing again. I pulled her paw back and gathered her into my arms, pressing my face into her soft fur. She yowled half-heartedly, but put up with the humiliation of public affection. For the moment.

"So, who would have access?" I asked through C.C.'s fur. That had to be the important question. I just hoped Felix had the important answer.

Felix tilted his head and stroked his mustache.

"Curare used to be a big friggin' wonder drug. Docs used the stuff for surgery. Poor suckers they worked on didn't move at all. But then the hoodoo-men found out it wasn't really a true anesthetic. That it just caused paralysis. Though the slice-and-dice docs still use it sometimes."

Damn, that made me think of Dean. I didn't want to think of Dean.

"Who else would have access?" I asked.

"South American blow-pipe wizards?" Felix hazarded.

I ran the suspects through a mental line-up. None of them were from South America as far as I could tell.

"So what else did you dig up?" I asked. Felix was on a roll and I wanted him to keep rolling.

"Vince Quadríni has more money than God," he answered. "Self-made zillionaire or something. He's a former plumber turned realtor. His wife bit the big one a few years back. He helped her with her homecare medication, if you know what I mean." He pantomimed an injection with his hand. "Now the guy's some kind of whoopdee-do philanthropist."

"Yeah . . ." I prompted. Keep his lips moving, I told myself.

"Phyllis Oberman is super-twink acupuncturist and herbalist. And get this, she used to be an emergency-room nurse." He paused. "And that little gremlin's husband, Lou Cassell, he does his time as an accountant for a chain of hospitals. And he's trained in all kinds of emergency whiz-bang.

"Then there's Dean Frazier, anesthesiologist extraordinaire." He paused dramatically.

"Give, Felix," I commanded. I had a feeling we were getting to the sparring part now.

"Dean was a friggin' paramedic in Vietnam." Felix went wild now, his hand imaginarily injecting a whole roomful of ghosts.

"And Ted Brown's kid was sick. Big Daddy spent all kinds of time in the hospital with him before he died. And Zoe Ingersoll's sick, too. Some wacko disease."

"So . . ."

"Man, everyone and their friggin' iguana had access to syringes," Felix summarized.

"But you want to hear the really gonzo part?" he added, smiling his Cheshire Cat grin.

I nodded nonchalantly.

Felix just kept smiling.

I hoped I wouldn't have to beg too much.

"What, Felix?" I asked softly.

"The Man himself, Captain Cal Xavier of the Verduras cop shop." He paused again. I made an experimental growling sound in my throat. C.C. leapt off my lap as Felix's smile disappeared. "Holy socks, you're getting weirder than a turtle on amphetamines," he told me.

I decided not to even try to understand his last sentence and growled a little deeper.

"Okay, okay. Don't have an exorcism or anything," he said, then smiled again. "Captain Cal is running for mayor of Verduras. It seems that the *chief* of the Verduras P.D. is planning to be there a long time, so Captain Cal's got no upward friggin' mobility. So the captain's just going to hop right over the chief before the chief caks in the saddle. Mayoralty is Captain Cal's game."

I nodded calmly and sagely, as my mind danced with the information. It did explain the smiles and the handshakes. Maybe.

"Does he happen to have a brother named Bob?" I asked Felix, stretching my luck. I just hoped Felix wouldn't stop to ask why I wanted to know. He didn't.

He leaned back and laughed instead. "Ah yes, brother Bob. Remember President Carter's brother Billy?"

"Yeah . . ."

"Well, that's brother Bob in a nutshell, or a plastic Baggie, as the legal case may be. The guy whose big brother is running for mayor . . . is a lawyer. And just for extras, he's a drug lawyer. You got a little problem with your drug empire, call on Bob Xavier. Captain Cal is going out of his gourd. He'd probably take a hit out on the kid if he could."

Now that was good news. Maybe angering Bob Xavier wasn't the same as angering Captain Cal Xavier. But you never know. Family loyalty suspends disbelief sometimes.

"So what's the poop from Scott Green?" Felix asked, leaning forward, eyes gleaming. I knew then that my run of receiving information was over. I was no longer the givee. I was the giver. And Felix was the blunt object to make it all happen.

Felix Byrne had wrung my brain dry and still wanted more details by the time Wayne came home from La Fête à

L'Oiel, looking tired. He took one furrowed glance at me and my companion before escorting Felix out of the house.

I was just feeling my brain come back to life, and mumbling my thanks to Wayne for the rescue, when Ingrid walked in the door.

I tried to think of it as yin and yang. It was tai chi night after all. A balance in all things. So I didn't resist as Wayne led me gently down the hall toward bed.

Tuesday morning, at four A.M., we woke to the smell of skunk. The gagging smell of skunk, poisoning the whole bedroom.

"Arghmrmp!" Wayne roared through the pillow he held over his face.

"Yemmmyuk," I replied, holding the covers over my own head and coughing.

Some hours later, we agreed to the skunk broker's terms by telephone. He'd take our striped friends away on Saturday, he assured us. Saturday was five days too late as far as I was concerned, but the skunk broker was booked every evening until then. And as far as ethics went, ethics were gone. I didn't care if the man was just moving the skunks a block away. As long as he moved them.

"But why can't he come earlier?" Ingrid complained nasally over morning Whol-ios. The nasal part I could sympathize with. The skunk smell was still strong enough to shut down the least sensitive nasal cavities. And Ingrid was nothing if not sensitive.

"Make him come earlier," she ordered.

Wayne and I just looked at each other, rose in unison, and took a ride in my Toyota.

Luckily for Wayne and myself, Vince Quadrini's secretary informed us, Mr. Quadrini was an early riser and at his office when we arrived. She showed us in, over an expanse of plush carpet, where Mr. Quadrini sat behind a leather-topped desk big enough for a tennis match. Except that there was no net. Three cats sat in military precision in front of his desk.

One of the cats stood up as we entered.

"Down, Stan," he ordered. The cat sat down.

I looked at Vince Quadrini with new respect. And with suspicion. He had given the cat an order and the cat had obeyed. Now it was our turn.

"Please, take a seat," he said, standing up from his own throne and gesturing formally toward two deep leather seats that looked like they could swallow us without a trace. His voice was slightly less authoritarian than it had been with Stan. But just slightly. So we took our chances and lowered ourselves into the chairs. I felt like a rabbit in a boa constrictor as the chair slurped me up.

Once we were consumed by leather, Mr. Quadrini took matters in hand politely, but firmly.

"I asked you here today because certain information has come to my attention." He paused, narrowing his eyes in our direction. "Information that might prove useful in your investigations."

"Yes," Wayne said neutrally, respectfully.

Mr. Quadrini sat back down in his own executive chair. Was it my imagination, or was his chair at least two feet higher than ours?

"Ms. Phyllis Oberman went to high school with Shayla Greenfree," he told us. "A fact the police seem to find insignificant, although Ms. Oberman claimed no former connection with Ms. Greenfree."

I mulled over his words. Phyllis Oberman, acupuncturist, former emergency-room nurse. Why would she have kept the relationship secret?

"Maybe Phyllis didn't recognize Shayla," I suggested.

Mr. Quadrini's eyebrows rose fractionally, but he made no comment.

"I found out why Shayla called out my name," I told him. "And why *I* didn't recognize her."

And then I poured out the story, the story I hadn't even told the police yet, under Vince Quadrini's stern gaze. It wasn't until I was at the end of the story that I thought to wonder how Mr. Quadrini had found out about Phyllis Oberman's former association with Shayla Greenfree.

"Excuse me, sir," Wayne said politely. "But may I ask the source of your information?"

Vince Quadrini smiled then. He really was handsome in his statesmanlike way, with strong solid features and a magnificent head of wavy gray hair.

"You may certainly ask," the realtor replied just as politely. "But I'm afraid I can't answer."

He rose from his seat again. All three cats rose with him. I had a feeling we were about to leave. If we could get out of the chairs.

"Did you give your wife injections when she was . . . um . . . sick?" I stammered out.

"No," he answered simply, his voice trembling, whether with anger or sadness I couldn't tell. "A visiting nurse gave her the necessary injections."

He drew up his shoulders and smiled again.

"It's been good talking to you both," he said. "Thank you for coming."

"But—" I began.

But what? I didn't even know what to ask this man.

He walked around his desk and his cats triangulated themselves to surround him like a miniature honor guard. Or the Secret Service. I wondered for a moment if they carried weapons as they moved in lockstep with their master. And then we struggled out of the leather chairs and left Vince Quadrini's office.

"Well, at least he told us something," I said to Wayne a few minutes later in the Toyota.

"But why?" Wayne asked.

That was a question neither of us could answer over our brunch at the Dancing Carrot Cafe. Not to mention who'd killed S.X. Greenfree. So we satisfied ourselves with blue tortilla, tempeh enchiladas with a habanero sauce that could blow a person's head off. But it didn't seem to clear our minds, though it did clear the skunk right out of our sinuses. Ivan Nakagawa, Marcia Armeson, Ted Brown, Yvette Cassell, Lou Cassell, Zoe Ingersoll, Dean Frazier, Winona Eads, Vince Quadrini, and the unforthcoming Phyllis Oberman. Wayne and I could make a case for each and every one of them. Envy, blackmail, spurned friendship . . . The possibilities were endless. Well, maybe not endless, but at least they lasted until we finished our final bites of spicy rice and beans.

Then we went home to the smell of skunk and the artillery of Ingrid's voice.

Wayne lasted less than ten minutes before leaving for work. Early. Very early.

I decided to go to the library for the rest of the day. I wanted to study poisons, and the library still had books. Despite tax cuts. They even had phones, at least at the county library in the Frank Lloyd Wright Civic Center. Usually I avoided the Civic Center because it was too easy to get lost there. But skunks and Ingrid were enough. Lost in the Civic Center was better than found in our skunk habitat.

I located the phones in the Civic Center lobby by the elevators. The Marin County Superior Court was located in the same building, so I had to wait my turn behind a line of briefcases. But then I was on the phone, dialing the number of the emergency-room nurse whose name Ann Rivera had given me.

I took a big breath, ready to ask questions. And ended up talking to her answering machine. Right, she was probably working, like any sane person would be doing in the middle of a Tuesday. Any sane person without skunks and Ingrid to contend with.

I dialed again, this time the local emergency poison-control center.

"So, how would someone get hold of curare?" I dived right in, not wanting to waste an emergency person's time.

"Why do you want to know?" she asked reasonably enough.

"Well . . . there's been a murder and—"

"Do the police know about this murder?" she demanded, her voice growing louder.

"Well, yes—"

"I want you to know we're tracing this call," the woman told me. There was a new tone in her voice now, anger. Anger flavored with anxiety.

"Oh, well, thank you anyway," I said politely. I reminded myself that working with the public could be wearing.

Then I relinquished the telephone booth to the next brief-case in line, hoping his fingerprints would obliterate mine.

After that, I headed for the library. Quickly. But something funny happened on the way. I got lost. Now, there are those who swear that there are two parts of the Civic Center that don't match up, each set of floors being on a different level than the other set of floors. And then there are those who say that it's not a physical phenomenon at all, but a space/time warp that is only applicable to certain human beings. And some people just tell me I'm directionally challenged.

Like the Marin County Sheriff's Department where I ended up.

They all had a good laugh.

"Whenever we get a missing persons report, the first place we look is the library," a pleasant woman in uniform told me.

"And then we check the spaceships," a much less pleasant person in street clothes added, fah-hahhing and slapping his leg.

At least they told me how to get back to my car.

I came home sniffing for skunk. And Ingrid.

"You stoooo-pid bitch!" someone shouted before I even got to the front stairs. "Keep your nose out of my business or you're gonna be real sorry, do you hear!"

It wasn't Ingrid. It wasn't even a skunk.

FOURTEEN

꙳

I raised my eyes quickly. The woman on my deck was Marcia Armeson, Ivan Nakagawa's bookstore manager. And she was angry. More than angry.

Her delicate features looked tight and skeletal, her thin lips nearly invisible as she screamed. And she *was* screaming, not just raising her voice or straining her lungs. The volume and pitch that emerged from her slender, designer-jeaned body seemed to pound the whole deck, not to mention my eardrums.

I stopped at the bottom of the stairs as she screamed on.

". . . and what right do you have to be sticking your nose into my business!? I have sensibilities, you get it? Sensibilities . . ."

As I took each stair carefully, one by one, I wondered if she might be physically dangerous, this woman of sensibilities. Does a bear relieve itself in the woods? Was Felix Byrne a reporter?

I reminded myself to be relaxed and soft, suddenly sorry

I'd missed tai chi class the night before. And alert, don't for-get alert. Lessons of tai chi past reverberated in my head—*be so relaxed and soft that there will be nothing for an opponent to hit*—as I finally stepped onto the landing, my eyes on Marcia.

"You just don't understand!" Marcia shouted as she lunged at me.

And by the Tao, I *was* soft and relaxed. Just as Marcia would have hit me, I made a deep right turn from my waist and stepped back, so that she just brushed my hands and feet in passing.

"You bitch!" she shrieked as she came to ground in the geraniums at the other end of the deck.

Whoa, this stuff does work, I congratulated myself. Too soon. Marcia pulled herself out of the geraniums and came running at me from the other direction.

I reversed engines and turned to my left quickly, stepping back again and giving Marcia a light helping hand to en-courage her forward motion as she sped to the opposite side of the deck, finally hitting the railing with a thump to her midsection.

Unfortunately, the thump didn't knock all the air out of her. Though it did seem to knock some sense into her. She didn't run at me again. Instead she screamed from the railing.

"How did you do that!?"

"Marcia," I suggested, keeping my voice psychiatrically soothing with an effort. "Maybe if you calmed down, you could tell me what's upsetting you."

"Upsetting me!? You just keep out of my business, that's all! Or you'll be sorry, I swear!"

Then she crab-walked around me and skittered down the stairs.

I waited until I heard Marcia's car start up and accelerate away before I collapsed onto the deck. I was no longer the energetic softness of tai chi. Now I was the pudding softness of postponed fear. Or maybe Jell-O, quivering and covered in a sheen of moisture.

My ears were full of the sound of my own pulse. So full, I didn't hear Ingrid at first.

"Psst." The sound finally filtered into my consciousness.

"Psst, is she gone?"

I looked up. Ingrid's eyes were wide as she peeked through four inches of doorway.

"Were you there the whole time?" I asked her.

"Yeah," she whispered. "That woman was really scary."

"Did you call the police?" I demanded.

"No," she answered. "I thought I'd wait and see what happened."

I got up from the deck, dusting the remnants of fear from my pants, galvanized by new anger.

"Did it ever occur to you to help?" I asked Ingrid as I made my way to the door.

She began to close the four-inch gap in the doorway.

"Ingrid!" I shouted. "You can't shut the door on me. This is my house. I have keys!"

"Oh," she said and opened the door again.

"Are you gonna call the cops now?" she probed as I pushed my way past her into my own home.

"I certainly . . ." I stopped. If I called the local police, I wasn't sure what good it would do. And if I called Captain Cal . . . I shook my head. I didn't even want to think about it. And then there was Wayne to consider. If Ingrid kept her mouth shut, hopefully, he'd never hear about Marcia. "Probably not," I finished up.

Ingrid had her arms crossed now as she surveyed me.

"I thought you were my friend," she informed me. "But now I think you're dangerous." Then she stuck her bottom lip out. Probably trying to tan it to match the rest of her perfect body.

I was just working up my righteousness to tell Ingrid that it was time for her to rent a hotel room, when she pulled her lip back in.

"That weird leprechaun lady called," she told me.

I looked at my phone. The answering machine was turned off.

"Have you been answering my phone?" I demanded. As if I didn't know.

"Just in case Raoul called," she explained sullenly. Then she turned to walk back into the living room. "There were some other calls too, but I didn't understand them."

"Didn't understand them?" I asked her departing back.

But it was too late. Ingrid was humming to herself now. Loudly. Tuning me out. I was surprised she didn't stick her fingers in her ears too.

I called Yvette first. At least I knew she'd called me. Yvette wanted an evening meeting of suspects the next night at her place. I agreed to be there. It would get me out of the house. And I was all argued out, anyway.

"So what did Felix—" I began once I'd agreed.

The line went dead.

I decided not to even imagine what Felix had done and asked myself instead who else could have called. Judy from work? Wayne? My mother? My ex-husband? The President?

And then the name Perkin Vonburstig popped into my mind. It was worth a shot. I punched in his number.

And this time, I got the man himself, not his android. I identified myself, and stared at my index finger proudly as Perkin Vonburstig began to tell me a strange tale in halting, accented English.

He was a book fancier, he told me. A collector of sorts. And he'd begun his collection of recent collectibles some years back. His first great find had been . . .

"And . . ." I said, hoping to prompt more relevance from his story.

"I boughted a signed edition from an advertisement, in a magazine, you understand," he said. "A Smith. But the signature looked incorrect, eh, unauthentic. I perused at the earlier books I had boughten from the same advertisement and I beganed to wonder. I had the signatures, eh, examined by experts. They were forgeries, unauthentic. I called to an investigator, a P.I., do you say? And the books were traced to a place of sales named Fictional Pleasures. The proprietor seemed an honorable man but has certain worries about his employee, a Marcia Armeson. It was she, I founded out subsequently, who placed these advertisements . . ."

Now I was beginning to understand Marcia's anger. But why was I the target?

"I have spoken to both Mr. Nakagawa and finally, eh, Ms. Armeson," Vonburstig went on. "I have tolded them both that I would speak to you . . ."

Target practice was making more sense now.

Vonburstig told me, at length, of his theory that Marcia was not only stealing books from Ivan, but forging author signatures to increase their value, and then selling them as collectibles through ads. He seemed quite pleased with his discovery, but was not quite ready to go to the police. Maybe he was having too much fun. By the time I hung up the phone, I wasn't having fun, though. I wanted to talk to Ivan. Why hadn't he warned me?

I called Fictional Pleasures, but it was Marcia who answered the phone. I hung up without a peep, not even a yelp. Ingrid was right about one thing, Marcia was scary. And probably a thief and forger. But my mind couldn't make the leap to murderer. If Marcia was a murderer, wouldn't she have tried to keep a lower profile? Misguided deck attacks did not seem like an intelligent strategy. And the person who had loaded Shayla Greenfree's bracelet with curare had been an intelligent strategist. One capable of a better attack than Marcia's. On the other hand, she could be—

The phone rang, cutting off my musing mid-doubt.

"Hi, Kate," a familiar voice greeted me. "This is Jade." Right, now I had the current name too. My number one Jest Gifts employee, my main warehousewoman, and I'd already forgotten her latest name. "Listen, you might want to call the police," she told me.

"Huh?" I said. I hadn't told Judy/Jade about the murder, much less about Marcia. Was she as psychic as Barbara now?

"'Cause somebody else is answering your phone," Judy—maybe I could call her Jadey—went on.

"Houseguest," I explained briefly through clenched teeth.

"Oh, that's cool," my warehousewoman said graciously and then began the daily recitation of Jest Gifts crises.

I had to get back to work. The towers of paper on my desk loomed. I needed to contact errant suppliers, financially re- calcitrant customers, not to mention my frantic accountant. But Shayla Greenfree's death loomed too.

Just one more little whodunit call, I promised myself. Then I called Phyllis Oberman's office. I wanted to hear her own explanation for omitting her former relationship with Shayla Greenfree from her police statement.

But Phyllis didn't talk from her office. She only did acupuncture. And I didn't have her home number. So I told her receptionist my sinuses hurt and made an appointment. Then I sat down at my desk and worked hard. Long and hard. When Wayne came home late that night, I was still at my desk, having stopped only to eat, and to wonder where an acupuncturist stuck the needles for a sinus treatment.

I was still wondering about the needles the next day as I dutifully continued Jest Gifts crisis-stifling and bookkeep- ing, a virtual telephone abuse and paperwork sponge.

Wayne had agreed to accompany me to Yvette's that evening, and Ingrid was at work. And the skunks hadn't sprayed during the previous night. If it hadn't been for the unsolved murder, life at my desk might have been paradise. Or close anyway . . . if my back weren't so sore . . . if I could forget Marcia's threats . . . if I could forget my upcoming acupuncture treatment . . . if . . .

Many hours later, when Wayne finally walked in the door, barely in time to go to Yvette's meeting, I was more than ready to leave desk paradise.

We heard Yvette Cassell's voice ringing out from her open door before we'd even passed the first set of elves in her yard. Her actual words became piercingly clear by the time we stepped around the leprechaun statue.

"Shi-shick, we were all there," she was insisting. "Someone must have seen fuddin' something. Huh, huh? I mean . . ."

By the time we got past the sniffing Labrador retriever into the living room, she was still insisting, but no one was answering.

Ivan and Marcia sat next to each other in identical green velvet easy chairs under revolving posters of Yvette's books. Ivan was as still as a stone Buddha, with a marmalade cat in his lap and an English bulldog asleep at his feet. Marcia glanced up at us, though, once we'd shuffled through the open doorway, then whipped her head back around toward Yvette, but not before squirting a narrowed eyeful of vitriol my way.

". . . musta seen something, heard something . . ." Yvette went on.

Ted Brown sat farther back, near the Mr. Spock side of the bookcase, alone on a wooden chair. He raised his heavily lidded eyes briefly to us in greeting, then lowered them again. Lou Cassell and Dean Frazier sat side by side on a green tweed couch under a mobile of harps and shamrocks, apparently mesmerized by Yvette's words.

Who wasn't here? I scanned the room to see if anyone was hidden behind an oversized knickknack. Were the sane suspects the only missing ones? Zoe Ingersoll, Winona Eads, Phyllis Oberman, Vince Quadrini—

"Hey," Yvette greeted us, breaking into her own monologue. "You guys know what I mean, huh? The flickin' woman died and we were all there." She paused for a breath. "Goodies on the sideboard. Get some and take a seat. Then tell us what the hell-heck you think happened."

Getting the food, a variety of breads and spreads and sliced fruit, and arranging them on a china dish took a few minutes. The food smelled good against the must of animals and bric-a-brac. Settling ourselves on another green tweed couch near what seemed to be a bust of Nero Wolfe gave us a minute more. And then Wayne and I were under Yvette's intense tinted-glass scrutiny.

"You guys probably know what happened, right?" she prompted.

"Wrong," I answered briefly and took a bite of some kind of muffin dipped in tahini-peach spread. A big bite.

She wouldn't question a woman whose mouth was full, would she? Of course she would.

"Damn-darn, even if you don't know exactly what happened, you know a lot," she pressed. "You two have been asking questions. And getting fuddin' answers." She pointed her finger. "You're not going to tell me you don't know shick. No, you're going to tell me what you know right now—"

"Honey," Lou objected, his dark skin flushing under his wife's glare. "These two people are honest and professional. If they don't want to share what they've learned . . ." His words faltered, but his gaze lingered, shifting from my face to Wayne's. And back again. And his gaze begged us to talk.

Was this part of a good sleuth-bad sleuth act? If it was, it was tempting. Why not spill the beans about Marcia's scam, and Zoe's hurt, and Phyllis Oberman's omission—

"Don't even try to make sense when you talk to your

woman," Ted Brown burst in, his voice harsh. He barked out a laugh. "The last time I tried to have a lousy chat with my wife, she left. I got the divorce papers the next day. Injustice runs as smoothly as German trains."

"Oh, Ted," Yvette murmured, shaking her small head. There was affection in her softened tone. Or maybe just pity.

Her tone changed when she turned to Dean, though.

"Come on, Dean," she ordered loudly. "You knew the flickin' woman. You knew what made her tick. Don't you get it? If we all put our cards on the table, we can solve this thing."

"I've thought on this, believe me," Dean answered quietly. "And I just can't think of a thing that matters."

"Well then, what doesn't matter?" Yvette demanded, throwing up her hands.

But Dean just shrugged, slowly. Sadly.

I looked over at Marcia, wondering why she'd even shown up tonight. Or Ted—

"Kate?" Yvette demanded. Damn, she'd caught me thinking. I'd have to stop that.

"Kate?" she asked again, her voice softer. And I heard an echo of Shayla's pre-death "Kate" in her voice. Damn. My skin bubbled up into goose bumps like a pancake in a skillet. Yvette's tinted glasses zoomed in on my face.

"If we knew something relevant, we'd let you know," Wayne announced calmly.

I squeezed his hand gratefully, not even caring if Yvette noticed.

"Oh, yeah?" she challenged. Then she threw up her hands again. "Okay, I fuddin' give up. Eat, drink, and forget someone died. Have fun."

And with that, she turned on her tiny heel and left the room.

The sigh of relief that followed her was impossible to pinpoint. Maybe it was collective.

Slowly, some people began to stand and congregate.

Wayne walked over to Ivan. I stayed right where I was. I didn't want to get any closer to Marcia. A striped cat jumped and claimed a spot on my lap. She was heavy, but at least she wasn't clawing.

I was chewing on a second bite of muffin when Lou sat down next to me and the cat. I swallowed unhappily. Not that Lou Cassell wasn't a nice man. Gorgeous too, with those big brown feline eyes. But I didn't think he'd come over my way to chitchat.

"Yvette likes to take the initiative," Lou said by way of greeting. Nope, no chitchat. "She's a very courageous woman, but I'm worried that she's in over her head."

I nodded and looked past his shoulder.

Wayne, Ivan, and Dean stood in one corner, talking quietly. Marcia and Ted were in another corner, speaking in animated whispers, their heads darting back and forth like chickens pecking. I just wished I could hear what they were saying.

"You two have experience in these things," Lou went on.

I brought my eyes back to his concerned face. I looked closer. He really was concerned. It showed in the tightness under his cheekbones. Had he lost weight in the last few days? And in those beautiful eyes.

"Look," I told him. "Yvette is smart. She'll be careful."

Lou shook his head emphatically.

"My wife is intelligent, yes. And creative. But she doesn't seem to see the danger in this thing. She's an innocent—"

"Humph!" a voice snorted from our side.

Once again, Yvette had snuck up on us. How could such a loud woman be so quiet?

"An innocent?" she demanded, her head tilted to one side. But she didn't really sound angry.

Now Lou looked guilty as well as concerned. Yvette bent

to kiss him on the forehead. She didn't have to bend far despite the fact that Lou was sitting and she was standing.

"Only innocent for you, my darling," she murmured huskily.

Phew! Pheromones filled the air, and the room went into action. Ted was the first out the door. Then Dean walked up to say his goodbyes. The striped cat jumped off my lap. After that, Marcia left without a word.

Then finally, Wayne and Ivan came trudging up together. I was struck once more by the similarity of my sweetie and his friend. Their bulldog faces were both impenetrable. And yet I knew they were each softer inside than most. At least I knew Wayne was. Did an inner softness necessitate a hard shell?

"Looks like Ted and Marcia are getting pretty cozy, huh?" Yvette said to Lou.

Lou put his head into his hands.

"Please, Yvette, no more matchmaking," he begged. "Remember Paul and Joan and his ulcer—"

"Ah, come on, honey," she put in. "Ted could use some cheering up."

Marcia didn't seem exactly the cheery type to me, but I was keeping my mouth shut. Yvette turned to Ivan.

"And your son, Neil, and that Winona character," she added, raising her eyebrows over the rims of her glasses.

"Excuse me, but my son isn't even old enough—" Ivan began.

"Hey, get ready for the wedding bells," Yvette laughed and slapped him on his massive shoulder.

Ivan and Lou groaned together this time.

It seemed like a good time to leave. So Wayne and I did. We could still hear Yvette cajoling, Lou murmuring, and Ivan sputtering as we walked out the still-open door.

Wayne and I sat in my Toyota for a few moments after we got in, just holding hands. And breathing in the cool night air as we felt each other's warmth through palms and fingertips. And we thought.

"Kate," Wayne murmured into the silence finally. I guess he'd done the most thinking. "Wonder if we've done enough here. Woman's dead. Ivan's ready to let it go . . ."

I thought I heard a rap on the car, maybe a bird, but I ignored the sound.

"Worried about you," Wayne went on. "This isn't so simple as—"

A dark hand reached in the open window and Wayne's words came to an abrupt halt. Along with most of my vital signs.

FIFTEEN

✦

I felt the hand touch my shoulder, and my head vaulted toward the car ceiling. My vital signs were definitely coming back. Fast.

And then I heard the whisper.

"Sorry to startle you."

I looked out into the night and saw Lou Cassell bent uncertainly over our car, his hand withdrawn now. I could feel Wayne vibrating at my side. Had he just started to breathe again, too?

"Fine, no problem," I assured Lou. Only the words came out in a squeak.

"Sorry," Lou whispered back again. "I was just trying to get your attention. I tapped the roof of your car, but you didn't hear." He paused. "A strange hand on a dark night. Everyone's nightmare."

I forced a laugh, uncomfortably.

"Listen," Lou said urgently, looking over his shoulder

nervously. "I need to finish what I was trying to tell you in the living room."

"Want to get in the car?" I asked when he glanced over his shoulder again. Yvette was good at unexpected appearances. And it looked like Lou was trying to avoid one.

"Thanks," he murmured gratefully and climbed into the back seat.

"I have to leave on a business trip," he said, once he was settled in behind us. "I'm new at the company. I can't afford even a hint of unprofessionalism. So I can't back out of the trip now. I *am* professional. Or at least that's what we call it." I could hear an easing in his voice. Was he smiling behind me in the dark? "Actually, like a lot of 'professionals,' I'm one of the new homeless. Instead of pushing around a shopping cart with all of my belongings, I push around an airport cart with all of my luggage. I've flown to practically every state in the country."

His tone deepened again. "Usually, it's fine. But I'm worried about Yvette right now. Really worried. Please, will you two watch out for her?"

I didn't have an instant answer. Yvette? Watch out for Yvette? Was this going to be something like trying to catch a cat and give it a bath? Or would it be even harder?

Wayne groaned next to me, though the sound was so soft that I felt it more than heard it. Lou probably didn't even hear it. Poor Wayne. He was ready to pull us both out of the murder investigation business, and now an honorable man was begging for our involvement.

"Yvette just won't leave it alone," Lou explained sorrowfully.

"I know," Wayne muttered sympathetically. "I know."

I glared at my sweetie in the dark. Was he talking about Yvette or—

"She gets an idea in her head and you can't stop the woman—"

"Yeah," Wayne agreed fervently.

Me! Wayne *was* talking about me.

"But I love her."

"Right," Wayne conceded, his voice a little softer, then added gruffly, "We'll do what we can."

"Can't ask more than that," Lou replied. "Thanks, you guys."

I heard another rap on the car roof. This time I looked out the window, once my heart began beating again. Ivan Nakagawa was standing by the car door, his bulldog face barely visible.

"Come join the party," I invited, nodding toward the back seat.

Ivan climbed in one side of the Toyota and Lou climbed out the other, with more effusive thanks on the way. But before I even got a chance to say goodbye to Lou, Ivan started in on his own speech.

"I would like for us all to just get along," the bookseller stated for the record.

I waited a moment for Ivan to go on. He didn't.

"And . . ." I prompted. It appeared our back seat was taking on a new role as a virtual reality crisis hotline.

"Marcia Armeson appears to be a thief and a forger," Ivan murmured, and sighed. "If she would only talk to me, we could find some point of agreement, I'm sure. But she seems angry."

"No kidding," I replied.

"Oh, dear," Ivan whispered. "Did she bother you?"

I looked at Wayne, hoping he wouldn't be angry at my previous nondisclosure. Then I babbled. About Marcia's visit. About my call to Vonburstig. About how scary a woman Ivan's assistant was.

"Why didn't you tell me?" Wayne demanded when I got to the part about Marcia's final threats on her way down the stairs.

"I wanted to wait until tonight," I lied. Or maybe I didn't lie. It was tonight and I had just told him.

"But I'm most concerned about Winona Eads and my son," Ivan interrupted providentially. "She's too much older than Neil. Why, he's not even out of high school." He lowered his low voice even further. "And what if she turns out to be a murderer?"

I wanted to tell him Winona Eads couldn't be a murderer, but I didn't know that. Actually, I didn't really know very much about her at all.

"She seems to be a very kind young woman," I offered tentatively.

"But my son—"

All three of us jumped when we heard another tap on the car roof.

Dean Frazier was standing out there now.

I wondered if Yvette had noticed that her party was taking place in our car? Probably not. At least Lou was back with her again.

"Are you all okay?" Dean asked quietly.

"Oh, sure," I answered, trying to keep the sarcasm out of my voice. "Want to join us?" Maybe there was something he wanted to get off his chest too.

"Lord, no," Dean replied. "Not that I wouldn't like to, I mean. I just wanted to say goodbye."

And then he was gone. But my suspicions weren't. What had Dean wanted? Had he really just wanted to say goodbye again? Or was he worried that Ivan was holding us hostage? Or that we were holding Ivan hostage? Or was Dean spying? Or—

"Perhaps we could go back to the store and talk there," Ivan suggested, cutting off my speculation. "I'm hungry myself. How about you two?"

"Yeah, food," my mouth said before my brain engaged. I was hungry, hungrier than I'd realized. I hadn't ever eaten a

proper dinner. And two bites of muffin weren't near enough
to count as a meal.

"Why don't you go to the bookstore and I'll meet you
there with some take-out," Ivan went on, "from the health
food store."

"No reason for you to provide the food," Wayne objected.
And then the two men sparred ever-so-politely to see who
could be more generous. I just sat back and let them duke it
out. Finally, they agreed that we'd pick up some drinks, and
Ivan would pick up the food, since he was the one who
wanted to talk.

I looked at my watch. It was past eight.

"But is your store still open?" I asked. I was ready for
home—Ingrid, skunks, and all.

"Certainly," Ivan assured me. "Fictional Pleasures is open
until nine o'clock weeknights. For the community. And
Marcia is probably there. Neil was holding down the fort till
she came back. But she must be back by now."

Oh joy. More talk. And Marcia to boot.

Ivan whizzed away in his Buick. I waited a few tense moments for Wayne to say something, but he didn't. I started
up the Toyota.

We were halfway to the nearest grocery store to get
Wayne's favorite apple juice, my favorite carrot juice, and
Ivan's favorite iced tea, when Wayne finally exploded. At
least as much as Wayne is capable of explosion.

"Why didn't you tell me about Marcia?" he growled.
"She's dangerous—"

"I am not Yvette Cassell," I answered, feeling a spurt of
anger tingle through my own body. Actually it was more like
a gusher than a spurt. But I tried to keep my voice steady.
And to keep my hands steady on the wheel. "I can handle
myself. I am not irresponsible—"

"No one can handle themselves if a murderer is determined—"

"You just think I'm as goofy as Yvette—"

"Yvette has nothing to do with this—"

"She's only a murder suspect—"

"Exactly what I mean, Kate—"

We were off and running, the Toyota going faster and faster as our words escalated.

We got to the grocery store a lot faster than we should have. And I was shaking with anger. After all this time, Wayne still didn't trust me. And anyway, how was I supposed to know Marcia would show up on my doorstep? Was that my fault?

"I'll get the drinks," Wayne muttered when I parked the car.

"I'll call home and see if my answering machine's on," I muttered back. There was a pay phone at the entrance to the store. I might as well make use of it. And I didn't feel like walking down *any* aisle with Wayne right then.

Once I'd locked all the car doors, showing just how responsible I could be, I walked to the pay phone and dialed my own number. I didn't get my answering machine. I got Ingrid.

"I'm not Raoul," I informed her.

"Oh," she said.

"And I'll give you five seconds to turn my machine back on," I added. It was all too easy to infuse menace into my tone. I just hoped she could smell my anger over the phone. I just hoped she'd turn my answering machine back on. But I wouldn't have bet on it.

I glared at the phone for a while after I hung up, just for good measure. But I didn't call again. Active avoidance of disappointment can be a good strategy in times of stress. Not to mention complaining.

I was all set to complain about Ingrid when I got back to the car. But Wayne's stone scowl stopped me. He stood patiently with two bags full of drinks waiting for me to unlock the door. He'd probably bought enough beverages to drown a small nation, just to show Ivan how generous he was. It was then that I remembered Wayne wasn't carrying a key to the Toyota.

The remainder of the drive was quiet. And slow. I curbed my accelerator foot and mouth with an effort. I parked the Toyota on the street next to Fictional Pleasures and waited for Wayne to say something as we sat there. He didn't. And I just couldn't stand it. I'd never be able to resist real torture. Silence is enough to make me talk.

"I'm not like Yvette, am I?" I asked Wayne finally.

He didn't answer me right off. Then he growled, "No, you're taller," and got out of the car.

He stalked up to Fictional Pleasures and disappeared through its doorway before I could even think of a reply. Wayne could be aggravating at times, but the man was not stupid.

PMP was screaming when I followed Wayne into the store.

"Cash or charge, *scree, squawk!* No literary merit! I have pictures! God, paperbacks are expensive, *scree!*"

It was good that PMP was doing some screaming. Because I was ready to join in.

"Taller?" I said to Wayne. "Taller!"

"Sorry," he murmured, looking at his feet. Wayne was rarely mean at all, and when he was, it didn't last more than an instant. "Cheap shot, Kate. You know I care—"

But by now, PMP had taken up the refrain. "Taller!" she shrilled. "Want a bag? Will you shut up!"

I looked around the store, suddenly self-conscious. Why were we having this ridiculous argument? But I didn't see anyone watching us. As far as I could tell, there was no one in the store to hear our argument, ridiculous or not. The tall wooden bookshelves were all full and leaning toward us in apparent readiness to serve. But PMP was the only live being behind the counter.

Wayne and I must have realized it at the same time. We looked at each other and shrugged in unison.

"Pretty bird," PMP tried. "I understand. Anything with cats?"

But it was still spooky there without anyone else in the bookstore, for all of PMP's efforts.

The store heater roared into life, and Wayne and I both jerked in our shoes.

"Do you think there's something wrong?" I whispered to Wayne, petty arguments forgotten for the moment.

But before Wayne could answer, Ivan bustled in the door, a brown bag complete with grease spots in his hand.

"The health food store wasn't open," he told us. "So I got Chinese—"

"Where's Marcia?" Wayne asked.

"Marcia?" Ivan said, eyes widening as he looked around him. "Isn't she here?"

"I don't think so," I began slowly.

"Marcia?" Ivan shouted.

"Marcia!" PMP echoed. "Stooo-pid parrot. Will you shut up!"

"She must be in the storeroom," Ivan told us and lumbered down the center aisle.

I waited for a moment, then followed Ivan. Just as I pushed the door open at the end of the aisle, I heard his cry. It was softer than PMP's, but more urgent.

I burst through the door, afraid that Ivan had been attacked. But he hadn't. He stood stock-still in the center of the small storeroom. Just as before, books were everywhere. In carts, and piles, and boxes stacked to the ceiling. But the handcart I'd seen before was no longer on top of the highest stack of boxes.

The handcart was on top of Marcia Armeson.

Sixteen

✦

I looked closer. I shouldn't have. Marcia Armeson lay face down on the floor. The handcart lay at a haphazard angle to her body, its scoop end mashing the back of her head. I turned away, but not before the image of pulp and blood stamped itself indelibly on the retina of my mind's eye.

As I turned away, I saw Wayne coming through the door, registering the same picture I had. I pulled him into my arms in less than a moment. Yes, I was taller than Yvette Cassell. And shorter than Wayne. And none of it mattered. Just that we were alive and could hold each other.

I absorbed the intensity of Wayne's body: its heat and vibrating energy, and sudden dampness. And smelled the taint of fear in his perspiration. I could even feel his convulsive swallowing in the stillness of the storeroom. I concentrated on my impressions of *his* body, ignoring the one I was no longer facing, though I imagined I could still see Marcia Armeson through Wayne's eyes. Or maybe I really could.

"Might still be alive?" he suggested, so softly that I barely heard it over the roaring in my ears.

Oh God, he was right. Someone had to check. To take her pulse at least. To touch her. My body stiffened with resistance.

Ivan sighed, and then I heard him move. Even without turning, I was sure the rustle of cloth meant he was bending over Marcia now, the intake of his breath that he was touching her. Then I heard cloth rustle again.

"No pulse," he announced, his gentle voice thick. "Harmony," he added. I wasn't sure what he meant until I heard his tears. "Be one with all, Marcia."

And then silence. And the sound of a series of squawks from PMP that seemed very far away.

The interim between Ivan's words to Marcia and his next words felt endless and momentary at the same time. Something like meditation. I would have preferred meditation in my living room. But the three of us stood silently in the storeroom, there with Marcia for an infinite duration.

Then Ivan spoke again.

"We need to take proper care," he whispered. "We need to call the police."

And suddenly I was awake. Police. Marcia. Murder.

The three of us stumbled back into the main room of the bookstore all too quickly, united in our desire to be gone from the storeroom. Gone from the obvious presence of death.

Wayne and I set up a half-dozen folding chairs as Ivan called the Verduras Police Department. We had to do something. Anything.

I plopped onto one of the chairs with a sigh and wiggled uncomfortably on its slats. I had a feeling it was going to be a long time before we smelled skunk again at home. I almost missed the smell now.

"I understand," PMP sighed with me. "I understand."

It was good someone understood.

The first two men in uniform from the Verduras Police Department certainly didn't. Ivan led them down the aisle to the room where Marcia's body lay, and one of them came lurching back out, his face pale beneath its freckles. He looked young. Very young. I offered him a seat and he took it, then put his pale face in his hands. His partner stayed manfully on the spot as PMP squawked, merrily offering all forms of genre fiction to the assembled guests. Then Captain Cal Xavier and a tall female officer arrived. The pale, young, uniformed man leapt up from his chair. And the show began.

"So good to see you three again," the captain greeted us, his smile in place, but looking frayed now.

He even kept his smile pasted there on his trip to the storeroom and back again. Not frayed, I decided—his smile was more feral than frayed. Savage, actually. The store heater blasted more hot air into the room, and I realized I was already sweating.

"Accident or murder?" Ivan asked quietly.

"You tell me," Captain Cal answered and lowered himself onto a folding chair. His descent was slow and deliberate, his gaze intent. He might have been taking his place on a throne.

Then the questioning began. I was surprised that he didn't separate Ivan, Wayne, and me, but it appeared that Captain Cal had no time left for ritual. Within minutes, he'd established Wayne's movements and my own after Yvette's party. And Ivan's.

Or at least Ivan told Captain Cal his version of what he'd done after the party. He said he'd gone to the health food store, only to find it closed, and then to the Chinese restaurant next to it. He had the greasy bag to prove his story. The mixed smells of garlic and ginger and oil drifted over from behind the counter, mingling with the overheated air. But the smells that would usually make me salivate were making me queasy now. Because I wasn't sure that Ivan's tale was the truth. What if he'd killed Marcia first, then rushed out for food, with us as convenient almost-alibis? Or patsies, even.

". . . my son, Neil," Ivan was saying quietly, his voice as low as PMP's was high. "He was scheduled to work until Marcia came back, and then to hand the store over to her. They got along well—"

"Get the kid down here," Captain Cal interrupted. He wasn't smiling anymore, feral or otherwise. And the anger in his dark eyes wasn't an improvement. I shifted in my chair. Now he looked like his younger brother, Bob, good-looking . . . and scary.

And his questions went on. And on. Like a medieval artist's patron, he had us draw the sketches of our movements with our own words first, then encouraged us to supply the colors and the finer shadings. And like those artists of old, we knew we were in trouble if we couldn't supply the exact pictures the captain wanted.

". . . I think Yvette was still at her house when we left," I was telling Captain Xavier, about twenty PMP scree-scraws later. "But I couldn't say for sure. Anyway, she had plenty of time *after* we left to get here before us. Everyone did—"

The front door opened, with a whoosh of cool air that chilled my moist skin, and a bigger whoosh of verbiage.

"Hey, Dad!" Neil Nakagawa interrupted, his young voice shrill with excitement. "What's the deal here? These Five-0 recruits want to put a snitch jacket on me—"

"Neil," Ivan put in, his voice heavy with fatherhood. "This is very serious. This is not a game. Cooperate, please."

"But, Dad—" came the teenage lament.

"Neil, listen to me," Ivan went on, unheeding. His voice didn't waver and his face was unreadable, but his hands were clasping and unclasping as if in interrupted prayer. "There's been a death—"

"That's enough," Captain Xavier told Ivan.

Ivan shut his mouth slowly, his hands still fluttering in his lap. He closed his eyes for a moment, then looked at his son, a plea on his face.

The captain looked at Neil too, but his eyes were the angry eyes of law enforcement.

"When did you last see Marcia Armeson?" Captain Cal Xavier demanded.

"Marcia?" Neil looked confused. "A little before eight, I think. She came in and I gave her the day's ledger and the keys, and then I went home." His eyes widened. "Marcia's okay, isn't she?"

The captain didn't answer him. He just questioned Neil as exhaustively as he'd questioned us. And listening to a teenager being interrogated wasn't any more fun than being interrogated myself. But Neil had been alone with Marcia. Of course, Wayne and I had been alone with Marcia too. True, she'd been dead at the time. But the police didn't know that. Only we did.

Had Ivan been alone with Marcia? I shook my head. I liked Ivan, damn it.

Someone else must have been alone with Marcia. Someone who'd followed and killed her after Neil had left and before we'd arrived.

Or maybe it just was an accident after all. But would the police ever be able to tell? I could imagine that precariously placed handcart falling. I even shivered when I saw it hit Marcia in my mind's eye. But still, my imagination had to ask what caused it to fall in the first place.

"I told Marcia to be careful with the handcart." Ivan had broken in now. "I tried to communicate with her, to let her know that she shouldn't put it on top of things. It was too big, too heavy. But she didn't always listen to me."

Neil snorted. "She never listened to you, Dad," he said. "No way."

"I saw it too," I put in. Captain Cal's eyes raced to mine in an instant. And in that instant I was sorry I'd spoken. But I had to tell the truth. "When I went to the bathroom," I finished up. "The handcart was on top of a stack of boxes. It could have fallen."

"Right," said the captain, smiling again. Maybe the plain old anger was better. "And wouldn't that be convenient for everyone?"

Unfortunately, Captain Xavier wanted me to explain why and when I'd been in the storeroom before. And then I was the artist again, shading here, adding color there as Captain Xavier prodded and probed. I told him what I could remember, leaving out the fact that I had been nosing around, looking for whatever I thought Marcia might have hidden back there. As far as the Verduras police needed to know, I'd just gone to the bathroom. And I didn't mention that the same Marcia who was lying dead in the storeroom had attacked me the day before. Wayne didn't either. Or Ivan. Should I?

"You can leave now," Captain Cal Xavier said as if in answer.

The captain's words jolted me out of my seat. And answered my unspoken question. He'd never asked me specifically about the day before. There was no reason to tell him. Not really. At least that's what I told myself.

Wayne kept one big gentle hand on my shoulder on the long drive back home, and around my waist as we passed Ingrid's sleeping form in the living room and tiptoed down the hall to the bedroom.

"Tall enough for you?" I demanded, once we'd closed the door behind us. Gallows frivolity.

"Perfect," Wayne answered.

And then he proved it.

• • •

On Thursday morning, Wayne left to catch up on restauranteuring, and I got back to work on Jest Gifts in my skunky, paper-littered office. I never wanted to see Fictional Pleasures again. Or any of its nonfictional inhabitants. Except Phyllis Oberman, maybe. I paused as my No. 1 pencil touched columnar tablet, thinking about the woman. She was the only one that I'd never really talked to. The elusive goddess of needles. My curiosity bubbled up. I tried to put a lid on it as I marked a number in a box.

A few hours and too many stray thoughts later, I'd waded through two months' worth of invoices, almost bringing that pile of paperwork into the current year, when the doorbell rang.

I went rigid in my chair. I didn't really have to answer, I told myself. If only my doorbell worked like an answering machine, I could screen my visitors. I *would* screen my visitors. Why not? I was just sneaking over to my office window to see if I could catch a glimpse of the person who'd rung my doorbell when Ingrid answered the door. I smacked my fist into my palm angrily. And painfully. How could I have forgotten about Ingrid?

Our visitor was none other than Captain Cal Xavier of the Verduras Police Department.

And Ingrid was all aflutter, grinning and wiggling in aerobics spandex. And looking all too good as she did so. I wondered if Captain Cal was single.

"Cal," she greeted the captain, her loud voice now husky with affection. My heart dipped down to stomach level. And it didn't like the ride.

"Why, Ingrid," Captain Cal greeted her, smiling pleasantly. "Looking good as ever. Bob told me you were staying here."

After a few more minutes of brotherly pleasantries, the captain turned my way.

"But it's really Ms. Jasper I've come to see," he told her apologetically, his smile changing from pleasant to predatory as his eyes met mine. "Gotta get the job done. You understand the situation."

Ingrid nodded, her eyes wide with admiration and understanding. But she didn't leave the room. She just lowered herself gracefully onto her futon—our futon—while the captain settled down in one of the swinging chairs and I took the other.

"Have a few more questions for you, Ms. Jasper," the captain announced. I'd hoped he'd shoo Ingrid out of the room, but he didn't. "About Marcia Armeson's death."

The captain was about ten minutes into his questions, and I was ten minutes into the hell of continued interrogation, when Ingrid jumped up suddenly.

"Marcia Armeson!" she yelped. "Kate, wasn't Marcia Armeson that really, really scary woman who you were fighting with the other day? You know, the one who came at you, but you pushed her over—"

"I didn't push her over," I objected. I wanted to explain that Marcia's own energy had pulled her over, but the subtleties of tai chi were wilting under the captain's suddenly rapt gaze. "She just missed," I finished.

"Oh no, Kate," Ingrid kept on. "You were really cool, you really pushed her around. It was like some karate movie or something—"

"Listen, Captain Xavier," I began. "Marcia Armeson did visit me two days ago. I guess she was mad at me because she was afraid I knew about her book scam—"

"Book scam?" the captain asked, his voice deep with something like pleasure. Or maybe greed. Or lust.

I'd wondered if Ivan had told the Verduras representative of law enforcement about Marcia's allegedly larcenous activities. I didn't have to wonder anymore. He hadn't. And that was going to look suspicious in itself.

So I took a big breath and started in, about Perkin Vonburstig's call, about Marcia's reaction, about Ivan's reaction.
And about my bookseller friend's reticence to speak of Marcia's possible fraud and thievery once she'd been killed.

"Respect for the dead," I called it.

"Withholding information," the captain corrected me.

It went downhill from there, the captain pulling details
from me like an exorcist yanking out bad spirits. It was more
than half an hour before Captain Cal Xavier left, replete
with the feast of incriminating information that Ingrid had
helped to supply.

I listened to the captain of the Verduras Police Department drive off. Then I turned to Ingrid.

"Find another hotel," I told her.

"But Kate!" she objected. "I thought you were my
friend . . ."

"Another hotel," I repeated and turned on my heel.

"But that's not nice!" Ingrid yelped as I found my purse.
"It's . . . it's gross!"

I didn't reply as I slammed my own door behind me.

Somehow it seemed wrong that *I* was making the dra-
matic exit from my own house. But I had an acupuncture appointment to go to.

Phyllis Oberman's office was located not far from me in
Mill Valley. And it was mellow. The sound of birds and
flutes swam harmoniously in the air as I entered. The walls
were tinted aqua, the furnishings a light peach. And the receptionist was blond and slight and spoke so quietly I could
barely hear her voice.

"I'm here to see Dr. Oberman," I told her, muting my own
tone. Phyllis was after all, as I could see from the diploma
hanging behind the receptionist's desk between two art
prints, a doctor of Chinese medicine.

"Please, sit down," the receptionist whispered as if sharing an important secret.

I sat. Unfortunately, I sat on some kind of box that let out a clanging of church bells. I jumped up. A New Age whoopee cushion? My heart was pounding like the church bells.

"Oh my!" the receptionist whispered as she ran toward me. "The Sound Soother. I wondered where it had gone."

Within moments, she flicked the proper switches and the box was silent. We were back to flutes and birds. And intimate whispers as she sat down on the couch next to me.

"My name is Juliet," the receptionist told me. "And I'm terribly, terribly sorry to have upset your balance."

"No problem," I assured her, sensing a possible point of entry as my pulse returned to normal. "Juliet, how long have you worked for Dr. Oberman?"

"Oh, my," Juliet answered. "Five years at least. It's so soothing here."

I was beginning to feel drowsy myself, even after the church bells. Was it the birds and flutes? Or a little something extra in the incense that filled the room? I roused myself to nosiness.

"I'm a little worried," I told Juliet. "I've only met the doctor once and she seems a little, well . . ."

"Brusque," Juliet filled in helpfully.

I nodded, trying to look scared. It wasn't hard. The doctor was going to stick needles into me, after all.

"Oh, she's much more compassionate than she seems," Juliet assured me. "She really cares. And she's really beautiful, isn't she?"

I nodded sincerely, remembering Phyllis Oberman's tall, lush body, a body that cried out to be painted in an age when large women were better appreciated. That along with her big hazel eyes and creamy white skin—

"I wish I could be that big and beautiful," Juliet went on. "And you should see her boyfriend. He's a huge man, over six feet and three hundred pounds, but so sexy, so graceful. They're such a pair. He's a bail bondsman."

"Wow," I said, imagining the two together, on Mount Olympus. Then I got back to work.

"Did she see Shayla Greenfree much?" I asked innocently.

"Who?" Juliet asked and drew her head back from mine.

"Shayla was an author—"

"Oh, you mean that weird little woman who wears tinted glasses and looks like a leprechaun?" Juliet asked.

It was then that I remembered that Wayne and I were supposed to be watching out for Yvette Cassell. So far, neither of us had been doing much of a job on that assignment.

"When did the little woman come—" I began.

"Juliet?" came a questioning voice from above us. I flinched. The acupuncturist was in. And looming. At least there were no needles in her hands. Yet.

I swallowed and followed Dr. Phyllis Oberman into her office.

"Juliet tells me you have a sinus problem," she led off once we were seated.

"And a murder problem," I added. I wasn't going to put anything over on Phyllis. I was pretty sure of that.

Phyllis glared at me from those beautiful hazel eyes.

"Shayla was always difficult," she admitted.

All right! She was going to talk.

"You know that I was acquainted with Shayla in school, I suppose?" she said. "When she was still Shirley?"

I nodded.

"I will say this, and this only. Then I'll do your treatment," Phyllis announced. She stared into my eyes for agreement.

"All right," I conceded.

"In my view, which is many years old, since I've hardly seen Shirley since high school, Shirley was a woman of great internal integrity, despite her apparent ruthlessness. She did what she felt she had to do to give her life meaning. It wasn't easy for women our age. I must be at least ten years older than you. And what a difference in culture those ten years meant. I went the traditional route: got married and had kids, worked as a nurse. Good work, but not my life's work. Once my children were grown, and my husband had left, I began to see the human potential in alternative medicine. I went to school while I did nursing, here first, and then, once I'd saved the money, in China."

Phyllis went silent, her hazel eyes on the wall behind me, brooding.

"Shirley?" I prompted.

"Shirley was smart," Phyllis said as if she'd never stopped speaking. "I only talked with her maybe a dozen times over the years, but often enough to know she was on her own track. Her paradigm was different than mine, but no less valid. And her exceptional writing proved her worth."

I waited for more.

"It's time for your treatment," the doctor said.

In minutes, I was lying on a couch, listening to birds and flutes, staring at a fuzzy picture of waves, with a set of needles inserted under my eyes, and another above them, and a couple alongside my nose for good measure. They hadn't actually hurt too much going in, but my own fear was tensing every muscle in my body, for all the relaxing music. I was afraid to move my face, even afraid to move my toes, in case I'd jar the needles. I lay there, stiff as a corpse until Phyllis came back to release me, and then she was gone. I paid Juliet for the treatment and flew out of the office.

On the way home in the car I sniffed experimentally. I could breathe better. But maybe that was just fear opening my nasal passages.

I walked into my house, pondering the enigma of Phyllis Oberman, a woman who valued integrity, yet she'd neglected to tell the police of her relationship with the murder victim. And then I came perforated-face to face with Raoul Raymond.

"What the hell are you doing here?" I demanded impatiently.

"Ah, the beautiful Ms. Jasper!" he cried. "I am but a cad. I can no longer say I love you."

"Really?" I asked cautiously. Hopefully.

"I love Ingrid," he finished.

"And I love Raoul," Ingrid added from behind me.

"Wonderful." I congratulated them both.

I moved closer to Raoul than I liked to. But it was necessary to whisper in his ear.

"Show her you really love her," I advised him. "Take her away tonight."

SEVENTEEN

✦

Raoul's boiled-egg eyes widened spectacularly. Even the unruly curls on the top of his head danced as he stared at me.

"You don't mind?" he yelped in astonishment, so astonished his accent slipped for a moment.

"Look, are you rich?" I asked him. Usually I'm not so direct, but Ingrid's disappearance was riding on my rudeness.

"I have a certain, um . . . inheritance," he answered, his accent and charm back. He waved his hand gracefully. "From my late father."

"Yeah?" I prodded suspiciously.

"He was in the carpeting business," Raoul whispered into my ear. I was pretty sure I was hearing the truth now, sans accent. "Old fart made a bundle. And just me and Ruthie—you know—Ramona, to leave it to."

"Ramona's your sister?" I shot back. Now, *he'd* surprised *me*.

He looked over my shoulder, suddenly nervous. Was Ramona his excuse for not becoming too involved with the series of women he fell "in love" with? I decided I didn't care. I just wanted him to take Ingrid off my hands.

"Ingrid," I announced, swiveling my head to look at her where she stood behind me. "Raoul is rich. You are now homeless. Let him be your new hotel. Go for it." I felt like a minister at a wedding. A happy minister.

But Ingrid stuck out her lower lip. Perhaps I'd been a bit too insensitive? A bit too . . . gross?

"Raoul loves you," I corrected myself quickly. "Let him sweep you off your feet."

But when I turned back to Raoul, I could see that *he* was beginning to look panicked now. Maybe I shouldn't have mentioned homeless. Maybe I should have just left them alone.

"Poor Ingrid is just temporarily homeless," I backpedaled desperately. "A romantic affair, you understand?"

"Ah," Raoul breathed. He brought his hand to his heart in comprehension. "The romance. It is everything."

He looked longingly over my shoulder at Ingrid. Romance lived.

And then I did leave them alone, tiptoeing to my office to sit at my desk and beat back the paperwork jungle with my No. 1 pencil.

Wayne rolled on home in time to fix me a late lunch. I told him about Ingrid and Raoul over a quiet repast of non-Whol-ios, as the two lovers communicated in coos and murmurs from our living room. Wayne told me the two had been holding hands when he'd passed them.

"Good," I said, feeling hope warm my chest for the first time. The feeling went perfectly with the toasty soba noodle salad that Wayne had fixed. The salad that Ingrid hadn't even sniffed out in her current state of bliss. Or anticipatory bliss, or whatever she was feeling in her predatory little heart.

"Think he's really rich?" Wayne whispered.

"Probably," I answered judiciously.

"Then she'll be all over him like an opportunistic affection," Wayne predicted.

I chortled and leaned forward. "I told her to get a hotel," I confided.

Wayne smiled. And the whole room felt lighter. The sunlight was shimmering in through the slats of the window in the back door. And it was beautiful, glowing in fuzzy lines on the grainy wood of the kitchen table.

"If that doesn't work, there's always the skunk broker," he said. But then, suddenly, the smile left his face. "Why'd you tell her to go to a hotel?" he asked.

Sometimes I wished Wayne was just a little dumber. Only sometimes. And just a little.

But he wasn't, so I told him about Captain Cal's visit, his friendly relationship with Ingrid and Ingrid's blathering about my "fight" with Marcia. My sweetie didn't look happy anymore. So I told him about Phyllis Oberman too. Might as well make his day.

He glared, and opened his mouth. Mental tai chi time.

"We forgot about Yvette," I reminded him.

He shut his mouth and his eyes flickered guiltily beneath his lowered brows.

"Do you think she's all right?" I asked quietly. "We did promise Lou—"

"Okay, Kate," he growled. "Message received."

He pushed himself away from the table with the warm soba noodle salad. Away from the lines of sunlight. And went to the telephone to call Yvette Cassell. But of course, she wasn't home.

The phone rang the minute Wayne set the receiver back in its cradle. He picked it up.

He grunted and uh-huhed a few times and then whispered "Ivan" my way as he kept on listening.

"Ivan's for dinner?" he asked me finally, his hand over the mouthpiece.

I thought about the danger of pursuing this investigation any further. Then I thought about all the paperwork I had to do.

"Sure," I told him.

"Well?" I prompted after Wayne hung up the phone. I knew twenty minutes of grunting and uh-huhing weren't necessary for the acceptance of one dinner invitation.

"At least we know where Yvette Cassell is," he answered. "Or was."

"And where was that?" I continued to prompt, wishing I was Captain Cal Xavier for a minute. He'd probably be able to get information out of Wayne faster. Or maybe not.

"Ivan's," he answered. "At the bookstore, nosing around. Alive and well when she left."

"Should we call to see if she made it home?" I asked.

But there was no answer at the Cassell residence when Wayne phoned. And there was no answer an hour later when I called, in the midst of trying to figure out why the bank thought I had $26.72 more in my business account than I did. Or an hour later, when I'd finally found the error in my own ledger. Or another hour later, when I'd found another mistake. And then it was time to go to Ivan's house for dinner. At least we'd been invited to visit his home. I don't think I could have tolerated another evening event at Fictional Pleasures. Not after the previous evening's event.

"Just how are we supposed to keep an eye on Yvette Cassell?" Wayne demanded as he steered his Jaguar toward Ivan's house in Tiburon. "Move in with her?"

"Have Ingrid move in with her?" I suggested innocently.

Wayne barked out a laugh, then swallowed it again. He was right. It wouldn't be very funny if Yvette became the third fatality while Lou was away on his business trip. But how the hell were we supposed to watch over someone we couldn't even find? Neither of us had an answer by the time we drove up the long winding driveway to Ivan's home.

Ivan's decorator-beautiful home in Tiburon never failed to impress me, set atop a peak that allowed a visitor seated in the elegant living room a view not only of the Golden Gate Bridge, but of the Bay Bridge and everything else in between. Or maybe I should have said Nancy's home in Tiburon never failed to impress me, because the home was much more his wife's than his. In almost all ways. Not only did Nancy make far more money as a busy Tiburon dentist than Ivan made as a quiet bookseller, but Ivan didn't actually seem to notice much about his own home, except for the bookshelves and their contents. The sweeping views, vaulted ceilings, and original works of art that set off the white-on-white living room might have been invisible to him. The only room where he ever seemed comfortable was his own den, which was as stuffed with books as Fictional Pleasures. And the kitchen.

Because Ivan could cook. And that's exactly what he was doing when Nancy met us at the door.

"So good to see you two again," she greeted us, smiling her perfect smile and waving us into her perfect living room. I wondered whether a smile really meant friendly on Nancy Nakagawa's face. I wondered if she got free dentistry or fixed her own gleaming teeth. Nancy shared Ivan's Japanese-American ancestry and seemingly little else. Where Ivan's face was thuggish, Nancy's was delicate and attractively oval with wide-set eyes. Where Ivan smelled of wool and books, Nancy smelled of a sweet cologne too expensive for me to identify. Where Ivan was heavyset, Nancy was petitely stylish in a crimson miniskirted business suit and matching heels. The color made me remember she was a dentist. Was the crimson to match the color of—

"Ah, my friends," Ivan called out from behind his wife. "Want to follow me into the kitchen? I'm still cooking."

The smells could have pulled me into the kitchen on their own. Aromatic tai chi. I marched into the well-heated paradise of tile, wood, and copper, and breathed in lemon and garlic and curry and herbs and the almond smell of something baking. Wayne took a more aggressive interest, lifting the lids off pots and sniffing, peeking into the oven, discussing ingredients, grunting happily with Ivan as they put the final touches on the feast. No wonder the men were friends. They could talk cooking.

Nancy, who followed us in, stood with me in silence as our men communicated the best way they knew how. And all of my being cried out that Ivan not be a murderer. He was Wayne's friend. He could have been his brother.

"We're worried about our son, Neil," Nancy finally announced once we were properly seated at the dining room table on silk brocade chairs, sampling the eggplant dip on crusty whole-wheat bread. I made an effort to listen as my mouth embraced the flavors of garlicky capers and lemony herbs. "He's infatuated with this Winona Eads woman, and she's far too old for him." She paused with a significant look across the long rosewood table at her husband. "Among other things."

There was a short silence, and I noticed for the first time the soft background music. Violins so faint, I couldn't even catch the melody. Probably the same music Nancy piped in for her dental patients.

"Winona seems to be a serious young woman—" Ivan began.

I took another bite as Nancy retaliated.

"A serious young woman!" she snorted. "A serious mental case, if you ask me. And Ivan is actually considering offering her a job at the store."

"I need someone now that Marcia's gone," Ivan replied quietly. "And Winona truly loves and knows books—"

"Books aren't everything, Ivan," Nancy interrupted. A hint of affection actually stretched her face into something like a smile for a moment, but then it was gone. "The girl is trouble. Even her own mother won't speak to her—"

"Why?" I mumbled through a mouthful of eggplant and bread. Though I was fairly sure I knew the answer.

"Well, because . . ." Nancy's skin colored to more closely match her crimson suit. "Because of the child."

"Winona Eads is a single mother," Ivan put in. "But she cares for her son, Neil tells me, cares very well and very much. We aren't living in Victorian times. There is harmony possible—"

"Well, we're not living in the Age of Aquarius, either," Nancy countered. "Neil is our child." She slapped her well-manicured hands on the rosewood table, palms down. "And that's all that matters."

The war continued through the asparagus-and-watercress soup, and the curried yam salad. I was surprised Ivan was even capable of such military spirit. But in his own quiet way, he kept up with his wife.

It wasn't until we were devouring the main course, a deceptively simple linguine with fresh basil and vegetables, that Nancy's voice softened.

"My son's special," she murmured. "He's diabetic, you know. He has to give himself shots. Can you imagine that, our poor sweet kid . . . ?"

I was imagining all right, because shots implied syringes and Ivan had never mentioned his son being diabetic when we'd talked about access to syringes.

"The police suspect Neil," Ivan said, his gentle voice rising in pitch. "My own son."

"Neil, for God's sake!" his wife threw in, as if we hadn't understood.

For the moment, Nancy and Ivan seemed united, united by fear, but united all the same.

"Neil told me he said goodbye to Marcia before he left,

but then he just drove away," Ivan went on. He pushed his hands together. "He didn't see anyone hanging around—"

"He wasn't looking," Nancy put in angrily. "Why should he have been?"

"But he's okay," Ivan answered, reaching out to his wife with his gentle voice. "He's alive."

Nancy sighed, a sigh not unlike Ivan's. Or PMP's, for that matter. "That's right," she agreed. "At least he's alive. When I think how Ted's son died—" She shook her head slowly.

"Ted Brown?" I asked, alert now.

"Yeah," she answered, tilting her head my way. "Some weird disease. God, it was sad."

"Do you know Ted?" I asked.

"Yeah, I know Ted," she answered, her tone louder now, almost defensive. "I'm his dentist. I was Shayla's dentist too. I know the best teeth in town."

I glared over at Ivan, adding to my list another little thing he hadn't bothered to tell us. First, his son's syringe-use, and now, his wife's role as Shayla's dentist.

Ivan got up to clear the dinner plates. Quickly. And refused any offers of help.

Nancy ushered us into the living room on cue. She might not know why I was glaring at Ivan, but she seemed to know enough to back up his retreat. Maybe they had more in common than I thought.

Wayne and I were admiring the view of the Golden Gate and Bay bridges, lights twinkling against the darkness now, when Ivan brought in dessert, a platter of homemade almond biscotti and raspberry dipping sauce. He set it on a white lacquered coffee table shaped like an oversized lap tray. We took our places on the long sofa behind the coffee table, also white with throw pillows in blush and aqua. It was a long reach to the platter. I really wanted to sit on the floor. The plush white rug would have been plenty comfortable. And it was cool in the expansive living room, too cool. It would probably be warmer on the rug. But I looked at Nancy in her miniskirted suit and decided against the floor.

I'd snagged a biscotti and made the long-distance dip into the raspberry sauce when Ivan spoke again.

"I found the camera and film that Marcia shot during the signing," he announced. I jerked my head around to look at him. And dripped raspberry sauce onto the pristine white carpet. "I got the pictures made up this afternoon. I have the prints."

"Have you looked at them?" I breathed, bending over to absently swipe at the splatters of sauce with my napkin. All that filled my mind was Marcia. Was there a clue in her pictures?

"Don't worry," Nancy said.

"What?" I replied.

"The sauce, I'll take care of it," she explained.

Even then, it took me a moment to bring my mind back. Back from the storeroom at Fictional Pleasures. Ivan squatted down and laid a blue cardboard box of prints on the coffee table next to the platter of biscotti. He closed his eyes for a moment and then slid the top off the box.

"I was afraid to look," he answered belatedly. "Afraid of what I'd see. Or what I'd miss."

I nodded and sat down on the floor next to him. Wayne crowded in next to me and Ivan lowered himself from his squat to sit, too. Even Nancy knelt down across from us, on the other side of the coffee table, miniskirt and raspberry sauce forgotten.

Ivan pulled out an envelope of negatives and a stack of glossy prints. I recognized the first one right away. It was a picture of the authors' table, from the authors' side: neat stacks of books and pens for each author, three glasses of water, and one open book. An open book with Shayla Greenfree's signature. Nothing more, nothing less.

"So she could copy the signature?" Wayne suggested aloud.

Ivan grunted, turned over the print, and laid down another photo of the authors' table, this one a close-up of Shayla's signature. As Ivan flipped the prints over, we saw more and more shots of Shayla's signature. And then, finally, a few close-ups of Ted Brown's and Yvette Cassell's signatures. Then a couple of shots of Ted Brown, S.X. Greenfree, and Yvette Cassell trooping down the aisle from the storeroom, and a few shots of the audience, including Wayne and myself. And one of Winona Eads lurking behind a bookshelf. That was all. No surprises.

We passed around the pictures and scrutinized them one by one. But I didn't see any clues to the murder. Only to Marcia's scam.

"Where'd you find the camera and film?" Wayne asked as he looked at a shot of the authors.

"In the storeroom, behind some books," Ivan told him.

I shivered involuntarily. Was that camera what Marcia had been hiding in the back room of the store? But why? Because the film might show her all-too-evident interest in author signatures? I ran my eyes over the pictures again.

"Would the books be more valuable once Shayla was dead?" I asked Ivan after I couldn't look at the glossy prints anymore.

"Probably," he answered simply.

"But—" Wayne began.

"I know, I know," I finished for him. "Marcia is dead too. So she's not likely to be the murderer." I didn't bother to add that I'd ruled out murder/suicide in my own mind. Self-inflicted handcart injury wasn't a likely method of suicide.

"Why were the books already signed?" I tried.

"We like to accommodate the people who can't make events," Ivan explained, his voice tired, disappointed. I didn't blame him. I'd hoped there would be an answer in the prints too. "The authors sign some books ahead for them."

I took one last look at a shot of Shayla, S.X. Greenfree, a

swan in elegant blue silk. If I squeezed my eyes and thought back, I could just see the former Shirley Green beneath the smooth exterior. I sighed, too. It was too bad PMP wasn't there to join us.

Wayne and I scarfed down more almond biscotti without the appreciation that Ivan's baking deserved, then took our leave. Nancy and Ivan Nakagawa stood at the door as we left, with identical looks of hopelessness on their faces. Why had I thought the two had nothing in common? They had their son in common, if nothing else. And then Wayne drove back down the winding driveway, through Tiburon, and toward home.

"Should we drive to Yvette's and see if she's there?" I asked as we were almost home. It had taken me that long to remember her again. To remember our promise to Lou.

"Maybe call first so we don't startle her," Wayne suggested as he turned the car into our driveway.

"Right," I said. We sat in the car for a moment.

Then we left the Jaguar's warm leather womb and climbed out into the cool night air.

We had walked halfway up the stairs before we noticed that someone was waiting for us. Someone seated quietly in one of the chairs on our deck. Was it Ingrid? My heart beat a little louder. Or Bob? Or one of our murder suspects? I tried a long, cleansing breath to calm myself down. Or was it Felix? Or maybe an overgrown skunk? Or were Felix and an overgrown skunk one and the same?

The silent figure didn't speak as we took the next stair. And its identity didn't become any clearer. In part, because the figure was dressed in black, from its headdress and veil to its long black robe. Dressed in black with its head lolling back over the top of the chair.

Had Death come to our house for a visit?

Eighteen

✦

"Whaa?" the figure in the chair mumbled, jerking its head forward. "Damn, fu-fuddin' . . . guess I fell asleep."

It wasn't Death. It was Yvette Cassell. And for once, I was actually glad to see her.

Or at least to *hear* her through the heavy black veil she wore.

She jumped out of her chair, stretched out her black-robed arms like an oversized crow in the starlight, and then yawned.

I walked up the last few stairs and gave her an impromptu hug. Lou would be happy. Not only was his wife alive, I had her in my grip. For the moment.

"Whaa?" she repeated, suspiciously this time, and I released her from my embrace. Her costume smelled of must and mothballs anyway.

"Been here long?" Wayne asked from my side.

"Shi-shift, no. No more than half an hour, I guess," she answered, pulling the veil up and tossing it over the rest of the headdress. Sure enough, there she was, sharp nose, tinted glasses, and all. "I rang the doorbell, but no one answered."

"Why are you wearing that . . . that stuff?" I asked. With the veil and black burnoose, if it was a burnoose, she might have been a combination sheik/nun . . . or something.

"I'm in disguise," she confided, lowering her voice mysteriously.

"I can see that," I told her slowly, suddenly not as happy to see Yvette as I had been. How do you protect a woman who disguises herself in outfits that wouldn't even blend in on Halloween? "But *why* are you in disguise?" I finally asked.

"That's for me to know and you to find out," she replied, her voice a falsetto now.

Ugh. Not only was she speaking in the language I remembered as noxiously peculiar to high school, but I couldn't even remember the ritual response. I hate it when that happens.

"So anyway," she went on, "I gotta talk to you guys. I think maybe I've got a lead, you know. Whaddaya think, huh?"

"About what?" I asked carefully.

Yvette looked around her as if for eavesdroppers. I found myself following her glance nervously until I reminded myself that any eavesdroppers out here were likely to be non-human ones, and probably black with white stripes. Yvette pulled the veil over her face again.

"Let's go on inside," I suggested.

"Yeah, yeah," Yvette agreed impatiently, looking around her again as I opened the front door.

I didn't have to turn on the living room lights. Ingrid had already done that. She was folding a pair of jeans and placing them in her suitcase as we entered. And I was hoping that meant she was packing.

"Hey!" Yvette objected as she followed us into the living room.

I turned to Yvette, wondering what the problem was now. Was she upset by the lingering scent of skunk? But Yvette's eyes were on Ingrid. Ingrid folded a halter top in three precise rectangles and added it to the jeans in her suitcase. My heart executed a premature jump for joy.

"Were you here the whole time I was ringing the bell?" Yvette demanded, pointing her finger at Ingrid accusingly.

"Uh-huh," Ingrid muttered. I figured she'd have a hard time actually speaking while keeping her lower lip jutted out that far.

"Then why didn't you answer the figgin' bell?" Yvette shouted.

"I'm homeless," Ingrid answered briefly, then turned her perfect back on us as she continued to pack. Yes, packing. Her back was a beautiful sight in movement.

"Yeah, that's cool," Yvette replied, seeming to accept Ingrid's explanation. "Anyway, I think I've got it. It took a while, but now . . ." Her words trailed off suggestively. If she was trying to create suspense, she was doing a great job. If she was trying to drive me crazy, she was doing even better.

"What?" I prodded. "What do you think you've got?"

Yvette put her left hand up in the halt position, shaking her head. I was sure she was grinning under that veil.

"Not so damn-darn fast," she warned, plopping down in one of the swinging chairs and pushing off with her feet. Her veil floated in the breeze as she swung to and fro. "First we talk suspects. Huh, huh?"

"Fine," Wayne agreed, laying a restraining hand on my arm. He must have felt the micro-movements in that arm, urging it up and toward Yvette's neck. I willed my arm to rest, and Wayne and I took a seat together in the other swinging chair to wait for Yvette's murder-suspect review.

"First, you guys," she began.

Ingrid turned back to us with interest then, holding a piece of lime-green spandex in midair.

"Shayla called out your name—" Yvonne accused.

"But that was because—" I began.

"I know, I know," she cut back in impatiently. "But still, she called out your name and you were there. Even if I can't think of any motive, to tell you the truth."

"Me neither," I assured her, as my mind actually tried to think of one. My mind works that way, unfortunately.

Ingrid turned her back on us again with a small sigh of discontent.

"Marcia Armeson was up to something, some kind of scam, I'll bet," Yvette went on, bending forward eagerly. I wondered how much she knew. "But she's toast. Or scrambled eggs maybe."

Ivan's lovely meal flip-flopped in my stomach. The description was too apt. I wondered where Yvette had gotten her information. Or had she been there? Was Marcia's scrambled head—

"Now Ivan had the best opportunity. Talk about your man on the spot. Shick, he set up the whole fuddin' show—"

"But if he wanted to kill Shayla, would he have done it in his own—" Wayne began.

"Naah," Yvette agreed, waving a hand. "Probably not. Unless it was some spur of the moment thing. But it couldn't be, not with that bracelet. Though there's his kid and that Winona person."

Before I could ask what his kid and Winona had to do with it, her mouth moved on.

"Now Zoe's an interesting one . . ." Yvette's words faltered again. And I couldn't see her face under the veil. Was she torturing us on purpose?

"Why is Zoe so interesting?" I asked, keeping my voice

calm with an effort. Or at least trying to. A squeak at the end of my sentence ruined the effect.

"Well," Yvette whispered, pushing her veiled face our way, her chair suddenly stalled.

I leaned forward to hear her words. But I never got the chance. The expectant silence was pierced by the sound of a sudden hiss, a skittering of paws on linoleum, and terrified yips from the kitchen.

Apollo came rushing into the living room, a streak of upright fur followed by C.C., who stopped on one front claw as Apollo slipped behind Ingrid, then licked her other front claw smugly and exited the room. I was pretty sure that drop of red on her claw had been blood. I was afraid to look at Apollo. Though my racing heart beat with something like pride for a moment. My cat was tough.

"And Dean," Yvette went on unperturbed. Yep, Yvette was tough, too. "And of course, Ted—"

"And you," I countered. "And Lou."

"What the figgin' heck!" she objected. She yanked the veil back from her face, revealing the anger it might have hidden. "Whaddaya mean Lou?"

"Lou was there just like the rest of us—" I began.

"Well, Lou is no murderer," she cut in, crossing her arms and glaring our way. "You can count on that."

Right, I thought. That's all I needed, Yvette's word that Lou wasn't a murderer. And she hadn't even bothered to assure us that *she* wasn't a murderer.

"But which one had all three?" Yvette went on before I could voice those or any other doubts.

"All three what?" I asked as she paused for a moment to fiddle with her veil.

"Motive, means, and opportunity," she replied, pushing off the floor with her tiny feet and putting her chair in motion again. "Whaddaya think?"

"I don't know, who?" I said evenly.

"That's for me to know and you to find out," she answered.

I'll kill her, I thought. My pulse beat out the message like a war drum. *Kill Yvette. Kill Yvette.*

Wayne must have heard the drums from my side, because he spoke up again and quickly.

"Lou's worried about you," he said. "Wants you to be careful."

"Yeah, Lou's such a sweetie," Yvette murmured, a smile softening her sharp face. "He's so worried about his trip. But he's gotta make it." She smiled again, and pulled a couple of feet of wooden cudgel from the sleeve of her robe.

Wayne and I stopped swinging in our chair simultaneously. Was that thing lethal? It was a different cudgel than the oak one she had brandished at her house. Longer. Scarier. Yvette slapped the club in her hand. I thought about centering myself. Not easy to do in a chair that didn't touch the ground.

"See, I'm safe," she informed us. "Got my fuddin' shillelagh."

"Yvette," Wayne tried reasonably. "That shillelagh isn't going to do much good if someone is really determined to—"

"Huh!" she came back. "And anyway, I'm almost there. I've almost got it."

I wouldn't ask "what" this time. I'd just beat it out of her, shillelagh or no shillelagh. Verbally, I decided. There had to be a button to push on Yvette to get her to talk sensibly. Vanity?

"I should have known you'd figure it out," I began. I swallowed to keep from choking on my insincerity and plodded on. "You're so good at—"

The phone rang, interrupting me.

I ignored it, throwing pride and ethics to the wind. "Maybe we can help you, now that you're almost there. Maybe—"

"Kate, this is Zoe," the machine said hesitantly. "Zoe Ingersoll. There's some stuff I think you ought to know."

Damn.

I rushed to the phone as Zoe was apologizing for the call. I caught it just before she hung up. Maybe Wayne could suck the story out of Yvette, whatever it was. But Zoe had information. And I wouldn't have to beat it out of her, verbally or otherwise.

"Hello, hello!" I shouted into the receiver. "I'm really here."

Zoe's laughter greeted me over the line.

"I wish I could say the same," she told me. "I'm never sure if I'm 'really here.' Or if I want to be . . ."

I took a seat in my old Naugahyde comfy chair by the phone. I could still see Yvette and Wayne across the entryway, but I wouldn't be able to hear Zoe and them at the same time. In fact, I was barely hearing Zoe now, just watching them. I turned my back to the living room and pressed my ear to the receiver to really listen.

". . . being too existential," Zoe was saying.

"You said you had some stuff to tell me," I prompted, hoping I hadn't just missed the important stuff.

"Oh, yeah. Duh, sorry, did it again," Zoe reproached herself. "See, I talked to Dean." Her merry voice turned serious now. "He told me I was holding back on you. Holding back on my feelings. Self-denial, I'm an expert—"

"And?" I cut in, unable to resist the temptation to glance over my shoulder at Yvette and Wayne again. Yvette was waving her arms now. Wayne was nodding. I brought my head back around, bringing my mind and ears back to Zoe at the same time.

"See, I told you that Shayla really cared for me." Zoe's voice raced now. "That she really believed I could get well. You know: creative visualization, white light and coffee enemas. Would you like your coffee with white light? Anyway, there's a part of me—okay a lot of me—that doesn't believe that. About Shayla, I mean, not the white light."

Then silence. I could still hear Zoe breathing, but she wasn't talking anymore.

Yvette was, though.

"You guys hafta come, get it?" Yvette was demanding. I wondered if Wayne was agreeing to her demands. I pulled my mind back to Zoe again.

"What is it exactly that a lot of you doesn't believe?" I asked her cautiously. Was talking with Zoe going to be as frustrating as it was with Yvette?

"That she really cared." Zoe sighed. "Dean told me it was important to be honest about Shayla. And, oh phooey, I think all the stuff she said about how I should throw away my medications and heal myself was just to piss me off enough so I'd stop being her friend, her insignificant other. You know, so it wouldn't be *her* fault. I think she wanted *me* to break it off. So she could still see herself as the great and compassionate goddess, you know." Zoe laughed, but her laughter was maniacal now. "Only it didn't work, 'cause I'm too big a wuss to blow up. So then she just stopped talking to me altogether."

"So, you think she wanted to end your friendship, but didn't want to be the guilty party?" I summarized slowly, trying to understand, hoping this had something, anything, to do with Shayla's murder.

"See, that's what Dean wanted me to explain, I think," Zoe went on eagerly. "That's how Shayla operated. She wanted to be a good person. To think of herself as a good person. And basically she was, I guess. But when she wasn't, she always found ways to rationalize her ruthlessness. That's why she didn't have many friends. It was just too hard for her, too risky, you know. 'Cause it was too hard to be perfect and she wanted so much to be perfect."

I was nodding like a fool. Zoe couldn't see me over the phone.

"But in a weird way, Shayla really was an okay person. She might have been into twenty ways of creative denial, but it was 'cause she tried so hard to be good that she got all tangled up. She couldn't bear to realize she hurt people. That's why she was so unapproachable. Oh, phooey, I don't know. But in spite of everything, I want to help you guys find her killer. Because *I* really did care about *her*. And I know Scott trusts you."

There was another silence while I wondered if I trusted Scott Green. He was Shayla's husband. Didn't husbands kill wives? Or his lover, Dean Frazier. Or Zoe Ingersoll for that matter longing to be part of the magic circle. Was it more toxic than magic?

"So how do I help?" Zoe asked.

"Um . . . uh," I answered. Her question caught me off guard. When someone asks how they can help at a party, it's easy. They can put crackers on a tray, or cut up vegetables, or make a dip. But how can someone help solve a murder?

"Outside of confessing," she added.

I took a deep breath. Was she confessing?

"Just kidding," she assured me quickly. "Even on steroids, I'm too big a wuss to actually kill anyone."

I sat there in my Naugahyde chair and tried to think of a way for her to help. But I couldn't. Unless . . .

"All right, you're an artist," I suggested finally. "Think of this as a puzzle, as a great big piece of art. You have all the pieces, how do they fit together? Help me think."

"I can do that," Zoe answered slowly. Then her voice took on speed. "At least most of the time, I can think. Duh. Maybe if I cut out pieces of fabric, like each one is a suspect and then . . ."

I hung up the phone after at least fifteen more minutes of hearing Zoe's creative process unfold aloud. I'd never look at artwork the same way again. But at least Zoe's investigative process was safe. Unlike some of ours. I turned to look at Yvette.

But Yvette was gone. And worse yet, Ingrid wasn't. She was still folding pieces of clothing while Wayne sat in the hanging chair, swinging slowly back and forth.

I walked over to the living room and waited until his chair swung to the rear. Then I kissed the back of his head. Ingrid wasn't looking, anyway.

"We're going to a meeting of science-fiction writers tomorrow," Wayne announced quietly, turning his head my way as he stilled the movement of his chair.

"What?" I demanded.

"Yvette's suggestion," he explained. "Shayla was a member of the organization. People there knew her. Yvette thought we might learn something by going."

"And that way we can keep an eye on Yvette," I added, suddenly realizing why he'd agreed.

He nodded. "Just a couple of hours, okay?" he asked, looking over his shoulder at me, his vulnerable eyes peeking out from beneath his brows.

"Of course," I agreed and kissed him again, this time on the mouth.

Ingrid sniffed, loudly.

How could I have forgotten Ingrid? Wishful thinking?

"Bedtime?" I suggested to Wayne.

Ingrid sniffed even louder. I thought I heard her murmur "homeless," and "no one cares," among other things.

Wayne pulled himself out of the swinging chair and walked around it to put his hand in mine. I thought of romance. And then of Ingrid. And then the doorbell rang.

I opened the door cautiously, but not cautiously enough. Felix Byrne passed by me like a torpedo. Like a small projectile that explodes when meeting a hard object. The hard object was Wayne.

Felix was halfway into the living room, ranting about his "so-called friends," "potato brains," and unexplained "stiffs" when Wayne blocked his way.

"Another goner, mashed into glopperoo, and I get diddly!" Felix protested loudly.

Wayne stared down at him, like a man ready to pull an unsightly weed from his prized begonias.

"You guys are supposed to be my pals," Felix tried again, but the righteousness in his voice was fading.

"Calm down," Wayne suggested with all the friendliness of an execution squad. "Or leave."

"But," Felix objected. Then he spotted Ingrid.

He smiled her way unashamedly. "Hey, howdy-hi there, Ingrid," he called out.

And Ingrid smiled back.

Terrifying thoughts filled my mind. My mouth went dry. Felix and Ingrid. Ingrid confesses all. Banner headlines: I LIVED WITH A MONSTER MURDERESS— Then someone pushed the rationality switch in my brain. Because I wasn't sure yet that Marcia's death was necessarily murder. I wondered if our reporter pal knew.

"All we saw was a dead body," I told Felix. His eyes bounced from Ingrid to me like Ping-Pong balls. That was good. "Was Marcia Armeson murdered?"

He opened his mouth to rant a little more, looked up at Wayne, and visibly changed verbal direction.

"Not necessarily," Felix answered. "Guys at the Verduras cop shop say it could have been an accident. Ho, ho, ho— some accident. Like Dahmer just messed up with his lawn mower, you know what I mean—"

"And if it wasn't an accident?" I prompted.

Felix sighed. I was killing the melodrama. But he answered.

"Looks like this Marcia broad got herself pushed into a

pile of boxes and then the handcart fell on her. The pushing part being pretty essential to her little 'accident.' "

My mind went back to the storeroom. I could imagine pushing Marcia myself if she'd launched herself at me like she'd done before. And then she would have fallen into the boxes and the handcart would have tumbled down—

I wrapped my arms around myself to stop the shivers, to stop the image.

"But you guys were there," Felix went on. "What did you see?" His eyes were glittering.

"Time for a walk," Wayne suggested and grabbed my elbow. That shook me out of my thoughts. Because we were out the door, down the stairs, and tramping down the driveway before I had a chance to breathe, much less think. And then Wayne marched me up the dark and cold unpaved edge of the road. Wayne's walks belonged in triathlons.

I panted, but kept up the pace as Felix followed us, puffing loudly and calling out questions even more loudly. Questions that I didn't have enough air to answer. After about six or seven blocks, however, Felix tripped over something behind us. Hah, no night vision, I thought, and then slammed my foot into a slab of concrete.

"Holy socks, you guys," he pleaded as we passed the concrete and moved out of range. "You on some gonzo health kick or what?"

Neither of us replied. We just kept marching as Felix's dispirited mutterings grew fainter and fainter until they blended into the night sounds of cars and dogs and wind.

Wayne slowed down then, and we circled back, walking leisurely but our minds racing.

"Could it have been an accident, Kate?" Wayne asked me, his voice a quiet murmur in the cold night air.

I shrugged, then realized he probably couldn't see me.

"The scary thing is whoever killed her might have just meant to push her," I answered. "But the handcart . . ."

"Couldn't have planned the handcart, do you think?" Wayne ventured.

I put my arm around his waist in answer. He reciprocated with an arm around my shoulder and we shuffled the rest of the way home in the awkward embrace.

When we got there, all the lights were off. Even the living room lights were dimmed as we opened the front door.

"Do you think Ingrid's still here?" I whispered to Wayne.

But before Wayne could answer, a tall figure came barreling past us, nearly knocking us over on the way out the front door.

It wasn't Ingrid, that was for sure. But, if it wasn't Ingrid, who was it?

NINETEEN

My body remained frozen at the front door as my mind tried to figure out who'd just run past us. But Wayne's body wasn't frozen. He'd paused for about the time it took my brain to process the information that I wasn't breathing. Then he raced across the deck and down the stairs after the person or thing who was still running, frantic steps clattering on the gravel of the driveway now.

I ran after Wayne just before he gave up the chase. I heard the sound of some kind of vehicle starting up as I hit the top stair. A car? A truck? And then the screech of tires.

Wayne came shambling back up the stairs before I even reached the bottom one.

"Same VW van," he informed me briefly. "Could see its shape."

"The one that followed us before?" I asked, my brain still not processing very swiftly. It was too cold, too dark, to think. At least that's what I told myself.

He nodded and continued up the stairs. I climbed the last

three with him. We stopped on the deck, both lost in thought. Or shock. My mouth revived first.

"But who—" I began.

"Yeah, who was that guy?" a voice from behind me demanded.

I hopped a couple of inches into the air to keep up with my heart, even though I knew *that* voice couldn't belong to anyone but Ingrid.

"You guys are mixed up with some really, really icky people, you know," she continued defiantly. I turned in the dim light and saw her put her hands on her hips.

"Did you see the intruder?" Wayne asked brusquely.

Ingrid shrugged her tanned shoulders. How could she look so warm out here in the cool night air, wearing nothing but spandex shorts and a halter top?

"Yes or no, Ingrid?" I persisted. "It's not that hard a question. Either you saw him or you didn't."

"I don't know if I should even talk to you two anymore," she answered, or didn't answer. She jogged in place as she spoke. "This house probably isn't even safe." She tossed a significant look behind her at our home. *Our* home.

"And that's why you're moving out," I told her, smoothing my voice, hoping to work hypnosis into its tone. "You have money. You're all packed. Why not go to a hotel tonight? Wouldn't it be nice to feel safe?"

"Well," she pondered. She crossed her bare arms and chewed on her lower lip for a moment, considering. "The guy is already gone, so I guess it's safe, anyway."

I wanted to tell her that it wasn't safe, that we were probably more dangerous to her than the intruder. At least I was. And then I wanted to demonstrate that danger. Bodily. But Wayne wasn't through with his questions.

"It was a man, then?" he asked.

"Yeah," she admitted. Cooperation, finally. Maybe I'd let

her spend one more night. As if I could stop her if she wanted to. She was probably a protected species by now.

"What did he look like?" Wayne prodded, ever so gently.

"Oh, just some guy," Ingrid told him. "Tall, I guess, with a hat and maybe a raincoat. It was really gross. See, I heard the door open and I thought it was you two, but then this guy came in, like, tiptoeing or something. So, I hid real quick behind the futon."

And covered her eyes, I would have bet.

"Anything else you can tell us about him?" Wayne tried.

"He was really, really scary, sneaking around," she answered, her eyes widening in memory. "He was looking at stuff and walking toward the hallway when you two came back. I heard him run out."

Apollo began to yip from behind Ingrid before she could say anything more. The shrill canine bursts perforated my brain like a dentist's drill.

"Oh, you poor little thing," Ingrid murmured, stooping to pat the terrier's head. "You were scared too, huh, Apolly?"

"Was he behind the futon with you?" I asked.

"Uh-huh," Ingrid announced proudly. "And he didn't even let out a sound."

"Great watch dog," I commented.

Ingrid eyed me suspiciously, then wrapped her arms around Apollo to reward him for his bravery.

Fair is fair. I wrapped my arms around Wayne, and then shepherded him into the house and down the hall to the bedroom to reward *him* for *his* bravery. And Wayne didn't yip once.

My psychic friend, Barbara Chu, called me Friday morning, right after Wayne left for work. And Ingrid went back to packing. How long could it take to pack a few suitcases? Was she unpacking them when we weren't looking, like Penelope unraveling her weaving while waiting for Odysseus?

"Ingrid will finish packing when she's good and ready, kiddo," Barbara told me when I picked up the phone. "And it's up to you to make sure she *is* good and ready. But I think you're just about to do that."

I ignored the fact that Barbara had answered my unvoiced question. I hadn't ever figured out how she did it, but I refused to give her the satisfaction of expressing my annoyance aloud. Not that it mattered, since she probably knew when she drove me crazy without my saying so, anyway.

"About time you called," I put in before she could gloat. And then immediately regretted the words, remembering her cousin dying of cancer.

"He passed on," she told me.

"Oh, Barbara, I'm sorry," I blurted out. I clenched my pencil in my hand. I was sorry. Sorry for his passing, sorry for her pain, sorry for my uncharitable thoughts.

"No need to worry, kiddo," she answered, her voice muted. "He's in the light now." Then her voice took on more of its usual vitality. "So let's go for lunch."

"Lunch?" I thumbed through the stack of invoices I was checking off and listened to C.C. chasing a yipping Apollo around the living room.

"Yeah, I wanna hear more about your murder. Let's meet at that new place on Third and Quesco."

"The Cat's Meow?" Yipping and paperwork, or lunch with a friend? My grip weakened on my pencil.

"Yeah, that's the one," she told me. "But Felix and I call it the 'psychic cafe.'"

I opened my mouth to ask why, but she was way ahead of me, as usual.

"You'll find out why when you get there," she assured me. "See you at twelve."

Then she hung up.

It was a done deal. So my No. 1 pencil worked hard on paper, smudging my fingers with graphite, while my mind worked hard on a plan to dislodge Ingrid, smudging my core ethics with evil thoughts. Zoe's words about how people treated her as a sufferer of Crohn's disease came back to me. But most likely, Ingrid wouldn't even know what Crohn's disease was. Still . . .

By eleven-thirty, I had a plan. Maybe. If Ingrid would buy it.

I got up from my desk to leave for lunch.

"Oh, Ingrid," I said as nonchalantly as possible as I neared the front door.

"Yeah?" she muttered, her back to me.

"I'm going out for a while, but a group of people from the Fenestry Society are coming in a little while—"

"So?" she replied.

"Well, you know about fenestry, don't you?"

"No," she said, but she turned my way.

"Well, they're a really good cause. You know, fenestry is a little bit like leprosy—"

"Leprosy!"

"Only worse," I continued. "The poor guys, first it starts with this rash, this really, really icky rash. And boils. And then the body parts start falling off—"

"What!" she yelped. She began doing jumping jacks, her eyes still on my face. "They don't send out guys to your house *with* this disease, do they?"

I nodded somberly as she upped the pace of her exercises. Hot damn. She *was* buying it.

"It's important that you hand them something for me—"

"Uh-uh," she cut me off, touching her palms to the floor now, then stretching. "Are you crazy? Is it catching?"

"Well . . . sometimes," I said softly, shrugging my shoulders. "But it's important you don't act put off when you see them—"

"You *are* crazy!" she shrieked, raising her arms into the air in an exercise I couldn't identify. "I'm outa this place!"

I didn't laugh until I was in my car speeding toward the Cat's Meow, and giving my inner apologies to any real sufferers of leprosy or any other potentially disfiguring illnesses.

I found the Cat's Meow on the corner of Third and Quesco. A serious-looking young woman in a multicolored head wrap met me at the door. She stared at me for a moment.

"Party of two?" she asked.

I looked around me. Barbara wasn't here yet.

"Yes," I admitted hesitantly.

Barbara came in a few minutes later, after I was seated at a small but warm and sunny table with cartoon cats smiling up at me from the tablecloth.

"Hey, kiddo," Barbara greeted me, looking gorgeous as usual in a violet jumpsuit with matching crystal earrings that framed her elegant Asian face perfectly. I stood up and gave my friend a long hug. Damn, that felt good. I felt big chunks of the last week's anxiety and sadness and frustration seeping out of me, loosening my tense muscles as they went.

"Feels good to me, too," Barbara murmured after we finally dropped our arms. "I needed you, Kate."

"Me too," I told her, wondering what to ask her about her cousin's death.

But the serious young woman who'd shown me to our table was back again before I could even form a question.

"You'll be having the grilled polenta triangles with mozzarella," she told Barbara.

"I guess I will," Barbara agreed.

"And you . . ." The woman turned my way, a little frown creasing her forehead for a moment. "The tofu brochette over soba noodles."

"But—" I began. The tofu brochette sounded good, though. In fact . . .

The waitress turned and walked away.

I looked at Barbara. She was wearing her smug little Buddha smile.

"The 'psychic cafe'?" I demanded.

She just nodded.

"You set that up, right?" I asked.

She shook her head and grinned.

I grinned back. The psychic cafe indeed. And then I began laughing again. And Barbara laughed with me. Then we both started giggling, and kept on giggling far longer than the joke warranted. And I felt the remaining chunks of anxiety and sadness and frustration burbling out as we did. Primal giggling, the poor woman's psychotherapy.

By the time I was slipping grilled, marinated tofu and vegetables off my skewer and onto my noodles, Barbara had told me about her cousin's death. In detail. But oddly, her description had calmed me, even cheered me. I hoped Shayla's final transition to wherever she was headed could be as beautiful as Barbara's imagination.

"Don't worry," Barbara answered. "It will be."

"Okay, smarty-pants," I challenged. "Who did it? Who killed Shayla Greenfree? Who killed Marcia Armeson?"

As Barbara's habitual smile left her face, I felt my hopes sink like a crystal into deep water. I should have realized. Barbara always knew everything but whodunit.

"Felix thinks Yvette killed them," she told me, shaking her head.

"Why?" I asked, leaning forward eagerly, tofu forgotten.

"Because he has no imagination, Kate. Jeez-Louise, he figures she's weird, so she did it."

I flinched. My logic, exactly. "So who, then?" I prodded.

"The sick woman certainly had motive to kill Shayla, and the man whose ideas Shayla stole . . ."

"Did Felix tell you about them?" I demanded.

She shook her head no. Then she grinned again. "I read his notebook."

"You what—"

"He's still mad at me because I sent Ann to talk to you instead of to him," she explained cheerfully. Maybe reading other people's notebooks came easier to people who spent their days reading other people's minds.

"Too true," Barbara offered without apology.

"Okay, how about Ivan?"

"The bookstore owner?"

I nodded, surprised she needed to identify the name. But then she *had* needed to read Felix's notebook.

"Ivan's a good man," she told me. I relaxed into my chair a little. "Still, goodness doesn't preclude violence."

"But—"

"Same for the husband's lover. And for that brave young woman—jeez, it must be no fun having a kid when you're that young. And Yvette's husband. See, even if they're genuinely good people, it doesn't mean you can discount them as murderers."

"How about Phyllis Oberman and Vince Quadrini?" I asked, just for the record.

Barbara shrugged, the smile gone from her face again.

"I just don't know, damn it," she told me. She hit the table with her hand. "And I don't know why I'm always blocked when it's important. It's so frustrating! Because it *is* important. Someone out there is really mad—"

"Mad *angry*?" I interrupted. "Or mad *crazy*?"

"Both," she murmured soberly. And neither of us was laughing anymore. Anxiety clunked back into place. I was sure frustration and sadness would follow soon enough.

We ate quietly. The waitress was right. The tofu over noodles was perfect. The restaurant was bright and colorful. Even the warm sunlight on my back felt right. But in spite of all of that, Barbara's look when she hugged me goodbye chilled whatever warmth I'd felt.

"Be careful, kiddo," she warned once we were outside.

"I will," I told her as I turned to walk to my car. I was used to that warning.

"And Kate," she added. I swiveled my head back around to look at her. Her tone demanded it. "Be ready," she finished.

Unfortunately, that warning was a new one. But she was in her Volkswagen bug and backing out of her parking space before I could ask her for specifics.

My muscles were tense again as I drove home. Be ready for what? Did Barbara know something she wasn't telling me? Something she wasn't even aware of herself? I combed her words in my memory. Had she told me something important? Suddenly, I was convinced she had. But what?

I opened my front door and all thoughts of Barbara disappeared. Because one peek into the living room told me it was empty. Really empty. No Ingrid. No suitcases. Only the futon on the floor, wrinkled sheets bunched up in its center. Our home was ours again! Ours!

At least, it was ours and the skunks'.

I checked out each and every room in the house for Ingrid, Apollo, or suitcases, and joyously found none of the above. How to celebrate? Paperwork, the sergeant inside of me ordered. Paperwork.

I didn't waste any time arguing. I just trudged back to my desk, looked under the stacks of paperwork for Ingrid just to be sure, and then began dutifully filling out Jest Gifts forms. After a few hours, I asked myself why I couldn't solve a murder as easily as I'd dislodged Ingrid. And then I reminded myself just how difficult it really had been to dislodge Ingrid. It had taken work. And planning. So how could I work on finding out who killed Shayla and Marcia?

I could make lists, that's how. Means, motive, and opportunity. The one sensible thing Yvette had said. I pushed aside a stack of ledgers, pulled out a new pad of paper, and allocated a page each for Phyllis Oberman, Vince Quadrini,

Dean Frazier, Winona Eads, Zoe Ingersoll, Ted Brown, Yvette Cassell, Lou Cassell, and Ivan Nakagawa. I almost made one for Marcia Armeson, then shuddered, remembering her crushed body. How could I have forgotten? But filling in each page was harder than merely putting headings on.

I had written in a motive for Dean, and one for Zoe, Ted, and Yvette, when the front door rattled and opened.

I jumped out of my chair, wondering if this was the something I was supposed to be ready for. A murderer with a lock pick? But Wayne was the man who walked in, his eyes worried, harried, and hurried.

"Gotta go soon if we want to make the sci-fi meeting," he told me, not moving from the front door.

I pointed at the living room, but he didn't even seem to see my finger. Or the emptiness of the room. So I threw a jacket over my turtleneck and Chi-Pants and climbed into his Jaguar to go to the meeting of science fiction writers that Yvette had invited us to. The news about Ingrid could wait, to be savored all the more later.

The meeting was in San Francisco, over the Golden Gate Bridge, and all the way downtown in a neon-lit bar and restaurant that looked smaller on the outside than the inside. The waitress at the front just pointed upstairs when Wayne asked her for details. There was a little table at the top of the stairs where we paid our twenty-four dollars as nonmembers and got little, stick-on nametags as our reward.

The "meeting room" was a dark and smoky lounge with a bar, buffet, and scattered tables. The only thing interplanetary about it was the profusion of glowing beer signs and mismatched barstools and tables. And the writers. They weren't dressed as aliens, but they seemed as mismatched as the furniture: in torn jeans, cocktail dresses, beards, suits, overalls, jewels, cornrows, flattops, and bouffants.

Wayne and I stood for a moment by the door, surveying

the mixed crowd, searching for Yvette's pointy little head, and listening to the flotsam of babble floating our way.

"So my editor tells me space-time continuums aren't enough anymore, not with virtual reality . . ."

"Done before . . ."

"Heard the one about the agent and the nun . . ."

"Plagues, you gotta have plagues . . ."

"Hey, you guys, over here!" Yvette hailed us from a round table with three other humans. I hoped.

We elbowed our way through the mass of animation blocking us until we were at Yvette's table. She was dressed in a green sari, her narrow face bright with energy. She introduced her companions. I never caught their names in the overload of surrounding chatter, but nodded at an elderly woman with silver-and-purple hair, a middle-aged man whose features were covered by a blond beard, and a younger, good-sized woman in a red minisuit.

". . . tell you what you need to know," Yvette was shouting. "See you guys later." And then she was gone into the fuddin' crowd.

The older woman with the colorful hair motioned us toward the two remaining chairs at the table. I sat down carefully, wondering if my chair had a short leg the way it was wobbling. I took a deep breath, then thought better of it as I coughed recycled smoke.

"Okay to ask you some questions—?" Wayne began.

"Have to yell!" the older woman shouted in a good example. "Can't hear for all the freaks!"

So Wayne shouted out a request for some information about Shayla Greenfree.

"Too successful to hang out with us anymore," the younger woman in the red suit responded. Her voice was plenty loud, though she didn't seem to be shouting. Maybe she'd taken acting lessons and learned how to project.

"Ooh, that Shayla," the older woman added. "Had an ego

on her once the green stuff started rolling in! She sure chose the right name."

"But she was good," the bearded man put in, just loud enough to be heard.

"How about Ted Brown!" I threw into the stew of sound.

"Haven't seen much of him either," the bearded man replied, turning his head away as if uncomfortable. Uncomfortable about Ted Brown, or talking about colleagues, or—?

"Probably can't afford the twenty bucks!" the older woman added helpfully.

"His big New York publisher dropped him," the younger woman explained. "Now he's with a small press—"

"Small press!" the silver-and-purple haired woman yelped. "Great if you want earnest, dedicated staff, and doo-doo for money."

"Don't quit your day job," the three chorused in unison.

"Yvette?" Wayne bellowed.

"Nuts," the older woman summarized. "But she's doing pretty good for money."

"A true alien life form," the bearded man added, smiling a little now.

"Ted or Yvette a killer?" Wayne bellowed again when no one else added anything about Yvette.

The three of them just chuckled.

"Writers kill enough people on paper," the younger woman explained. "I've killed off whole planets. Don't have to do it for real."

That was pretty much it for the informational part of the science-fiction writers' meeting. We helped ourselves to some food from the buffet. Unfortunately, the colors of the vegetables weren't nearly as bright as the beer signs. After a few bites, we ditched our plates to mingle and ask about the three authors. One thing was for sure, I decided as we made our last round searching for Yvette, no one seemed to be mourning Shayla Greenfree very seriously. A few people seemed to feel her loss as a good writer. A few others were interested in her way of passing. But no one was missing her as a best friend.

Yvette found us just as we'd decided to leave.

"Well?" she said, crooking an eyebrow over her tinted glasses.

"Well, what?" I shouted back.

"Okay," she said, slapping my back. "Keep it to your fuddin' selves. We'll talk later."

We took the stairs back down to the street slowly in the faint light, then stepped outside into the bite of cold air. And breathed in big, grateful gulps.

Finally, we started walking back to our car. No matter how good the cold air felt, it was starting to rain. So we hurried around a man holding a large sign on a stick. It wasn't until we got in front of him, that I recognized the man as the one who'd been picketing Fictional Pleasures the night of the signing. I took a closer look.

It was him, all right. He had the same long beard, the same burning blue eyes, and the same sign.

The sign that read "Science Fiction = Demonic Poisoning."

ᕱWENTY

⏀

"ᕱey!" I shouted, conditioned into high volume by the bar upstairs. "Weren't you at Fictional Pleasures the night of the big signing?"

"Fictional Pleasures, must take measures," the man carrying the picket sign replied, staring back at me—through me—in the rain. "Books are the pleasures of Satan, creating disharmony where harmony reigned. Turning, churning, burning."

I took that for a yes. The raindrops were plopping down for real now. Maybe they followed the picketer wherever he went. And here we were, with him. Lucky us.

"The Bible is a book," Wayne put in, peering into the man's face.

"The Bible is *the* Book. No other need to look. Harmony, peace, salvation beyond—"

"And a good plot," I cut in.

He turned to me angrily, water spraying off his sign.

"God's truth has no plot. Only man's lot."

Uh-oh. That didn't sound like good news for man's lot, or women's for that matter.

"Did you know an author died that night?" I asked before he started up again.

The picketer's burning blue eyes didn't flicker. Only his mouth moved.

"Death, dying, lying. Mocking our Lord."

"She was poisoned, you know," I told him, upping my volume again. I wiped the raindrops out of my eyes. I wanted to see his reaction. "Was it demonic poisoning?"

"Poisoned?" His blue eyes finally flickered. He even stepped back. Had he really not known? He stared up into the wet sky as if for an answer.

"God is good," he concluded finally. "God is not fiction. God is kind, not of mind. Satan is fiction—"

"But if poisoning was God's work—" Wayne proposed, his voice deep with authority.

"No, no!" the picketer yelped, spinning toward Wayne, the sign spraying me once more, across the face this time. "It's Satan's work, not God's, poisoning our minds."

He must have been rattled. His words weren't rhyming anymore.

"But poisoning our bodies," I put in. "Wouldn't that take human intervention?"

"No, demonic intervention!" he shouted. I wasn't even sure he'd understood the question. Or any of our questions, for that matter. "God is good. As it should . . ."

We left him, versifying God's praise frantically in the cold, drenching rain. If I'd known how, I would have prayed for him in his own particular way.

My hair was as soggy as my brain by the time we made it back to the Jaguar's sumptuous embrace. I sank into the leather seat, feeling grateful I wasn't out in the wet anymore. And feeling guilty at the same time. Warmth came purring from the heater vents and I rubbed my icy hands together.

I'd make another donation to a homeless shelter when I got home. Visiting the city was getting more expensive all the time. Every time I saw someone on the street—

"Could he have killed her?" Wayne asked, interrupting my train of guilt.

"He was there, but he wasn't inside," I answered after an instant of reflection. "Was he?"

I assigned myself more homework. Beginning with a piece of paper labeled "nameless picketer, suspect."

"The man equates science fiction with the devil," Wayne muttered.

"And Shayla was a science-fiction writer, a famous one, it's true," I agreed slowly.

Motive filled itself in easily. But still, means and opportunity weren't so simple.

"He wouldn't have been able to get near the authors' table without attracting notice," I argued. "A lot of notice. And where would he get the bracelet?"

"And does he have the ability to plan . . ."

We talked about the possibilities all the way home. And by the time we got there, I wasn't even sure the man with the picket sign warranted his own suspect-sheet.

We walked in the front door and turned the lights on. Wayne let out the tiniest whisper of an indrawn breath, a gasp from anyone else. My body went rigid. Who lay in wait for us this time? But Wayne's indrawn breath wasn't about who was there. It was about who wasn't.

"Ingrid?" Wayne murmured, pointing to the empty living room.

I blinked, then grinned, remembering.

"Ingrid doesn't live here anymore," I told him.

His brows went all the way to the top.

"Was it the skunk broker?" he asked, and for a moment I thought he was serious. Maybe he was.

I never got to ask him, though. He had me in his arms and

was carrying me down the hallway before I could speak, whooping like it was New Year's Eve. Maybe it was New Year's Eve somewhere. And even if it wasn't, there was no one else home to dispute our early celebration.

Saturday morning I woke to the smell of Soysage, fresh-baked dairyless Danish, and stuffed apples. No Whol-ios in sight. And Wayne had already reassembled the living room, our old denim-and-wood couch back in its place of honor between the swinging chairs, the futon neatly folded across from it. Now it felt more like Christmas Day than New Year's.

I sat down at the kitchen table, stuffing my face as I filled Wayne in on the details of the Fenestry Society.

The phone rang mid-laughter, and I wondered if Christmas was over. Ingrid may have been gone, but Shayla's and Marcia's ghosts weren't.

"Vince Quadrini here," the voice over the phone informed me. Christmas was turning into Boxing Day now. And yes, the ghosts were alive and well, and living in my stomach along with all that good food Wayne had cooked. "I would be very pleased to have you and Mr. Caruso visit my home today."

"Yeah . . ." I murmured tentatively, waiting for more.

"Certain information has come into my hands that may be of use to you," he obliged.

"Well, I suppose—" I began.

"I'll send a driver within the hour," he told me. And then he hung up before I could even consider saying no, much less voice the word.

So Wayne and I finished our breakfast and our laughter, got dressed, and waited for Vince Quadrini's car.

And here I'd thought Wayne's Jaguar was embarrassingly ostentatious. Vince Quadrini's "car" turned out to be a lim-ousine, driven by a taciturn white-haired man who couldn't have been much younger than Vince Quadrini himself. Wayne and I sat in the rear and amused ourselves looking at the little bar and the little computer and the little phone, careful not to actually touch anything. By the time the car climbed the last long slope to reach its destination, the word *Mafia* had crossed my mind more than once. But the word *rich* was probably more to the point.

I wasn't sure about the first word, but at least the second one was proved correct when we stepped out of the limousine and were escorted up the marble steps to Mr. Quadrini's immodest mansion in the hills of Marin. Which hills, I wasn't exactly sure. Maybe that's why the limousine's windows were tinted, outside and in.

I took a moment at the entrance to glance at the formal garden surrounding the house, thinking that this estate really belonged in the English countryside, and then we were escorted past the fluted columns, through the double doors, to the foyer inside. Marble; scattered thick carpets; and spotlighted country prints from earlier centuries dominated the spacious room. I turned and took a step forward to look at one of the prints. Were they numbered? But our chauffeur shepherded us all too effectively, keeping us moving across the expanse of the foyer without any further dallying. Finally, he knocked on a thick wooden door and we were admitted to Vince Quadrini's private study.

Mr. Quadrini's study looked very much like his office, complete with a rosewood desk the size of a small soccer field and his honor guard of cats arrayed precisely in front of it. He clearly moved with his troops. But there were more country prints here, more books, more cat hair, and chairs upholstered in tapestry rather than leather. The room smelled pleasantly of must and potpourri. We quickly lowered ourselves into the tapestried chairs upon Mr. Quadrini's invitation.

Or had it been an order? I looked into the realtor's states-

manlike face and wondered if we had just been kidnapped.
Damn. And I hadn't even thought to ask exactly where we
were going in that limousine. As the thick wooden door
shut, I realized the study we were in was probably sound-
proof. I couldn't hear traffic, or children's voices, or dogs
barking, only the steady breathing of the humans and felines
in the room and the even steadier ticking of a clock behind
me. Hadn't Barbara told me to be ready? And now that Ingrid had left, there was no one to say where we'd gone. Not
that she would have told anyone, anyway.

"Please forgive me for inconveniencing you on a Saturday," Mr. Quadrini began smoothly. Were those the words of
a kidnapper? That rich tone the voice of a murderer? "But I
had information I thought you might use in your investigation."

I opened my mouth to say we weren't investigating and
then just shut it again. If Mr. Quadrini wanted to think we
were investigating, I had a feeling we weren't going to stop
him.

"You probably know already that curare was the poison
used in the bracelet," he stated, as if for the record. He might
have been a senator starting in on a cabinet appointee. A senator from the opposing party.

I nodded.

His gaze grew more intense on my face.

"Police contacts," Wayne explained quickly from my
side.

"And did those contacts tell you that Yvette Cassell has an
arrest record?" Mr. Quadrini inquired politely.

"He damn well didn't," I answered, turning to Wayne.
Why hadn't Felix told us?

But Wayne's poker face showed no anger with Felix.
Maybe he just didn't expect as much as I did out of our
friendly reporter. Maybe he didn't expect anything. Anything but aggravation, of course.

"May I ask what Ms. Cassell was arrested for?" Wayne questioned, matching his polite tone to Mr. Quadrini's perfectly.

"Protesting the Vietnam War," Mr. Quadrini told him.

Protesting? Maybe that's why Felix hadn't mentioned Yvette's record. A protest arrest was just as likely to be a badge of honor as a stain for any woman who'd gone to college in the late sixties. And I figured Yvette had to be about my age.

"Perhaps your informant also failed to mention that one of our suspects spent time in an institution for the insane?" Mr. Quadrini threw in with affected nonchalance.

I flipped through my mental records frantically, finding no reference. Zoe? Ted? Winona?

"Need I tell you who?" Mr. Quadrini asked.

"Of course, you need tell me," I shot back, wondering why Wayne wasn't as excited as I was. Maybe I was being a trifle gauche? I modified my words. "I mean, please do."

"Ivan Nakagawa," Mr. Quadrini proclaimed.

I whipped my head around to look at Wayne. He rolled his shoulders. I could hear the crackling sound his tendons made in the nearly silent room. Had he known about Ivan's stay in a mental hospital? Of course he had. I brought my head back to the front. And he hadn't bothered to tell me.

"You probably know that almost everyone there that evening had some kind of experience with syringes," Mr. Quadrini ground on.

"But how do *you* know?" I demanded, suddenly fed up. With Felix. With Vince Quadrini. With Wayne.

Mr. Quadrini's handsome features reddened slightly. He coughed in his hand. His cats bristled in front of his desk. I was surprised when he finally did answer my question.

"I've hired a private investigator," he admitted.

"You what . . . ?"

Of course a rich, *sane* man would hire an investigator.

That made sense. My brain twitched. Something else was making sense now too.

"Does your investigator happen to drive a red VW van?" I asked.

Mr. Quadrini's face grew even redder.

"And does he happen to break into people's houses—?" I went on. Or tried to.

"You must understand, Ms. Jasper," Vincent Quadrini said, his voice as rich and smooth as ever. "I cared a great deal for Shayla Greenfree. I want her killer to be brought to justice. And the Verduras Police Department, well, they are not . . . perfect." He shrugged. "In this case, I believe the ends justify the means. Don't you?"

"I—" I stopped. I'd been ready to say no ends justified a man rummaging through my house. But two women were dead. "I don't know," I answered finally.

We were back in the limousine going home, very soon after that. Wayne and I conversed in hushed whispers in the rear seats, oblivious to the lure of the little computer and the rest of the toys. And I wondered if we were being taped, no matter how low our voices were pitched. For a man like Vince Quadrini, who felt the ends justified the means, it certainly wasn't outside the realm of possibility. Maybe that cute little TV was really a camera. But still, we had to talk. Or at least, I did.

"Did you know about Ivan being—" I began as the limousine moved smoothly down the slope of the driveway.

"Yes, I knew about Ivan's stay in a mental institution," he cut in quickly.

"But then, why didn't—"

"Should have told you," he growled. "But it was a long time ago. Would have told you if it was necessary, Kate."

I opened my mouth to give him a whispered piece of my mind, but thought better of it. That was just the way Wayne was. Loyal. Somehow, I couldn't even whisper at him in anger. Because I loved that loyalty. Anyway, I had more on my mind than Ivan's mental state.

"Quadrini's scary," I murmured in Wayne's ear. "Could he have decided Marcia killed Shayla and had Marcia killed himself?"

"*Could* Marcia have killed Shayla?" Wayne murmured back.

That topic took us all the way home. There could have been two murderers. Or one murder and one accident. Or . . . One thing was for sure, I needed to do up a suspect-sheet on Marcia Armeson after all.

The limousine driver dropped us off where he'd found us. We walked up our front stairs, happy in our knowledge that there was no Ingrid within. But the house was not completely intruder-free. The light on my answering machine was blinking intrusively, even aggressively, when we made our way inside.

"You guys there?" the tape asked when I ran it. "Huh? huh?" There was a silence. "Oh, shi-shift," Yvette finally babbled on. "I'm having another meeting tomorrow, lunchtime. Bring your goodies. Everyone will be there. You guys, Dean, Ted for sure, Zoe . . ."

"Well, at least she's still alive," Wayne commented. "Lou will be happy."

"Do you think those guys will really show up at her meeting?" I asked.

"Maybe they'll make up for our absence," Wayne muttered and then disappeared into the kitchen.

I could hear him pulling supplies from the cupboard. Bread, I decided. He was going to bake bread. And cook soup? I'd let him surprise me. I sat down at my desk, happy to push my pencil through the fields of paperwork, though my conscience kicked a little at the thought of Yvette's lunchtime meeting. Would *anyone* show up? I should call her back. I would, I told myself. But what could I say? I was sure she'd talk me into something, no matter what I said. So I just kept carefully out of phone range. Even Wayne seemed to have managed to forget Yvette as he clanked and tapped and hummed around the kitchen.

Good smells came from the kitchen within minutes, and even better ones after half an hour had gone by. Sweet yeasty smells floated delicately over the heavier aroma of onions simmering with bay and thyme and brandy. I inhaled happily. The doorbell rang. So much for the benefits of deep breathing.

I approached the door cautiously. But not cautiously enough. I opened it and Bob Xavier came barreling through, his dark eyes rolling from side to side. When they got to the living room, I decided to tell him the good news.

"Ingrid's gone," I announced.

And suddenly his angry eyes were panicked.

"Gone?" he said, stunned. I knew he was stunned. He wasn't shouting. "But where?"

"I don't know," I told him, glad my answer was honest. Though a tango was playing in the back of my skull.

"Look, if you know anything, you'd better tell me," he threatened. "You know who my brother is—"

"Captain Cal Xavier," I cut in, keeping my voice calm. "I know. *He* knows."

Bob's shoulders slumped. Bingo. He couldn't play the big brother card if his big brother hated him.

"I don't know why I even let her get to me," he muttered, shaking his head.

I was liking Bob a whole lot better now that Ingrid was gone.

"What do you see in her?" I asked, curiosity grabbing my tongue and twisting it into voice.

"Ingrid's simple, you see," he told me, smiling a little as his eyes went out of focus. "I know what she wants. No complications. No 'are we communicating?' No 'intimacy issues.' No 'privacy issues.' No, 'I think you're in denial of your female side.' "

I nodded. I was beginning to get the idea.

"Just money," he went on. "And fun. She's fun, you see."

I was beginning to feel some retroactive fondness for Ingrid. She was just childlike, I told myself. That's all. Had I failed as a mother?

"Does she really have a degree in math?" I asked aloud.

"Oh, yeah," Bob answered, nodding enthusiastically, reminding me of Apollo for a moment. "In the abstract things, she was really smart. She knew all this complex stuff, way beyond me. It was just her social skills—"

"Simple?" I put in guiltily.

"Simple," he confirmed.

And then I heard the sound of something coming up the stairs. A lot of something coming up the stairs. Footsteps and excited voices and a whirring sound that seemed all too familiar.

TWENTY-ONE

⚜

I looked over Bob Xavier's shoulder. A light flashed in my eyes, blinding me temporarily. Something kaclunked and whirred, and the sound of too many voices in imperfect chorus came flying at me like rotten tomatoes. My mouth turned dry as salt. The media had arrived.

"So, Ms. Jasper," a young woman with a halo of blond curls asked, thrusting a tape recorder my way. "How does it feel to be a suspect once again—?"

"How come you keep finding—?" another voice interrupted.

"Is it true that you fought with—?"

I stepped past Bob Xavier, onto the deck, blocking the front door with my body. Not one of these guys was going to set foot in my house. Not one! I rooted myself onto the redwood planks, through the redwood planks, ready to block any invasion. And closed my gaping, dry mouth. I would probably pass for a shark in the front-page photo. Or a wide-mouthed bass. I reminded myself not to look at any papers for a while. And reminded myself not to answer any questions.

A tall, well-groomed man pushed himself to the front of the crowd, then turned to look out at a small red-haired woman with a Steadicam slung over her shoulder.

"We are here at the home of Kate Jasper," he began. "A woman who always seems to be where the dead bodies are . . ."

Ugh. I clamped my jaw tight.

And felt someone trying to push around me as my teeth ground together. I centered myself, relaxing my mouth and my whole body, rooting even deeper, trying to imagine my stance both soft and impenetrable. But, wait a minute, they were pushing from behind! I stood my ground, not even turning to look. And then I remembered Bob Xavier. Damn. Bob was behind me and he wanted out. I swiveled my body ever so slightly to the left, creating a narrow exit for him. Once he'd slid by, I swiveled back and waited for him to talk as the reporters pushed microphones in his face. Waited for him to accuse. Waited for him to malign.

But all he did was slink through the crowd with what appeared to be a technique born of experience. Was this something drug-defense attorneys learned early on?

"Ms. Jasper?" the well-groomed man inquired smoothly, as he pivoted his glossy head my way, a slim microphone in his hand. "How does it feel—?"

Another light flashed in my eyes. And finally, one went off in my head.

"Did Felix Byrne send you guys?" I demanded, remembering my *ex* buddy reporter lagging farther and farther behind us as Wayne and I had marched on two nights before. Was this his revenge? I would have bet a box of Jest Gifts speculum earrings on it.

"What?" the well-groomed man said. Apparently, Felix Byrne wasn't in his script.

"My paper got an anonymous call saying you had new information about the Verduras murders," the young blond woman with the tape recorder told me. Suddenly I liked her despite her tape recorder. She was honest. Or at least doing a damn good imitation of being honest. "It said you knew a lot you weren't telling. And all this stuff about the previous bodies you'd found."

"Us too," someone else murmured.

"Felix Byrne likes to sic the media on me," I told the crowd, taking advantage of their sudden slackness. They weren't taking pictures or asking questions anymore. "It's his idea of a practical joke."

"You'll find that Mr. Byrne has done this sort of thing before," came Wayne's authoritative voice from behind me.

The reinforcements had arrived. I let myself lean into Wayne's solid body, wondering how I could have forgotten that he was within calling range. Wondering how I could have forgotten him at all.

"We suspect some kind of mental illness in Mr. Byrne's case," I put in solemnly, taking Wayne's cue. "Maybe you should interview him."

". . . guy *is* gonzo . . ." A high voice surfaced from the mutterings and rumblings of the crowd.

". . . probably she's telling the truth . . ." another called out.

"Let's get him," a deeper voice suggested.

And then the wave of people and light and sound retreated en masse. After five minutes, nothing remained but the echoes of their shouts and shoves and flashes.

"Hope they're on their way to see Felix," Wayne growled as the last news truck pulled away.

"What a lovely thought," I murmured and leaned all the way back into Wayne's arms. The air was clear and crisp. Wayne was warm and substantial. Somewhere a child was laughing. And I could smell . . .

"Something burning," Wayne muttered urgently. And then his substantial body was gone.

I dragged my feet back to my desk, suddenly exhausted, smelling burnt onions and herbs, and listening to Wayne's mutters from the kitchen.

As my pencil pushed through paperwork as efficiently as a lone lawn mower in the Amazon jungle, an idea occurred to me. And for once it wasn't about murder. It was about tai chi. And Jest Gifts. The acupuncture-needle earrings seemed to be selling much better than I'd expected through the professional acupuncture magazines. Phyllis Oberman jumped into my mind. I shoved her back out. Not now. I wanted the relief of creativity now. And I had an idea.

How about something for tai chi teachers and students? A tai chi magazine existed. I'd seen it. Yes! When I'd started tai chi some ten years ago, there had been a handful of classes in the Bay Area. Now there were a truckload. How about tai chi cups with the appropriate Chinese symbols, each handle a leg kicking . . . and earrings shaped like those ubiquitous Chinese slippers? My mind began to buzz pleasantly and my pencil sketched on the back of a ledger sheet. This was as good as it got. Creative bliss.

I breathed in deeply. The doorbell rang. Damn. Did I have to stop inhaling? Was that the trigger for those chimes?

This time I approached the door even more cautiously. And blocked Raoul Raymond quickly before he slithered his way into my home.

"Ingrid's gone, you know," I told him right off the bat. Or maybe it was off the beat of the tango.

"My Ingrid is gone?" he cried out, his hand slapping his heart. "My sweet, innocent Ingrid."

"Simple too," I added helpfully.

He looked at me suspiciously for a moment, then rolled his boiled-egg eyes tragically. At least that's the effect I thought he was going for.

"But where has my little dove flown?" he asked, his after-shaved face close to mine now.

"I thought she was with you," I told him honestly.

"But no," he declared, stepping back and waving a hand dramatically. "Family business took me to other places, other lands. I returned today, ready to offer Ingrid shelter. Shelter for her gentle soul as well as her . . . her . . . her gentle body. And now she is gone." He put his face into his hands.

"Where were you, anyway?" I asked.

"Wisconsin," he muttered. Then he got back in character. "But how will I find her? My little lost love. How will I find her in this big uncaring world?"

"She have your phone number?" I asked.

He nodded thoughtfully.

"She'll call," I assured him. If he was unlucky. But then maybe Raoul could handle Ingrid. Anyone could handle her better than I had. And Raoul. With his roving eye, and his hand-seeking lips, I bet he had a lawyer just loaded with prenuptial agreements. I didn't think mine and Ingrid's had been the only hearts he'd toyed with.

"Do you really think she'll call?" he asked plaintively.

"Your love will show her the way," I assured him. Actually, it was kind of fun to talk like Raoul. Maybe this was how it felt to be in a roving troupe of players. Without leaving home. And the romantic words did the job.

"Ah yes, my dear Ms. Jasper," Raoul gushed. "You are wise as well as kind."

He grabbed my hand and kissed it before I could grab it back. But then he was gone. I'd disinfect the hand later. I had gag-gifts to design.

I rushed back to my desk, sketching the little tai chi slipper earrings. They would be perfect. I could even picture them dangling from my own, usually unadorned, ears.

That is, if the doorbell would stop ringing. My pencil

ground to a stop when I heard the chime, the fourth in the hour. I hadn't even breathed deeply, as far as I could remember. Maybe I'd just have to stop breathing at all, at least until I was through with the tai chi gift project.

This time I didn't approach the door cautiously. I approached it angrily, flinging it open.

A short, balding man in aviator glasses stood framed in the doorway.

"Ms. Jasper?" he inquired.

"Yeah," I snarled back. What was it this round? Save the rocks? Save the moss? Save a solicitor's job?

"Skunks," he said.

"What?"

"Buy low, smell high," he added.

I just stared.

"A little skunk humor," he explained. "I'm the skunk broker."

"Oh, the skunk broker," I murmured. In fact I could smell the faint odor of eau-de-skunk emanating from his short body. This man was here to save us. I stopped snarling. Maybe I should throw myself at his feet. But the smell kept me at a distance.

"I've got the traps," he told me. "Just need to get under the house, rustle up the little fellows, and guide them away. And get my check, of course." He smiled and added, "Heh-heh." But all chuckles aside, I had a feeling the check was the real priority.

I showed him the way under the house through a hinged piece of plywood I'd used to cover the entrance in the early stages of the skunk wars.

"Will it smell?" I asked.

"Probably not," he reassured me. "The little guys are pretty sleepy during the day. I'll get them out of here before they know what's happening. I put a tarp over the cage and they don't even know where they're going."

Nor did I, really. To a game reserve or to the next neighborhood. As long as they were at least a block away, I
wouldn't worry. I stuffed a metaphorical cork in my bottle
of ethical objections and watched him disappear into the re-
cesses underneath the house. Then I ran back up the stairs,
waiting for the aromatic explosion. But it never came.

Fifteen minutes later, he was back. And his skunk scent
hadn't increased any as far as my aroma-meter could tell. I
could barely smell it over the tang of the meal Wayne was
still working on.

"Four skunks, two hundred dollars," he informed me. I
got my checkbook. As I filled out the check, I wondered
what he would have charged for Ingrid.

Just as I closed the door on the skunk broker, Wayne wandered out of the kitchen. Had he timed it that way?

"Think I saved the meal," he announced with all the grav-
ity of an emergency-room surgeon.

Before I could even say "yum," the telephone rang. At
least it was a change of pace from the doorbell. Yvette was
on the other end of the line.

"Lunchtime, tomorrow," was her greeting.

"No more meetings," was my reply.

"But I think the murderer will be there—"

And once again the doorbell rang.

"Gotta go," I told Yvette cheerfully, hung up the phone,
and ran to the door.

Winona Eads was standing on my doorstep when I
opened up. I surveyed her tall, gawky body and beautiful
face and decided it could have been worse. It could have
been Felix. But hopefully Felix was being grilled by his own
peers at this very moment. I shook the thought of manacles
and red-hot pincers from my mind reluctantly. Winona was
here, not Felix.

"Is it cool for you to talk now?" she asked me, her voice

barely a whisper. I balanced the smells floating in from the kitchen with the need in her widely spaced eyes.

Her eyes won. Barely.

"Come on in," I told her, trying to keep the sigh out of my voice. Of all my visitors, only a murder suspect had made it into my living room. I wasn't sure what that said about my social abilities.

"I've been . . . well . . . thinking," she told me once she was sitting on the denim couch.

I nodded encouragingly and lowered myself into one of the hanging chairs.

Winona wriggled uncomfortably, and pushed a hank of her long red hair back from her oval face. Was she uncomfortable on the couch or in her own body? My guess was her body.

"See, I gotta know who did it," she declared, thrusting her head forward suddenly. "Like I said before, S.X. Greenfree meant something to me. She was important. She wrote beautiful stuff. No way she shoulda been killed like that. No way."

Wayne walked in and lowered himself down next to me in the hanging chair. It wobbled for a moment with his added weight, then stabilized.

"Hello, Winona," he said politely, no clue on his face that he'd just saved our lunch and wanted to eat it while it was still in remission.

"Hi," Winona replied and then jerked her head away.

Was her sudden wariness because Wayne was male? I knew at least one male in Winona's life had treated her badly. Maybe all men were suspect for her.

"So you've been thinking," I prompted her as patiently as I could.

"Yeah," she answered, turning her head back slowly. "See, it had to be someone who really knew her. At least I think so. 'Cause no one else would go to that much trouble to kill her. It wasn't enough to just read her books, you see."

I nodded. She had just taken herself out of the running as a suspect. Very convenient. Convenient for Wayne and me as well, I realized. All right, convenient *and* logical.

"So, I've been thinking, like, who *really* knew her?"

"The other two authors," I offered. But my mind asked if indeed they'd really known her, either. No one at the science fiction writers' meeting had seemed that close to Shayla Greenfree. Why should Ted or Yvette be any different?

"Yeah." Winona bobbed her head up and down eagerly. God, she was vulnerable. I wanted to hug her. I wanted to adopt her and her son. I wanted—

"Dean Frazier," Wayne put in, bringing my mind back to the real question. The question of murder. And he was right. Dean had probably known Shayla better than anyone else who'd been there that night.

Winona bobbed her head up and down again, but this time she blushed. Was she embarrassed by the relationship between Dean and Shayla's husband? Even though she was over twenty, there was something about Winona that still seemed teenaged. She was probably embarrassed by the mention of anything with sexual implications.

"You know about Dean Frazier and Scott Green?" Wayne asked quietly.

I gave him a sharp look. Was he trying to embarrass her even more? Then I realized. He wanted to know how she knew what she knew.

"Neil told me," she whispered. Then her voice got a little louder. "Neil Nakagawa, you know. He's really cool. He told me a lot of stuff. About that crazy woman who worked for his father. The one who died. And how the acupuncturist lady knew S.X. Greenfree before. And about how the Zoe lady was friends with her. And that old guy was nuts over her. See, all those guys knew her. They had . . . well . . . motives. Or something."

"Possible motives?" I tried.

"Yeah," she agreed, repeating my words carefully. " 'Possible motives.' That's it."

"Or at least relationships with S.X. Greenfree," Wayne put in. His voice was thoughtful now. "Whether relationship translates into motive is another question. For instance, how would a long-ago school friendship qualify as a murder motive?"

Winona's milky freckled skin flushed again.

"Maybe she was mean to her," she answered diffidently.

Mean. Shayla was mean to a lot of people by some accounts. It was a simple word, but—

"Neil's been really helping me out," Winona went on. "He even got me a job in his father's store." She lowered her voice again. "After the other lady died."

"What does Neil think about Marcia Armeson's death?" Wayne asked.

"He thought she wasn't really . . . well . . . very cool, you see," Winona answered hesitantly. "But he couldn't see why anyone would want to kill her. He thinks she just fell into those books."

"Do you think that's likely?" Wayne asked, his voice a prosecuting attorney's now.

"No." Winona sighed. "It doesn't make sense. Not so soon after the other murder. Not that I really understand it all."

"And you like Neil," I prompted.

"Yeah," she admitted. This time her skin turned bright red. "He thinks I could really be a writer, you see. He read some of my stuff and he, like, thinks maybe I could get a scholarship or a grant or something to go to a real college instead of dental hygiene school. Neil's so smart. I keep telling him 'no way,' but he just keeps telling me to think positive. He really believes in me. I don't know why."

For all of Winona's twenty or so years, she had such an innocence. A real innocence, an innocence that— An innocence that sucked me in like a vacuum cleaner. Suddenly, something in me chilled. Could all that innocence be an act?

"Neil's real worried right now," she added, frowning. "About his father, you see."

Damn, Neil's father. Our friend, Ivan Nakagawa. I still didn't know the details. Why had Ivan been in a mental hospital? I'd worked in mental hospitals and I knew there were all kinds of reasons to leave reality that didn't lead to murder. But still . . .

"Like his father's real distracted now."

She looked up at us, her wide eyes seeming to seek guidance.

"Are you worried that Neil's father is the killer?" Wayne asked gently.

Bingo. Winona's body jerked on the sofa.

"No, no way," she objected, but her head was turned away from us. "Neil's father is really nice, you see. And he's Neil's father. No way—"

The phone rang just as she was objecting. I ran to the answering machine.

I heard Wayne prompt Winona gently from behind me.

"But?" he said.

I picked up the phone just before the canned message began.

"Kate," a voice said. "I'm feeling very uneasy." It took me a moment to identify the voice as Ivan's, a.k.a. Neil's father. "I need to talk to you and Wayne. Can you come by tomorrow?"

I wanted to say no. I wanted to hang up. But this was Ivan, Wayne's friend. Wayne's friend who had spent time in a mental hospital for unknown reasons.

"Why?" I asked.

"I can't concentrate," he told me. There was a faint note of hysteria in his usually calm voice that I hadn't heard before. Maybe I just hadn't been listening. "I can't seem to find the serenity . . . I just can't—"

He stopped mid-sentence.

"Harmony will be restored when we find out the reason for the deaths," he finally finished.

"The murders," I reminded him.

"The murders," he agreed solemnly. "Will you talk with me once more? Please."

"Of course," I told him. Why had I said "of course" to Ivan and "no" to Yvette?

But Ivan thanked me and hung up before I could answer my own question. Or change my mind.

I marched back into the living room, feeling suckered all around. Kate Jasper, the all-day sucker. The all-life sucker.

"But why didn't Neil's dad fire that Marcia lady?" Winona was asking. "I keep thinking about it. Why didn't he just fire her if she was that awful?"

The question stopped me with one foot still in the air.

TWENTY-TWO

I let my foot drop back to the carpet and then just stood there, staring at Winona. The ever-so-innocent Winona Eads who had come up with a nasty question that I hadn't even bothered to seriously consider before. Ivan's failure to fire Marcia *was* suspicious. And unfortunately, I could think of at least one answer to the question of why Ivan hadn't fired Marcia Armeson. Blackmail.

The word tunneled into my mind like a dentist's drill, vibrating with the threat of worse things to come. But my mind rejected the word. I shook my head. Shook it hard. In spite of all my doubts about the man, I couldn't believe that Ivan Nakagawa would allow himself to be blackmailed. Any more than Wayne would. But would Ivan commit murder? That was a different question. One I was starting to worry about.

"Maybe Mr. Nakagawa was too softhearted to fire Ms. Armeson," Wayne proposed.

Winona wriggled on the couch, thinking it over. My mind

wriggled with her. How softhearted did an employer have to be to put up with all the grief that Marcia had handed out? Not to mention the thieving.

"Don't have to worry about Mr. Nakagawa," Wayne went on gruffly. "He's a good man."

Winona looked over at Wayne, her lovely freckled face open with a willingness to believe his kind words.

But were Wayne's words really kind? I knew that's how he meant them. But what if Ivan Nakagawa *was* dangerous? If he was, it wasn't a favor to Winona to minimize that danger. Especially if Winona was going to work for Ivan at Fictional Pleasures.

"You have our phone number," I put in, trying to keep the urgency out of my voice. "If anything strange happens, just call us."

Winona turned her head my way now and frowned in confusion. No wonder she was confused. Talk about mixed messages.

"Just in case," I added, trying to soften the message. I manufactured a smile.

"Oh, cool," she replied and smiled back, seeming to relax the littlest bit.

My mind began reeling off disaster scenarios as I kept the corners of my mouth in the up position. Painfully. Worrying and smiling was like trying to chew gum and walk at the same time. Difficult for someone like me. I imagined Winona alone with Ivan. Winona discovering whatever it was that had gotten Marcia Armeson killed. Winona calling us . . . and getting our answering machine. My heart sank, but then struggled up to the surface again.

Winona Eads had a job. A job in the bookstore she loved. Was I going to ruin that for my imagination's sake? The chances that Ivan was a murderer were minimal, I told myself. Well—all right—maybe one percent, two percent?

I erased the percentages from my mental ledger and just

kept smiling, willing Winona to be all right. She'd had enough tragedy in her young life. She didn't need any more.

And then suddenly, she was on her feet, looking at the ceiling and rubbing her arms.

"Um, thanks, you guys," she said diffidently. Then she brought her gaze down from the ceiling and peered into my still smiling face as if seeing me for the first time. The rest of her words came out in a rush. "You've been really cool about this. And don't worry about me. No way anything bad's gonna happen to me. Not while I have Johnny to take care of. No way."

I wanted to hug her. She'd gotten the message. She'd take the job at Fictional Pleasures. But she'd be on her guard.

And when she started toward the door, I did hug her. Just long enough to feel her initial start and then her responding embrace. She almost knocked me off my feet with the enthusiasm of her response. I'd forgotten how tall she was. And how strong.

She was blushing as she galloped out the front door, issuing more thanks over her shoulder. And then she was gone.

"Did we do the right thing?" I asked Wayne when we finally sat down to the meal he'd rescued. Fresh-baked pumpernickel bread and onion soup with herbs. I waited for his answer before taking a bite.

"Hope so," he shot back, his brows low with what might have been thoughtfulness. Or maybe guilt. "Ivan's no killer, Kate. Can't be."

I suspended disbelief and took a bite of the warm bread. Molasses, lemon, and raisins nuzzled my taste buds first. And then the more subtle flavors kicked in. And the soup was even better, loaded with onions (burnt but delicious), bay, and brandy. Food heaven.

I gave Wayne a reprieve as we chomped and slurped, the soup and bread warming me from the inside out. Then I went for the jugular.

"Why was Ivan in a mental hospital?" I demanded
quickly, hoping to catch him off guard.

"Stress of being an attorney too long," Wayne shot back.
He'd been expecting the question, I could tell. And he'd prepared his answer. Well, his answer wasn't good enough. I
bent forward over the kitchen table.

"You know what I mean," I insisted. "What was wrong
with him? What was his diagnosis?"

"Nothing that relates to murder," my so-called sweetie
answered, staring down at the remains of his soup.

Stubborn. But I could be stubborn too. I crossed my arms
and narrowed my eyes, trying to look threatening.

"I'm not going to stop asking," I told him.

He sighed, a long, drawn-out sigh that seemed to blow its
way through the whole house like a gentle tornado. So much
for unwedded bliss without Ingrid.

"Wayne, you have to tell me," I bulldozed on. "I'm not
going to stop worrying about Winona until you do."

Wayne mumbled something beneath his breath. Something that ended with the word "whip."

A whip. It was true, I could have used one. But my mouth
would probably be enough.

"I'm not going to stop—"

"Okay," he interrupted, his voice rising an octave. He
lowered it again. "Okay. I'll tell you. But it goes no further,
understood?"

I nodded my understanding. And kept my arms crossed
for good measure.

"Ivan got very depressed working as an attorney," Wayne
began. He sighed again. "Very depressed. Then he got into
drugs—"

"Ivan?" I blurted out. I couldn't imagine it. Literally.

Wayne glared at me.

"Sorry," I put in swiftly. "I didn't mean to interrupt."

"Not much more to tell, anyway," Wayne growled.

"Nancy got him into a hospital. Luckily, it was a good one. He realized that the drugs were a cover for his depression. And that his depression was because he hated what he was doing. So he stopped practicing law. That simple. Nancy insisted. Ivan has family money. Nancy works. He didn't have to be an attorney."

I opened my mouth to ask if the drugs in question had involved needles, but shut it again when I saw the scowl on Wayne's face. He thought he'd told me too much already. He didn't have to say it. The anger and guilt radiated from him. If ice can radiate. I shivered, longing for a vest, maybe a lead-lined one. Wayne was loyal to his friends. And right now he was probably mad at himself for not being loyal enough. I was just getting the leftovers.

"I needed to know, sweetie," I told him softly. "It ends with me, I promise. And thank you."

The scowl disappeared. Now he radiated gratitude. Warm gratitude that melted the ice.

"Thanks, Kate," he murmured.

Damn, Wayne was an easy man to love. I reached over and laid my hand on his bigger one. He grabbed it for a moment, then let go. And if it weren't for his inherent goodness, there was always the food to sweeten the deal. I took another bite of bread. It tasted even better now that the interrogation was over.

Wayne and I hugged a lot for the rest of that day, at least until he had to go to the city. In between pencil-pushing, we'd each take turns slipping out of our respective offices for sneak attacks and then returning furtively as if the goddess of entrepreneurs might be taking notes on who was being naughty. And then Wayne left for San Francisco. Saturday night at La Fête à L'Oiel was always a busy one.

I spent the rest of the evening working in silence. No more doorbells, no more phone calls, only the buzzing of my own worried mind for my Saturday night entertainment.

• • •

¶ woke up Sunday morning with Wayne's warm arm resting lightly on mine as he slept. The sun was just beginning
to play on the wet skylights, shimmering through the drops
of leftover rain. But something was different. No fresh
skunk smell, that was it! And no Ingrid, I reminded myself.
I moved closer to Wayne, in a bliss of non-thought. And then
I remembered the murders.

"Whaa?" Wayne murmured sleepily. I must have stiffened.

"Ivan," I whispered. "We have to see Ivan today."

"Lunchtime," he told me, never opening his eyes, and
then he was asleep again. If he'd ever been awake.

By noon, I doubted he'd even remember his early morning words. But just as I'd filled in the last box on my sales
tax return, Wayne was behind me. I jumped in my seat when
his hands touched my shoulders. The man knew how to
walk softly, too softly sometimes.

"Time to see Ivan now?" he suggested. "Then lunch?"

"Could we drop in on Yvette afterwards?" I found myself
asking. Was I beginning to like the woman? No, that was
impossible. But still . . . "As long as we're out?"

"Good plan," he agreed. Though I could hear the sigh he
was stifling. "We did promise Lou."

Lou. I'd almost forgotten Lou and our promise to look
after Yvette. And then there was Shayla's husband, Scott.
And Winona. And Ivan. Too many people were depending
on us to solve a set of murders that were probably unsolv-
able. How had we gotten into this, anyway?

And that wasn't the only question on my mind as I drove
my Toyota toward the Fictional Pleasures Bookstore. Because I had no idea what Ivan and Wayne and I were going
to talk about when we got there. What had Ivan said on the
phone the day before? Something about feeling uneasy. But

what did that mean? Killing two women might make a person uneasy.

PMP greeted us as usual when we pushed the bookstore door open. "*Scree, scraw,* cats are good. Cash or charge?"

And then Winona waved at us from behind the counter. Her face was beaming. Even her shoulders looked straighter as she rang up book prices on the aging cash register. A middle-aged woman in a parka watched with suspicious eyes as Winona banged the keys.

"I certainly hope you enjoy them," Winona said when she'd totaled up the sale. She guided the stack of books gently into their bag. "And thank you."

"Well, thank you," the woman replied, handing over her credit card. Surprise flavored her words. Maybe Marcia had waited on her the last time.

"Thank you, *scree.* Thank you," PMP put in. She learned fast.

I hoped Ivan knew how lucky he was to have Winona behind the counter instead of Marcia. Then I remembered why Winona was behind the counter instead of Marcia . . . and a little chill went up my neck. Winona Eads had a motive. Maybe not for S.X. Greenfree, but for Marcia—

"Hi, you guys," the new suspect welcomed us enthusiastically. "Is there anything I can help you with?"

"Just here to see Ivan," Wayne told her.

"Oh, that's cool," Winona replied, her voice losing enthusiasm. Maybe she was hoping to sell us some books.

"There's a new Margaret Atwood in today," she said quietly.

She was trying to sell us books! I should have known that anything Winona took on she'd do her best at.

"In hardback or soft?" I asked, willing to be tempted.

"Hard, but it's, like, really worth it," she assured me. "I've already read the first few chapters," she whispered. "Here."

I bought the new Margaret Atwood and Winona had bagged it by the time Ivan came shambling up the center aisle to greet Wayne and me.

He hugged each of us with a rib-cracking grip, before sending a fond grin Winona's way.

"Ms. Eads has already doubled our annual sales in a morning," he told us.

Winona blushed.

"No way," she murmured, but she was smiling underneath the blush.

"Heard you needed to talk to us, Ivan," Wayne muttered.

Ivan's smile faded along with Winona's.

"I have a few chairs set up by the tea urn," Ivan told us. "Thought we could talk—"

"Kate, Wayne!" came a voice bursting into the store. "Whoa, good seeing you here."

Zoe Ingersoll came rushing up to the cash register, her moon face as usual looking too big atop her tiny body as she surveyed the store, her eyes receding from the rest of us. We might have all been invisible now.

"Wow," she murmured. "Wow. The murder scene." A few heartbeats later, her eyes refocused on us all, and finally on my eyes in particular. "See, I'm doing like you said, making it a puzzle, a cloth puzzle," she explained, her voice racing. "I made pieces for all the suspects, but I needed a bigger piece for the background, the gestalt, to weave it in, all the colors blending like a story—"

She cut herself off suddenly and slapped the side of her head.

"Duh," she muttered. "I guess I could have kept that to myself, huh? Oh, phooey! But it is coming together, a different kind of piece than I usually do, but I don't usually do death." She punched her palm this time. "Oops, I mean, I don't usually do *artwork* about death. Oh, phooey, I'm hopeless." Her eyes rolled wildly under her oversized glasses.

"There's a new novel in by Margaret Atwood," Winona suggested diffidently.

"Really?" Zoe caroled, turning toward the sales counter. "I love her stuff. She's so complex, but not complicated, you know what I mean . . ."

Ivan motioned us over to the chairs set up by the tea urn while Zoe and Winona talked. We slunk away under cover of the high, bright tones of Zoe's voice underlined by the occasional murmur of Winona's.

And then finally the three of us were seated. With nothing to say.

Ivan sighed first. Then Wayne. I turned, waiting for PMP to join in, but apparently she was too enthralled by the closer conversation.

"So why is Zoe in here?" I asked Ivan. Much as I already knew the answer. After all, I'd been the one who'd suggested she put the puzzle together, even if she'd thought of doing it in fabric. But at that point, I would have asked anything to get Ivan's mouth in motion.

"Harmony," he answered, his rough, round features solemn, his eyes almost closed. "The violence, it's too much. There are demons to be exorcised."

He wasn't talking about Zoe, I realized. He was talking about himself.

"Reason isn't always enough," he went on. The note of hysteria I'd heard before in his soft-spoken voice had risen again. "I . . . I . . . I'm sorry," he finished.

"Sorry for what?" I asked quickly.

But before he could answer, Zoe was waving and shouting her noisy goodbyes across the store at us. She carried a heavy-looking bag of books. Winona had sold her more than the Margaret Atwood.

"Sorry about what?" I repeated once Zoe had exited the store, leaving relative silence behind her.

Ivan put his hands together and squeezed.

"Sorry this all happened at my store," he explained. "Could I have stopped it? What could I have done? I keep wondering. Shayla was bad enough, but Marcia?"

I didn't wait for another opening. "Why didn't you just fire Marcia?" I asked.

Ivan drew in a sharp breath, still squeezing his hands together.

"Of course, I should have fired her. But I just couldn't," he said. His eyes finally opened to stare into mine beseechingly. "That's why I was such a terrible attorney. I like to get along. In peace. I don't like to argue. Confrontation makes me . . . makes me ill."

I could well believe it. He looked ill now, just talking about it, his skin graying beneath the brown, his lips robbed of natural color.

"When Marcia first worked here, she did an adequate job, but then . . . then she became abrasive. I began to hint that she might work elsewhere, but she didn't take the hint. And she needed the money. I felt too guilty. It's easy to talk about firing someone, but to actually do it?" He shrugged. "Even when I thought she might be stealing books, I still couldn't bring myself to force her to leave."

I nodded involuntarily. How could I have doubted Ivan when neither Wayne nor I had been able to force Ingrid to leave our own home?

"So I gave Marcia the benefit of the doubt," Ivan finished up. "It was all I could do. And now she's dead."

No wonder he looked so sick.

"So you need to find an answer," Wayne put in gently.

He believed his old friend now. He hadn't been sure before, I realized.

"Yes," Ivan hissed, nodding his head violently as he kept

his hands locked together. "Why did Marcia die?" he asked. "Was she murdered?"

"Could Marcia have guessed who Shayla's murderer was?" I asked. I had a dim memory of her insinuating that she knew. Had she shared her guesses with the wrong person? No, knowing Marcia, she would have accused, not shared.

"That's what I've been afraid of," Ivan admitted. Finally he unclasped his hands and leaned forward. "Marcia told me she knew more than I did about the murder," he whispered. "She teased me about it. She said she was going to make more money with that knowledge than she did selling books."

"Blackmail?" I whispered back.

He nodded. "I knew that's what she meant. I told her that blackmail was dangerous. I pleaded with her to go to the police if she really knew something. But I wasn't sure if she was just trying to upset me. She did that sometimes. I didn't know . . ." His words faltered and he stared at the floor.

Ivan was blaming himself for Marcia's murder, but I didn't think he was the killer. Not anymore.

"Okay," Wayne put in, his voice brusque. "Enough of the guilt. Let's go over this analytically."

Ivan looked up, a flicker of hope in his eyes.

"Start with everyone who was here that night," Wayne ordered.

"Well," Ivan began. "I suppose I knew Yvette the best. And Ted. You know about his son."

"Not everything," I prompted.

"Well, Ted's son had a terrible illness. He needed a liver transplant. He was on a waiting list. Ted kept saying he could save his son's life if he had enough money to bribe the right person. I don't know if it was true. But he didn't have the money. His books weren't selling as well by that time.

His original publisher had dropped him and he'd gone with a small press. He was desperate."

"Poor guy," a voice from behind us put in. Winona. I hadn't heard her walking our way. Ivan didn't even seem to notice her presence. He was too caught up in Ted's story.

"Ted's son died before he ever got a liver transplant."

Winona gulped. I looked up and saw tears in her eyes.

"No wonder he's bitter," I muttered.

"It was terrible," Ivan agreed. "I think of my own son. God, how could Ted bear it? And then his wife left him. I would have never expected her to leave. But all that held them together was their son. They'd quit the jewelry business a long time ago—"

"The jewelry business," I interrupted. "Ted was in the jewelry business?"

TWENTY-THREE

✦

"Are you telling me that Ted was in the jewelry business, as in *making* bracelets, not just selling them?" I prodded, my voice gaining speed along with the pounding of the blood in my temples.

"Well . . . yes," Ivan admitted slowly, tilting his head as he looked at me. Could he have really missed the connection?

"So could Ted have made *the* bracelet?"

Blank-faced silence was my only answer at first. It probably wasn't very long before Ivan finally reacted, but it felt like decades.

And then Ivan gulped. I could hear the sound just as clearly as if I'd gulped myself in the stillness of the bookstore. Ivan's face grew even grayer than before. I hoped he wasn't going to pass out. I hoped *I* wasn't going to pass out.

"No way," Winona whispered.

The heater seized the moment to kick in with a roar of hot air.

We all jumped simultaneously. Even Wayne. Even PMP.

"Scree!" the parrot screamed. "Shut up! Shut up! Thank you."

"Tell me about Ted's business," Wayne ordered, standing abruptly. "Did Ted actually manufacture jewelry?"

"Well, yes, he did," Ivan answered, blinking urgently. He squeezed his hands together again. "He and his wife made necklaces and earrings." His voice lowered. "And bracelets. They sold their stock to jewelry stores and boutiques. It was a good little business. They worked very well together. But when Ted's writing actually began to pay him enough to live on, they shut down the jewelry operation. I don't know about the equipment . . ." He faltered. "I didn't even think of it. I thought of Ted only as a writer. I . . ."

"You're not just talking about stringing beads on wire for bracelets?" I asked. I'd done that myself in college for a few extra bucks. So had half the women I'd known.

"No, they had a professional workshop and everything," Ivan assured me. Not that it was an assurance I particularly wanted. Though at least Ivan's face was getting some color back now. "I don't know what was involved, but they used precious metals and gems, and did some lovely, intricate designs—"

Damn. Now I was out of my chair too. Ted *could* have made the bracelet.

"But wait," Ivan put in, frowning. "Yvette made jewelry at one time too." But then he shook his head. "No, no, that's not right. I think it was Lou, when he was in accountancy school. His mother or his aunt—or someone—was in the jewelry business. Something like that. Oh, I can't remember the exact details." He made his hands into fists as if to force the information out. "I just remember Yvette talking about how beautiful Lou's pieces were. So it must have been Lou. I think."

Yvette. My mind shrilled a warning. Yvette was having a

meeting. Lunchtime, she'd said. And she'd said Ted would come. Like Ivan, I was having a hard time remembering exactly. Hadn't she said Ted would come "for sure"? Why would she say that? Why hadn't I asked?

"But making jewelry doesn't necessarily imply—" Ivan was saying.

"Wayne, they're meeting now!" I interrupted. And suddenly I was shouting. "Lunchtime, Yvette's house!"

"Oh no," Ivan groaned. "I'd forgotten. Yvette's having another meeting."

"Gotta go," Wayne growled and headed toward the door.

I was right there with him, until Winona blocked me.

"Kate, let me come too," she begged. "Yvette asked me. Let me help."

I looked at Winona, hardly able to focus on her freckled, oval face with Yvette's narrow, sharp one floating in my mind. I tried to center my nagging thoughts. We had to hurry.

"No," I said firmly. "You've got Johnny, remember?"

Winona's shoulders slumped. But she nodded in agreement as I ran past her to catch up with Wayne.

"It's probably no big deal anyway," I yelled over my shoulder as we passed through the doorway.

But one last, backwards glance told me that neither Winona nor Ivan believed me.

"No big deal," PMP echoed cheerfully as the door closed behind me. "No big deal."

Once we were on the highway, I pushed the Toyota to its limit. Unfortunately, my aged Toyota's limit with two people inside wasn't quite seventy miles an hour.

"We promised Lou," Wayne murmured as I prodded the Toyota over a steep hill by pure force of will. My hands were sweating and slippery on the steering wheel.

"Maybe we're just overreacting," I told him. At least I was. My pulse was doing everything the Toyota couldn't.

"Lou might have killed Shayla himself. Or Yvette might have, for that matter. If Lou knew how to do whatever you have to do to make jewelry, she probably did too. And who knows who else could make jewelry?"

"But why Yvette?" Wayne shot back. "Why Lou?"

"What if Yvette was jealous of Shayla?" I proposed. "What if she was just nuts?"

"Lou could have been trying to protect Yvette somehow, but . . ."

Wayne's voice faltered as I skidded around a curve. Honking greeted the brief intrusion of my rear wheels into the next lane.

"Or Lou and Yvette together," Wayne muttered.

"Or Ted Brown." There, I'd said it. "Ted. He had the means. And his son died. Maybe he blamed Shayla somehow. She stole his ideas."

I let my words float through the car as I swung off onto the exit ramp, minutes away from Yvette's. What would be there when we arrived? Nothing, I told myself. Nothing but the usual chaos of bric-a-brac and animals. And weapons, I remembered suddenly. Daggers, swords, and shillelaghs among the teacups and posters and African masks.

I rammed my car up to the curb and over in front of the house. I didn't stop to parallel park. And just as I yanked open the gate to the Cassells' green, leprechaun-encrusted yard, Wayne spoke again.

"The film," he whispered. "Marcia's film. There was no bracelet on the table before the authors came in."

The photos that Ivan had shown us flashed through my mind. Wayne was right. No bracelet. But which author had come in first? I didn't have time to remember as we rushed to Yvette's front door. But when I tried to open the door, it was locked. I twisted the knob furiously. It couldn't be locked. Yvette was having a meeting. It had to be open. But it wasn't. A dog barked somewhere inside the house. Then I heard a human voice.

"If you're Demetrius Douvert, then I'm a fuddin' leprechaun." Yvette, that was Yvette speaking. Her voice was high and loud, but calm.

Douvert, my mind sorted urgently. Wasn't Demetrius Douvert Ted's protagonist?

"I take the lives of those who are evil," another voice answered. A deep voice. Was it Ted's voice? It sounded something like Ted, but it lacked its usual brittle, jerking quality. This voice was deep and slow. Ted Brown playing Shakespeare. One of the tragedies.

"Listen for a damn-dang minute here, Ted," Yvette said. "Shayla wasn't evil. Absolute good and evil are only illusions. Shi-shick, she had her good points, her bad points—"

"She was evil," the deep voice answered. Ted's voice. It had to be, unless Yvette was talking to herself.

I twisted the doorknob again. But it was well and truly locked.

"Well, was Marcia evil, then?" Yvette inquired. I didn't hear fear in her voice. But I felt it creeping up my own body. Hadn't Ted just said he took the lives of those who were evil? Wasn't he saying he'd killed Shayla?

It was quiet inside the house for a few heartbeats, then the deeper voice answered.

"Ted didn't mean to kill Marcia. Marcia thought she had it all figured out. Ted thought she was coming on to him sexually, but she just wanted to blackmail him. He shoved her and the handcart fell. An accident."

"Okay, okay. It was a figgin' accident. But am I evil, Ted?" Yvette asked, her voice that of a professor posing an important question to a student.

"Not Ted, Douvert!" he roared.

The sound of dogs barking obscured all other sounds for

a moment. But the dogs weren't near Ted and Yvette, I realized. Their barking came from the rear of the house.

Damn. Yvette wasn't evil. She was crazy. Did she want this man to kill her? I looked for a window to break.

I moved away from the door just as Wayne hurled himself at its oaken surface. But his large, muscular body just bounced off.

Yvette still sounded calm as Wayne stepped back to try again.

"Okay, *Douvert*, am I evil?" she rephrased her question.

"Hey, guys, um . . ." A new voice. Was that Felix Byrne? "You know, this gonzo stuff is really far friggin' out and all, but—"

"Felix, open the door!" I shouted.

"You defend an evil woman," the deep voice went on. It sounded like a judgment.

Had anyone even heard my shout? I looked around me. The ceramic harp by the door looked sturdy enough to break glass.

And then the door opened.

Felix was the first person I saw in the maze of Star Trek, Ireland, Africa, and the mysteries that defined Yvette Cassell's living room. Fear had widened Felix's dark, soulful eyes, but excitement was lurking there too.

Wayne rushed through the door one pulse ahead of me.

"Hey man," Felix whispered, grabbing his arm. "This Ted guy's from outer space, you know, another planet . . ."

I stepped around the two men, surveying the room, and there, past the *Enterprise,* past the needlepoint, and past the poster-size blow-ups of Yvette's book covers, I saw Ted Brown. He wasn't wearing his cowboy hat, but his dark ponytail was in place, his posture ramrod-straight now as he faced Yvette.

"Earth to Ted," Yvette said, her hands resting on her tiny hips as if in exasperation. "I keep telling you, Shayla wasn't fuddin' evil." Yvette stared at Ted through her tinted glasses, her head back as if trying to figure something out. Too late. Ted grabbed a bust of Nero Wolfe and advanced on her slowly. The dogs began barking again. But the dogs were in another room.

"Evil," he repeated. "Evil must die."

"Oh, come on, Ted," Yvette cajoled, but she was reaching in the long pocket of her green jacket. For her shillelagh? She'd never get it out in time.

My mind didn't have anything to do with the next instant. I was just running and kicking. My foot circled and knocked the Wolfe bust from Ted's hand. No cerebral assistance was necessary.

But then he turned his face to me. And my mind returned and was chilled. Ted's face was no longer morose. It was filled with hatred. He reached a hand toward me. My mind urged me to move. To move fast.

I stepped backwards, out of reach. And centered myself, ready.

One breath was all I took, and Wayne was behind Ted, one arm around his neck, the other holding his arm behind his back in a classic hammerlock. As if Wayne and I had been a team. Maybe we had.

My own body went slack with relief. And my brain buzzed. The science-fiction writers had been wrong. It wasn't always enough to kill on paper. At least, not for Ted Brown.

"I knew it was Ted," Yvette announced. She threw her little hands up in the air. "But would anyone listen?"

"Why didn't you just say so?" I demanded, feeling cold and clammy now. And resentful. Didn't this woman know I'd just saved her life?

"I tried—" she began, but Ted, or Douvert, wasn't finished.

"Shayla's success made Ted broke," he said, his voice a monotone, his eyes disappearing inward. "No more health insurance. Then Ted's kid got sick. Ted heard you could bribe someone at the national transplant registry. He tried the coordinator's assistant, but he wanted lots of money. More money than Ted had. Ted's son died. Ted's wife left. Ted almost killed himself, but I promised to revenge the evil done. I, Douvert, made the bracelet. I talked Ivan into the signing. Shayla ruined Ted's life. She killed his son. Wouldn't lend Ted money. And she didn't even need the money. Her husband was wealthy. She was evil, evil—"

"Ted didn't mean to off Marcia," Felix threw in helpfully. "But Shayla . . ."

I tuned him out. Because Ted was still speaking. Or was it Douvert?

"Shayla could have helped Ted out. She had money. She could have saved Ted's son. She owed it to Ted. She stole his ideas, made him a pauper. But she just ignored his son's illness, like everyone else ignores illness . . . and death."

For a moment, his eyes burned with rage again.

"You know what she said when Ted begged her? She said, 'Oh, I'm sure the boy will get better.' The only thing that could have made him better was a liver transplant—"

"But why Shayla?" I broke in. "Why didn't you kill the coordinator's assistant? Why didn't you kill the person who denied your—" No, not *your*, I reminded myself. This man is Douvert now. "Why not kill the guy who denied Ted's son a transplant?"

"I did," the man held before me in a hammerlock replied. And then the rage was gone from his eyes, disappearing inward once more. "I did."

ＴWENTY-FOUR

✦

"Shick, it was easy to figure out whodunit," Yvette was saying. Her high voice cut clearly through the sound of the rain pounding her bric-a-brac house. "Fu-fuddin' deduction, you know. Holmes was right. Deduction is everything."

"Especially tax deductions," muttered Lou over her head. He gazed down at his wife fondly. The nomadic accountant had come back from his business trip early this morning and had been glad to find his wife alive. Very glad. He must have thanked Wayne and me more than a dozen times. Of course, Yvette hadn't thanked either of us once. But if you counted them as a couple, the gratitude quotient seemed reasonable. Not that the same could have been said about Yvette.

"Pretty damn-darn obvious if you think about it, huh?" she went on. She stuck her tiny hand in the air and counted off the fingertips of her kelly-green gloves. Green gloves to match the green tights and minidress she wore as the star of her own self-celebration. I hoped she was warm. I wasn't. It was too cool from the many openings and closings of the front door. "Motive, means, opportunity . . ."

I looked around the room, trying to ignore the Star Trek memorabilia, Irish kitsch, African mementos, and the weapons. Especially the weapons. The police had taken away the Nero Wolfe bust, but swords and daggers and cudgels still lurked in the chaos of collectibles.

The English bulldog at my feet gave a low growl as if he were remembering the Nero Wolfe bust, too. I took a deep breath. And smelled wet wool and the sweetish remainders of the tea and pastries that Yvette had fed us earlier.

"Holy moly, only you could have gotten the skinny on this gonzo case," Felix gushed. I was sure there was a tape recorder keeping pace in his pocket. "Jeez-Louise, presto-pronto, whiz-bang . . ."

Felix. Felix who had done nothing to defend Yvette against Ted Brown's attack the day before, but who was nevertheless celebrating Yvette's deductions along with the rest of us on that rainy Monday evening. Because you'd better believe all the suspects had answered Yvette's summons this time. Ivan had come with Winona. Even his son, Neil, was here. I wondered who was minding the store. PMP probably.

And Zoe had rushed in the front door a few minutes ago bearing the wall hanging she had pieced together from the suspects floating through her steroidal mind. It was glorious. And I was jealous. Especially since I was the one who'd suggested the puzzle motif in the first place. The shimmering silk tapestry lay over the back of an easy chair now. I was sure it would be lost soon in the jungle of Yvette's living room, peeking out from behind some twelve-foot blow-up of a book cover or something. It would have been given top billing in my living room. Not that I could see any suspects in the sparkles and colors that swirled mysteriously through its stitched sections. Maybe that took deduction.

"Poor man," Phyllis Oberman commented. "A profoundly tortured soul."

Vince Quadrini and Dean Frazier nodded earnestly across from her. Well, she ought to be an expert on torture, I thought, nodding beside them, remembering my own acupuncture treatment.

"Yeah, yeah," Yvette conceded. "But he wasn't very careful, you know. Uncool procedure all the way around. Anyone could have seen him. Shi-shick, if I were going to kill someone . . ."

"How's Scott?" I whispered to Dean under the cover of the sound of rain and Yvette's continuing analysis of her own acumen.

"Scott's doing better, thank the Lord," Dean whispered back. "Now that he knows—now that he's thought on it—I do believe he's come to accept a little. Just a little for now, but . . ." He shrugged his shoulders to finish his sentence, fingering the amulet beneath his shirt.

I nodded. I was doing better myself. No more murder to worry about. And the skunks seemed to be gone permanently. But Ingrid? I clenched my teeth. Was our uninvited guest planning a return engagement? It hadn't even been a consideration until this morning. Until Wayne had watered one of our mammoth potted plants and found a backpack tucked neatly behind it. The pack contained two pair of spandex pants, two halter tops, undies, a toothbrush, and a bag of cosmetics. Not quite a bomb, but Wayne and I were still trying to decipher its meaning. I unclenched my teeth. There was good news, I reminded myself. My warehouse-woman Judy had definitely, absolutely, changed her name to Jade. Actually, I wasn't too sure about that either.

"So this Marcia woman was doing a fuddin' book scam, right?" Yvette asked, turning her tinted lenses on Ivan.

I forgot about Ingrid as Ivan's head popped up guiltily.

"It appears so," he admitted. "But she's at peace now, so—"

"Peace, shmeece," Yvette interrupted. "The woman was a menace. How come—"

"Mr. Nakagawa did everything he could," Winona threw in unexpectedly. She even reached out and touched her new employer's shoulder diffidently. "No way he could have done better."

"Yeah, no way," Neil chimed in, gazing fondly at Winona and his father. Ivan folded his hands together and a gentle smile settled on his thuggish face. He wanted harmony. And it looked like he was finally getting some. At least for a little while.

"Hey, Ivan," Zoe put in, her voice fast and nervous. "I was putting the suspects in place, you know, for the tapestry, and I just kept wondering about everyone. Like who had needles and stuff. Like me, for instance. Duh? And like who was really mad and stuff. And I was going to ask you, but I forgot." She tapped the side of her head with the heel of her hand, propelling more words out. "Who suggested the signing in the first place?"

Ivan's solid body jerked back, his eyes widening for a moment.

"Ted," the bookseller answered finally. Then he sighed his trademark sigh. "It was Ted originally. He suggested a mystery/sci-fi crossover signing. And then I invited Yvette and Shayla. Ted must have known Shayla would be invited." He hung his head. "I never even thought about it. The planning stages were so long ago."

"See!" Yvette said, stamping her foot to better make her point. "It takes a real detective for deduction. Phooey, if *I'd* known Ted was behind the signing—"

"Honey, you're not a real detective either," Lou reminded her gently as Winona and Neil closed ranks physically and emotionally on either side of Ivan and glared Yvette's way.

"Yeah, yeah," she said, looking up at her husband, affection softening her sharp features. "You just want to keep me out of trouble. But I am a detective now. I just proved it."

Lou sighed, a beaten man. But a loved one. Yvette stood on tiptoe and kissed his gorgeous chin.

"But the guy in the trench coat and the red VW van was a real detective, wasn't he?" I threw in, turning toward Vince Quadrini. Mr. Quadrini had been awfully quiet all evening. Was he revising his absolutist views on Saint S.X. Greenfree upon consideration of her treatment of Ted Brown and his dying child? Or was he just feeling guilty for siccing his private investigator on us?

Mr. Quadrini reddened under my look, then cleared his throat and drew up his shoulders as if to give a speech.

"I must beg everyone's forgiveness for any intrusion on the part of Mr. McClanaha—"

"Who the hell-heck is Mr. McClanaha?" Yvette demanded.

"Mr. McClanaha is a private detective Mr. Quadrini hired," I answered in triumph. I might not have nailed the murderer, but at least I'd spotted the *real* detective.

But no one noticed my brilliance in the turmoil that followed.

"The guy in the red van?" Zoe muttered, hitting her head again. "Whoa—"

"Do you mean to tell me that the man who came to me requesting an acupuncture treatment was really an investigator, invading the integrity of my office?" Phyllis demanded, pinning Mr. Quadrini with a scowl.

Mr. Quadrini just nodded. Manfully, hands held behind his back.

"I wondered why he wouldn't take off his trench coat," Phyllis murmured, subsiding into an unfocused frown. "How the man imagined I was going to insert needles while he still had his coat on—"

"Was he the sleazeball that scared me that night?" Winona put in.

Ivan put *his* hand on *her* shoulder now, murmuring consolation. Then dawn broke on his own face.

"He parked across the street from Fictional Pleasures," the bookseller said slowly. "He even came in—"

"Good Lord, he parked across from my house too," Dean said in wonderment. "I thought he was just some poor homeless soul."

"But did he figure it out?" Yvette asked loudly, silencing the buzz. She threw her hands in the air. "Shtick no. These hard-boiled guys don't have any class. No brains. Ted was angry. He knew how to make jewelry. And . . ." She smiled widely. "And he was the first one to reach the authors' table, in the perfect position to leave the bracelet. Deduction. Fuddin' deduction."

"Yvette told Ted he was deep in doo-doo," Felix piped up, returning to sycophancy. "Then Ted went totally gonzo, locked the front door, even locked the dogs in the kitchen."

The bulldog at my feet straightened up, laid back its ears, and growled at Felix. Yeah.

"Why didn't you do something?" I demanded of my so-called friend.

"Holy socks, I'm a reporter," he huffed, his eyes widening with apparent hurt. "I observe objectively. It was a *story,* man. Get it?"

The bulldog looked up at me as if asking whether to tear the reporter's leg off. Objectively, of course.

"Down, Marple," Lou ordered and the bulldog lay on his—or her—back. Too bad.

"So was he, like, a multiple personality or something?" Winona asked tentatively.

"No," Yvette replied, returning to center stage. "He was just a writer. See, you really have to be your own protagonist to write a good story. Ted just went a little overboard."

A little?

"So why don't you kill people, then?" Winona asked.

"I, I mean my protagonist doesn't kill people," she reminded us. "Lovell is a peaceful leprechaun . . ."

Her mouth was off and running again, this time extolling her protagonist's virtues in loving detail.

"What I don't understand," Ivan whispered beneath the hum of Yvette's voice, "is why he didn't just go back to making jewelry to get the money he needed."

"It was too late," Dean returned his whisper. "His boy needed the liver transplant then. A child's body is less likely to reject a liver transplant than an adult's. But he needed it immediately." Dean paused and shook his head. "The poor man. I believe that's why Scott is beginning to forgive him."

"Vigilantism versus forgiveness," Wayne put in. "Should have seen it in his books. What Ted thought was righteous execution was murder. Forgiveness was beyond him."

"Yeah!" Felix's voice broke in, ecstatic now. "Man, everyone down at the cop shop is smiling. Verduras has got him for Shayla and Marcia. And the San Ricardo P.D. has got him for Steve Sanders—"

"Sanders?" Yvette interrupted.

"Sanders was the potato-brain from the national liver transplant registry. He tried to scam Ted outa a bundle to put his kid higher up on the list for a liver. He didn't really have the power. But Ted thought he did. When Ted couldn't come up with the moolah, he blew him off, told him to go away. So ole Ted put curare-tipped pins between the keys of the potato-brain's word processor. Tap, tap, tap, clunk!" Felix mimed collapsing over a word processor.

"No way," Winona and Neil murmured together.

Felix nodded eagerly, enjoying his moment in the spotlight.

"Yeah, Ted is out there, man. Cops found the space cadet's diary. Tells the whole gonzo story. Ted Brown thinks he's Demetrius Douvert, right from outer space. That's where he is now anyway. He said 'astral travel,' and they haven't heard another peep from the perp since."

"Shi-shift, dogs or no dogs." Yvette took up her story again. *Her* story. "I could have handled Ted with my shillelagh. Right between the eyes, you know. Though Kate here did do a pretty impressive kick."

Warmth filled my body. And my mind. She had noticed. I opened my mouth to thank her, graciously. But I wasn't fast enough.

"Not that it was necessary," she amended. "You see—"

The doorbell rang. I looked around, wondering who was left that wasn't already at the party.

Lou opened the door and my question was answered. Captain Cal Xavier, that was who. I flinched in spite of myself. In spite of knowing that Wayne and I weren't under suspicion anymore. Something about the captain's shining teeth still gave me the third degree. Was he here on his brother's behalf?

"Hello there, Mr. Cassell," he said, extending his ever ready hand to shake Lou's. "I wanted to thank each and every one of you for your help in clearing up the unpleasantness—"

"Shick, murder is more than unpleasant," Yvette interrupted him mid-speech.

His smile dimmed for a nanosecond. Then he turned on the high beams. "Especially you, Ms. Cassell," he said. "Quite the hero, or should I say heroine?"

Yvette smiled back, caught off guard. I tried not to gag. Meanwhile, Lou glared.

"Well, I did do pretty damn-darn well," Yvette caroled. "Even if I do say so myself."

After a nauseating tribute to Yvette, the captain made his way around the group to congratulate me on my minor in Ted's capture.

He winked as he shook my hand. "I hear you practice some pretty mean tai chi, Ms. Jasper," he said, his voice hushed as Yvette continued her analysis of her own astute detective work. "Ms. Cassell ought to be thankful."

Now *I* smiled. Maybe this man would win his election bid after all.

"How's Bob?" I asked and then wished I hadn't. Because the famous Xavier smile had dimmed again at the mention of his brother's name.

"Well, Bob's given up on your friend Ingrid," the captain answered. "Ingrid came and spoke to me just yesterday. She told me she's living with a tango teacher now. I checked him out. The man calls himself Raoul Raymond, but his real name's Ralph Robinson. Turns out he's a very wealthy citizen. He teaches tango for his own entertainment, along with his sister, Ruth."

Ramona, I translated in my mind. That's right, Ramona was Ruth. And I hoped the captain of the Verduras Police Department wasn't going to blame me for the phony Raymonds.

"An interesting man," Captain Xavier went on. "Especially to your friend Ingrid." He winked again. I tried to wink back, not quite sure what we were supposed to be communicating, but hoping it was friendly. "By the way, Ingrid did ask me to tell you she wants her backpack returned if I were to see you."

"Really?" I yipped. Happy endorphins flooded my brain. "That's great. I mean—"

I flinched again.

"Sorry about your brother—" I started over.

"Hey, what sorry?" the captain whispered in my ear. "Don't tell the voters, but I never could stand my little brother. Except battered and fried maybe." This time at least, I knew what he was winking about.

Then he smiled his Xavier smile, and proceeded to shake

my hand in his smooth one, before making the rounds, shaking everyone's hands and saying his goodbyes.

A warm, rough hand grabbed mine not long after Captain Xavier had abandoned it. But it wasn't the captain back for seconds. It was Wayne.

"You heard the man," my sweetie muttered.

"What?" I said, still too dazed from my encounter with the man who I was sure would soon be mayor to understand my sweetie's meaning.

"Ingrid is tangoing with Raoul," Wayne whispered. "She's really gone. Forever."

"And?"

Wayne was trying to tell me something. I could feel it in his urgent grip. I could even taste it on his pastry-sweetened lips pressing my own suddenly.

"We can go home now, Kate," he added after a moment of sugar-coated bliss. "Home."

"Well, shick, a deduction," I said in awe. "What a wonderful fuddin' deduction."

We beat Captain Cal out the door by a step, and ran through the rain to our car.

LEPRECHAUN SAUCE

Ingredients:

1 large onion
1 tablespoon minced garlic
1 bunch parsley, chopped
1 teaspoon each dried basil, sage, rosemary and thyme
4 ounces crumbled soy sausage or minced, marinated
    tofu
1 15-oz can vegetable broth
1 tablespoon dark sesame oil
1 tablespoon Worcestershire sauce
2 tablespoons maple syrup
1 tablespoon hot prepared mustard
Leftover vegetables (optional)
1 tablespoon cornstarch dissolved in 2 tablespoons
cold water

Directions:

1. Cook onion, garlic, parsley, herbs, soy sausage or tofu in sesame oil and 1/2 cup of vegetable broth until wilted. (5-10 minutes)

2. Stir in Worcestershire, maple syrup, hot mustard, remaining vegetable broth, and leftover vegetables if desired.

3. Thicken with cornstarch.

4. Serve over rice, pasta, or 1 boiled leprechaun.

Yield: 4 servings

(Note: No leprechauns were harmed in the preparation of this recipe.)